SILENCE IS DEADLY

SILENCE IS DEADLY

LLOYD BIGGLE, JR.

 millington

All of the characters in the book
are fictitious, and any resemblance
to actual persons, living or dead,
is purely coincidental.

An entirely different version of SILENCE IS DEADLY appeared as a short story in the October 1957 issue of *If Worlds of Science Fiction*. Copyright 1957 by Quinn Publishing Co., Inc.

Copyright © 1977 by Lloyd Biggle, Jr.

All rights reserved

ISBN o 86000 106 7

First published in Great Britain in 1981 by
Millington Books
an imprint of
Davison Publishing Ltd
54 Elgin Avenue
London W9 2HA

Printed in Great Britain by The Anchor Press Ltd
and bound by Wm Brendon & Son Ltd
both of Tiptree, Essex

Map of Storoz by Pamela Whitlark

Illustrations by Steven Carpenter

SILENCE IS DEADLY

STOROZ

CHAPTER 1

The pursuit was almost upon them before Jan Darzek became aware of it.

Above the rhythmic clumping of the hurrying draft nabrula and the screaming racket pronounced continuously by their cart's ungreased axles, Darzek's impaired hearing caught a faintly muddled overlay of hoofbeats. He turned and looked back.

The three knights were a mere thirty meters behind them and riding hard: black capes whipping in the wind, mustaches streaming, whip arms ascending and falling rhythmically, leather armor flapping. The ponderous riding nabrula were thundering along as fast as they could gallop.

For a long moment Darzek stared at them, his surprise mingled with fascination and disbelief. A knight of Kamm in full charge was a spectacle, and these three specimens were priests, notorious black knights of the Winged Beast.

He touched Riklo on the shoulder and pointed at the knights. She glanced backward, shrugged, and returned her attention to their own three rushing nabrula. Their only possible action now was to drive straight ahead in a splendid presumption of innocence.

The surlane was narrow here—scarcely wide enough for two carts to pass abreast. Tall, bulbous-topped stalks of the sponge forest crowded it on either side. Sporadic eddies of sponge scent enveloped them as their steadily laboring tandem set a brisk pace over the deeply rutted lane—one moment pleasant and faintly aromatic; the next, chokingly pungent. The cart bounced and swayed, and its pegged boards added an irregular polyphony of creaks and groans to the incessant squawking of the axles. From behind them, under the gaily colored tent that sheltered the cart box, came the continuous tinkle and clatter of rattling glass and pottery.

Darzek looked again at the knights. Their aura of bristling menace made him think nostalgically of Keystone Cops. Each rider clung desperately with one hand to the massive folds of skin that curled about his nabrulk's neck. His absurdly elongated boot toes were locked under the ugly beast's flabby stomach. These nabrula were a blotched yellow in color, a variety much favored for their riding qualities, and though the beasts were hairless, their mottled skin made Darzek think of the mange. With saliva pouring copiously from gaping, toothless mouths, with bulging noses aquiver, with double-hinged legs laboring furiously, with each beast's club-like horn lowered farcically as though for the kill —the horn projected backward, over the creature's rump, and served a procreational function Darzek hadn't believed even after he'd seen it— the nabrula seemed specifically designed for populating nightmares, though they were awkward, stupid beasts, disgustingly gentle and affectionate.

But the menace was real enough. The knights' free hands held their whips ready for action, the deadly lashes coiled and poised to strike. Darzek had seen a victim cut to the bone at eight paces, sliced open as though with a meat cleaver, and he hoped that these knights were merely intent on overtaking them.

He turned to Riklo and spoke with his fingers. The caterwauling of the cart wheels made vocal conversation difficult; also, Darzek needed the practice.

Why would black knights be waylaying innocent travelers in the Duke Merzkion's province? he asked, trying not to lisp with his awkward sixth finger.

Her hands were busy with the reins. She dropped a shoulder negatively—she was as mystified as he.

Before Darzek could grapple further with this unexpected wrinkle in Kammian intrigue, the first knight drew close enough to strike. His whip curled around the horn of the trailing nabrulk, which came to a rearing halt, buckling the harnesses, dragging the other two nabrula to a stop, and almost overturning the cart. Darzek and Riklo scrambled to the ground and sank to their knees.

But they kept their eyes on the knight who confronted them. For this was Kamm, the Silent Planet, the world of the deaf, and no one humbly averted his gaze when he was about to be spoken to.

The knight's fingers flashed. *Who are you?*

I am Lazk, Darzek's hands explained. *A skilled purveyor of scents. A guarantor of delicious dreams and memorable love nights, of sharpened senses and prolonged appetites. From Northpor I come, traveling these eleven days and dispensing happiness at wayside forums. OO-Fair is my destination, may the Winged Beast prosper it and me.*

He plucked a vial of perfume from an inner pocket of his cape, unstoppered it, and offered it to the knight for sampling.

Simultaneously, Riklo was shaping her own carefully prepared identity. *I am Riklo, a keeper of secrets. I read the future in reflected star-*

*light and fashion amulets to change it as the Winged Beast may assent.
I reconcile lovers and restore friendships. I accompany my mate.*

They finished, and the knight sat looking down at them stonily. Watching him, Darzek pondered this strange Kammian ability to absorb multiple conversations. The notion that some Kammians could "listen" to as many as four pairs of hands speaking at once confounded him, but he had seen it done.

One of the knights had ridden up to the cart and opened a tent flap, and he was poking about among the flasks and vials and crocks and the stocks of herbs and essences. The third knight dismounted and slowly began to circle the cart. He held something cupped in his hands, and Darzek wished he dared turn his head to see what it was.

The first knight continued to scrutinize them. Suddenly he bent forward, snatched the unstoppered vial from Darzek's fingers, and sniffed deeply. Then he emptied the contents onto Darzek's head.

Scornfully he flung the vial aside. *A quality product,* his fingers announced, *but some of your dabblings are less well formulated, perfumer. Your most recent concoction stinks. If you don't mend your fumbling ways, you'll lose custom.*

Blinded in one eye, dazed by the overpowering scent, Darzek nearly toppled over. As he regained his balance, the peripheral vision of his untouched eye caught a flash of light.

At the same instant, Riklo cried out. "Pazul!"

Darzek leaped to his feet. On a neck thong he wore a carved amulet, an image of the grotesque symbol of Kamm's death religion, the Winged Beast. He pointed the gaping, toothed snout at the knight on foot, who now held a gleaming light cupped in his hands and was regarding it with astonishment. Darzek pressed the Beast's breast, and the knight collapsed abruptly. He whirled to see Riklo calmly shoot the first knight from his saddle with her own amulet. The third knight's whip already was in motion when Darzek sent him and his nabrulk to the ground in a paralyzed tangle.

Darzek hurried to the knight who had held the light. It lay in the lane beside him, a milky, egg-shaped crystal with a blunted black end. He picked it up cautiously, examined it, and finally repeated the knight's maneuver in walking around the cart with it.

Only when he thought to point the black end at the cart's concealed compartments did it suddenly blaze with light.

"It's not a pazul," he called to Riklo. "It's only a metal detector."

He sat down on the cart step and contemplated it. Almost from the moment he first heard of Kamm there had been panicky references to a pazul on this world, and he was becoming tired of them. The ultimate death ray was a theoretical possibility, but it wouldn't be invented on a world with Kamm's level of primitive technology.

But neither would a metal detector, and Darzek found this one almost as disturbing as a pazul would have been. Its milky white, translucent case looked like synthetic crystal, and the inner workings had to reflect a considerable skill in microelectronics. The instrument was sensitive enough to respond palely to the infinitesimally fine wiring of Darzek's amulet.

"The question," Riklo announced, "is whether they're really knights of the Winged Beast."

She bent over one of them, opened his tunic, and slid it down his arm. On his shoulder was an ugly red tatoo.

Darzek abandoned the metal detector for this new perplexity. "Why would the Duke Merzkion be disguising his knights in his own province?" he demanded.

Riklo smiled enigmatically and did not answer.

Darzek lifted a tent flap, folded back the exquisitely woven carpet that covered the bottom of the cart, and opened a concealed panel. He placed the detector in a padded compartment, wondering as he did so what kind of shielding would be required to protect them from further harassment.

When he emerged, Riklo had grabbed the legs of one of the knights and was dragging him into the forest. "Where are you taking him?" Darzek called.

She answered over her shoulder. "Do you have a better idea?"

Darzek fretfully rubbed his head where an ear should have been. It was at times like this, when he was faced with a limited number of highly undesirable alternatives, that he missed his ears the most. "I suppose not," he said reluctantly.

She vanished into the forest with the knight. When she came out again, she said, "I'll bury their clothing and armor separately and disguise the bodies. You go on with the cart. Pull it into the first crosslane you come to, and take their nabrula into the forest and find them a grazing place. After I clean things up here, I'll wait for you at the cart."

"All right," Darzek said.

She hauled the second knight away and returned for the third; and Darzek straightened the cart's twisted harnesses, helped the paralyzed nabrulk to its feet—the charge that knocked out a knight for an hour or more only stunned this mammoth beast for a few minutes—tied the three riderless nabrula in tandem, and set off along the surlane.

At nightfall, Darzek and Riklo were striding boldly through the forest, and every footstep sent clouds of winking lights soaring into the air, or leaping aside, or scurrying away.

For this was Kamm, the world where no life form possessed a sense of hearing, and darkness transformed it. It became a fairyland to the eye and hell to the nose. The world's night creatures existed in a multiplicity of forms and sizes, and without sound to claim their territories, or attract their mates, or just exuberantly announce their presences, all of them did so with light or with pheromones. The lights were spectacular pulsations of sparkling, multicolored luminosity. The odors were equally dramatic but unfortunately were as likely to be spectacularly nauseous as exquisite. Darzek never took a night walk without longing for a gas mask.

The peculiarities of Kamm's night creatures posed a serious problem for the alien agent. No one, and no thing, walked about secretly during a Kammian night. The creatures dodging his footsteps often supplied sufficient light to read by, and his path was a streak of illumination that could be seen for kilometers. In compensation, the natives of Kamm rarely were around to see it, because they shunned the night. They actually seemed to fear darkness; but even if they hadn't, there was nothing for a nocturnal native to do in a sponge forest, so Darzek and Riklo strode along boldly.

Suddenly Riklo burst into laughter. "Some of your dabblings are less well formulated, perfumer," she sputtered. "Some of your dabblings—"

"What the devil did he mean?" Darzek demanded.

"It's the most cutting insult one could direct at a perfumer—to tell him he stinks."

"Thank you. Now tell me a few cutting insults that can be directed at knights."

She turned quickly. "Are you still brooding about those knights?"

Darzek said nothing.

"They would have done the same for you, cheerfully, and with far less provocation."

"I know."

"I find it appropriate that the last blood on their hands should be their own. They've washed often enough in the blood of innocents."

"I know."

"If we'd turned them loose, they would have set off a search such as Kamm has never known, and every perfumer on Storoz would have been subject to arrest, torture, and probably death."

"I know."

"Then why are you brooding? You Earth people are strangely tender-hearted."

"I don't like the idea of cutting a creature's throat when it's helpless."

She turned and scrutinized him. "Did you speak truly when you said that your features are your own, and that you had hearing flaps which the surgeons removed to make you look like a Kammian?"

"Of course," Darzek said irritably. "They removed the flaps and covered the openings."

She tittered. "I don't believe it. Where would the hearing flaps go? No natural process would produce a life form looking that absurd."

"I wore the hearing flaps on my posterior," Darzek told her. "When I didn't want to listen, I sat down."

They walked on. Some minutes later she announced, "I don't believe it. I don't believe any of it."

Darzek thought she was rather unbelievable herself. On Earth she would have been an extremely attractive young female with an outlandish hairdo. On this world of Kamm, where all the females seemed extremely attractive and all of the hairdos were outlandish, she was an ordinary commoner wearing the cloak of a dubious occupation.

What perplexed Darzek was the fact that her appearance was synthetic. She wore an ingeniously contrived artificial body that perfectly represented the appearance of a Kammian native, and within it was concealed the utterly alien life form that was an agent of the Galactic Synthesis.

What that utterly alien life form actually looked like, Darzek had no idea. He knew that she was a native of the world of Hnolon, but he had never been there and couldn't recall meeting one of its inhabitants before. Perhaps the Hnolonians were giant slugs. Or spiders. Or octopuses. Darzek had spent no small amount of time in watching Riklo and speculating as to what manner of creature was concealed under her synthetic Kammian exterior. Thus far, he had been too polite to ask her.

At the moment he had something more important to worry about. The previous night their young colleague, Wenz, had invaded the castle of the Duke Merzkion. Wenz had a peculiar talent that Darzek found incredible even after seeing it demonstrated. He could walk up a sheer wall. He had entered the castle at its weakest point, the highest window in the tallest turret, and his plan was to explore the building by night and hide by day. If he got into any kind of difficulty, all he had to do was step out the nearest window and walk around on the outside of the castle or perch on the roof until the uproar diminished. For the ultimate emergency, he wore a Winged Beast amulet like those of Darzek and Riklo.

Ten Synthesis agents had vanished on Kamm, several from the province of the Duke Merzkion. These inexplicable disappearances had further fueled the rumors of a pazul. Wenz was to search the castle for traces of the missing agents, while Darzek and Riklo combed the surrounding countryside on the same mission. On the previous night, they had seen Wenz signal his safe arrival at the upper level of the castle. Tonight, he was to signal how much longer his search would take.

It was the metal detector that worried Darzek. He wondered what other instruments of detection guarded the duke's stronghold.

When finally they reached the edge of the forest, they stood for a long time looking upward at the looming castle. It perched on the cliff high above them, silhouetted against the richly starred sky and looking like a bulgy, many-pronged finger pointed at the infinite.

It was a finger rising from a sewer. The foul odor that clung noisomely to the foot of the cliff left both of them gasping, and above them the cliffside was a smear of lights. The nobility of Kamm was no more fastidious about its environment than the nobility of Earth had been in earlier times. It built its castles on the edge of hills or chasms or cliffs and disposed of waste and refuse by pitching it out of the appropriate windows. What they were seeing and smelling—luminously delineated by the night creatures that came to gorge on it—was the Duke Merzkion's garbage heap.

They waited, watching Kamm's swift-moving small moons, and each time an inner moon come into conjunction with an outer moon, they stared intently at the castle. But no light flashed in any window.

After the third conjunction, Darzek stirred uneasily. "Is it possible that he's finished and left already?"

"Maybe he's signaling from a window we can't see from here," Riklo said.

"Then let's move."

They walked along the edge of the forest on a path that took them directly under the garbage heap, and the overpowering stench enveloped them like a corrosive cloud. It became a tangible thing, and Darzek wanted to seize it with his two six-fingered hands and shove it aside so he could breathe. They stumbled forward, keeping their eyes on the castle.

Suddenly Riklo halted. "What's that?"

There was a scraggly sponge growth at the foot of the cliff, and something had crashed into it and was caught there. A limp arm dangled perpendicularly; a twisted leg was entangled in the sponge fronds. They hurried toward it, ignoring the foul squish of garbage underfoot. Carefully, tenderly, they lifted the body down and carried it to the concealment of the forest.

The soft bark had cushioned its fall, and most night creatures had found it not yet ripe enough for their liking. Darzek and Riklo stretched out the body and examined it with a hand light, flicking the beam from time to time to make it look like one of the night creatures scurrying among the sponge stalks.

Wenz, agent of the Galactic Synthesis. Young, good-looking, intelligent, well trained, skilled, highly capable. The Duke Merzkion had inflicted upon him the final indignity that the Dukes of Storoz reserved for enemies and victims alike: his body had been thrown out with the garbage.

At least that final indignity had been painless. The evidence of what came before it sickened Darzek. The teeth were set; the face was twisted gruesomely; the hands and even the feet were clenched; every body muscle was tensed—not from rigor mortis, but from torture.

And yet the body was unmarked except for the trickle of blood that had caked in the nose and eyes and mouth.

Darzek and Riklo exchanged glances.

Wenz had remarked jokingly that if the Duke Merzkion actually possessed a death ray, he would find it. The duke did, and Wenz had found it; and it had killed him.

At the same instant, it had doomed a world.

CHAPTER 2

Jan Darzek first heard of the world of Kamm at a meeting of the Council of Supreme.

It was Interstellar Trade Day at the council. Supreme, the world-sized computer that governed the galaxy, gave birth to a mountain of economic statistics every ten cycles; and the Council of Supreme, which liked to think that it governed the galaxy, felt obligated to meet and consider them.

Old E-Wusk, the Second Councilor and the council's expert on trade, had achieved a formula of condensation that almost capsuled Supreme's report out of existence; but first he felt obliged to perform a statistical analysis. "The balance of trade in the neighboring sector, in contrast to the two sectors just cited—"

Darzek, the First Councilor and, under the name Gul Darr, a well-known interstellar trader himself, cared nothing for either statistics or economics. He suppressed a yawn and amused himself by watching his fellow councilors.

The large ball with an upper hemisphere bristling with eye stalks was THREE, the Third Councilor. When bored, its eye stalks twitched and intertwined. When bored to distraction, they began to tie themselves into knots. At the moment it was plaiting the stalks into rather complicated braids, the final stage before knot tying.

SIX, the Sixth Councilor, a gaunt, angular, nocturnal triped, was performing an involved plaiting of her own. Her three looping arms twined and untwined incessantly. Her expression was invisible behind the shaded translucency of her light shield.

FIVE was equally capable of fanciful plaiting, but she kept her multifingered tentacles in a state of perfect relaxation. Her massive, conical head was bent forward slightly in a posture of attentiveness; her twig of a body was concealed by the drooping tentacles. The Fifth Councilor always maintained a guise of polite interest, however boring the report.

SEVEN was listening silently, which meant that it was asleep. It was a massive lung in a slug-like body, and its regular wheezes were disconcertingly audible when it was awake. When it slept, its metabolism slowed almost to zero.

FOUR probably was asleep. He was the council's enigma, a faceless life form with a row of sensory humps located across his shoulders. He rarely spoke, and the only evidence of consciousness was the twitching and jerking of the humps as he focused and refocused his organs of sight and hearing to follow a discussion. Now the humps were motionless.

Darzek turned his attention to EIGHT, Rok Wllon, the council's Director of Uncertified Worlds. He had been watching the Eighth Councilor intermittently through the meeting, but now he scrutinized him with concern.

Rok Wllon's usual listening attitude was one of poised alertness as he waited to pounce on a contradiction or interrupt with a question. His knack for transforming an orderly meeting into acrimony with a well-placed interruption or two was exceeded only by his remarkable talent for interminable debate on inconsequential issues.

But today he was leaning far back in his chair, and his half-closed eyes seemed to be focused on the infinity of the jace-vaulted ceiling. This entirely unwonted silence worried Darzek. There was no visible sign of illness—the Eighth Councilor had a decidedly blue set to his complexion, but that peculiar hue was his normal color, just as his normal but unlikely looking silhouette was massively broad when seen from the front and improbably narrow when viewed from the side—but something was decidedly wrong with him. Never before had he permitted E-Wusk to rattle off economic statistics without challenge.

E-Wusk harrumphed twice and swung into his capsuled summary: The total volume of trade among the worlds of the Galactic Synthesis was up slightly. The trade of twenty-six and something per cent of the worlds had increased; the trade of twenty-eight and something per cent of the worlds had diminished. The trade of the others showed no significant fluctuation. A few worlds were experiencing unusual prosperity. A few were enmeshed in economic difficulties. Any councilor interested in either category could ask Supreme for a list of the twenty or thirty thousand worlds numbered therein. In E-Wusk's opinion, the decacycle just concluded showed no anomalies, and none were predicted for the decacycle to come.

The Second Councilor harrumphed to a conclusion and then sank back into a tangle of telescoping limbs.

Darzek opened the meeting to discussion or questions. There was no response, so he officially accepted E-Wusk's report with the council's thanks. "Is there any further business?" he asked.

The Third Councilor hurriedly unbraided its eye stalks and inflated its vocal sack. "I have a complaint," it hissed.

Darzek asked politely, "What is it that you wish to complain about?"

"*I'm* not complaining," THREE protested. "I have received a complaint. From compatriot tourists. They complain that they can't see the government."

Darzek reflected for a moment. "That's probably true."

"Of course it's true. They make a long and expensive journey in order to view Primores, the central world of the galaxy, home of Supreme, principal site of the governing bodies of the Galactic Synthesis. And when they arrive here, it's just another alien world and not as interesting as most. There are governmental structures, of course, but all worlds have governmental structures. There's nothing for them to see."

"What do you suggest?" Darzek asked.

"There should be displays. Festivities. Ceremonies, to foster pride in the Synthesis."

Darzek asked, "Are you suggesting that this council should place its meetings on public display?"

He sat back to enjoy the uproar. Objections erupted around the table, but FIVE, who spoke through an amplifier because her voice was almost non-existent, drowned them out with her sudden burst of laughter. She turned off the amplifier and laughed on in silence, with every tentacle and finger fluttering. "Nothing," she announced finally, "would do less to foster pride in government than placing the members of this council on display."

"Or any other council," Darzek murmured.

SEVEN wheezed its agreement. E-Wusk grunted his.

THREE sputtered indignantly. "I had no intention of suggesting that, and the First Councilor knows it."

"None of us object to ceremonies as long as we don't have to take part," Darzek said. "Would you like to look into the possibility of establishing suitable festivities, displays, and ceremonies for the edification and entertainment of tourists to Primores?"

"Certainly."

"Please do. Is there any further business?"

Rok Wllon snapped to alertness and leaned forward. He said, in a soft voice, "I desire your counsel."

Darzek turned instinctively to FIVE, the council's medical authority. She was gazing at the Eighth Councilor in consternation. Never in Darzek's recollection had Rok Wllon asked advice from anyone except when he was transparently attempting to manipulate it to some advantage.

"It concerns a poem," Rok Wllon continued apologetically. "I have translated it, and I will render it to you as a song—to capture the spirit of the original."

Now all of the councilors were staring at him. FIVE was completely engrossed. E-Wusk was flabbergasted enough to rise up out of his tangle of limbs and gape. SIX absently discarded her light shield and gazed at the Eighth Councilor with her three enlarged, tearing eyes. The others, including Darzek, were simply speechless.

Rok Wllon, still acting apologetic, looked about the table as though he expected someone to stop him. When no one did, he began to sing.

> Death's heavy shadow
> > unseen, unfelt, unsmelled
> > ripples no awareness
> > heeds no sanctuary.
>
> It enters and touches
> > and departs
> > leaving no mark of passage
> > except Death.

His voice was not unpleasant, Darzek thought; but the grunted inflections and breathy melismas made the performance one that would have held more appeal for masochists than music lovers.

The other councilors remained speechless. There was in fact nothing that could be said, but as First Councilor Darzek was required to say something. After a pause, he asked, "Is it a song from your world?"

"It is not a song," Rok Wllon said irritably. "I told you I had translated it and would render it as a song, but it is a poem."

"From your world?" Darzek persisted.

"No. From the world of Kamm. The Silent Planet."

Darzek had never heard of it. "What's silent about it?" he asked.

Rok Wllon told them. Then he pronounced the phrase again, the Silent Planet, and the touch of horror in his voice suggested that there must be something uncanny about a world where no one, where no thing, could hear.

FIVE, with her instant interest in anything with medical implications, wanted to know more. Medical literature, she said, was unaware of the existence of a world where no life form had developed a sense of hearing.

"But they did develop senses of hearing," Rok Wllon said testily. "And then they lost them."

FIVE was incredulous. "You mean all the life forms on the planet had senses of hearing that disappeared through atrophy? That's impossible!"

Rok Wllon was becoming increasingly agitated. Abruptly he got to his feet. "I only know what a scientist from my department told me. Perhaps he was—if you'll excuse me. There is no important business left to consider, is there? I have many—my own work, you know, those of you who have no administrative responsibilities can't be aware of how much—"

He turned uncertainly and walked away.

That, also, was unheard of.

There was a shuffle of feet, a twisting of torsos, a purring of motors as the councilors turned themselves or their chairs to look after him. E-Wusk struggled to an upright position and then sank back in astonishment. Darzek's eyes were on FIVE, who was watching the departing councilor with obvious concern.

FIVE said, "I'll call on him later today."

"And I'll see him tomorrow," Darzek said. He turned to the others. "At your conveniencies, I want each of you to pay him a courtesy call before you leave Primores."

"But why?" THREE demanded. "If the Eighth Councilor has lost his mental balance, Supreme should be informed. But surely there is no need for we seven to inconvenience ourselves."

Darzek silenced a babble of talk with a wave of his hand. "The Eighth Councilor has not lost his mental balance," he said. "We all know how he persists in seeing dangers where there are none, but we also know that he faces any danger with gusto."

"That is true," FIVE agreed.

"So I think all of us should call on him," Darzek went on. "Try to learn what is bothering him and let me know what you find out. As you are aware, I have shared many real dangers with the Eighth Councilor. This is the only time I have ever seen him frightened."

FIVE reported to Darzek later that day. She had visited Rok Wllon and asked if he had more poetry from the world of Kamm. He had promised to send her some. He seemed as rational and as stodgy as ever —which meant that he had returned to normal.

Darzek thanked her.

He went himself the following morning, but the Eighth Councilor was not at home. He returned that afternoon, and Rok Wllon received him in the vast study that ornamented his official councilor's residence.

In response to Darzek's questions, he activated a projection that filled the room: a shallow slice of the galaxy reproduced three dimensionally just above their heads. Darzek consulted the key and orientated himself; and then Rok Wllon touched a control and set one of the suns flashing on and off: Gwanor, whose only habitable planet was named Kamm.

"What's the problem with Kamm?" Darzek wanted to know.

"There's a Death Religion," Rok Wllon whispered.

"Surely there's nothing unique about that," Darzek said.

Rok Wllon hesitated. He whispered again. "I can't say more than that. Not yet. Not here."

Darzek studied him thoughtfully. This was the same frightened Rok Wllon he had seen at the council meeting. "When can you say more?" Darzek asked. "And where?"

"Perhaps tomorrow." Rok Wllon leaped to his feet and paced the floor excitedly, disrupting the pinpricks of light that wheeled about the room's axis. "Yes. Tomorrow would be better."

The following morning, when Darzek called again, Rok Wllon was not at home. Darzek went at once to the Department of Uncertified Worlds.

This was the anonymous service of the Galactic Synthesis. It attracted people with the peculiar temperament that was especially suited for world watching—a turn of mind and personality that enabled them to fit into an alien society and play a role there through their entire lives and simply observe.

The Uncertified Worlds were those planets that were, for one or more of a multitude of reasons, ineligible to join the Galactic Synthesis. Requirements for membership were based more upon the character of a world's inhabitants than upon their achievements, and the Synthesis demonstrated no official interest in whether any world attained membership or not. Non-member worlds were ignored unless their activities posed a threat to Synthesis members or seemed likely to.

As Director of the Department of Uncertified Worlds, Rok Wllon placed observation teams on such planets wherever or whenever he thought they were needed. These teams supplied voluminous and continuing reports on the worlds, and if through some evolutionary coincidence a world achieved eligibility by way of its own self-improvement, the department recommended it for membership. Rok Wllon performed a highly responsible and thankless job, and he did it superbly. For all of his petty idiosyncrasies, he was the government's best top level administrator.

Rok Wllon's young administrative assistant, a compatriot of his named Kom Rmmon, politely expressed his regrets to Darzek. The director had left that morning with a team of administrators for the world of Slonfus to attend a conference about something or other.

That seemed perfectly normal. The Director of Uncertified Worlds spent more than half of his time traveling.

But he did not normally leave for that kind of conference unexpectedly—especially when he had an appointment with the First Councilor. Darzek's uneasiness remained, but for the present there was nothing that he could do. He asked to be notified the moment the director returned; but Rok Wllon's trip proved to be an extended one, and Darzek had his own work to do, and eventually his puzzlement over the Eighth Councilor's conduct—and Kamm, the Silent Planet—faded.

Periodically Supreme divested its computer self of a list of worlds under the heading, "Potential Trouble Sources." The projected difficulties were sometimes monumental and sometimes unbelievably trivial, and the word *potential* not infrequently meant, as Darzek had discovered in the past, that even a computer's imagination could be overly active.

But Darzek felt obliged to investigate each world named. In most instances the action needed was obvious and easily taken: to avert a medical crisis due to inept public health measures; to prevent a looming economic catastrophe caused by a failing source of critical metals; to defuse an interworld dispute with timely mediation. Darzek's practice was to first skim through the columns, picking out those worlds he was familiar with.

On this particular list, his rapid skimming was brought to an abrupt halt by one word: Kamm.

CHAPTER 3

Darzek immediately asked Supreme for a posting on its councilors. Supreme did not know where Rok Wllon was.

Neither did the Department of Uncertified Worlds. The director was traveling, Kom Rmmon informed Darzek politely. Doubtless he would soon supply the department with a new itinerary.

Kom Rmmon had been trained superbly. He radiated efficiency and intelligence; but beneath the imposing veneer of those qualities, it seemed to Darzek that the youngster was as badly frightened as Rok Wllon had been.

As First Councilor, Darzek possessed an impressive portfolio of emergency powers. Although he disciplined himself to use them only in genuine crises, and as a last resort, he had little difficulty in persuading himself that the disappearance of a member of the Council of Supreme had to be investigated at once, with every means available to him.

Darzek went directly to the Eighth Councilor's official residence and had himself admitted by Supreme. He sat down at the communications panel in Rok Wllon's study and asked Supreme to show him, one at a time, the last things the Eighth Councilor had viewed before his departure.

A projection filled the room just above Darzek's head—an enlarged portion of the same shallow slice of the galaxy that Rok Wllon had displayed to him. Darzek picked out the sun Gwanor and its one habitable planet, Kamm; but the pinpoints of light told him nothing.

The star projection faded, and the desk screen came to life. The beautifully drawn calligraphy shown there was Rok Wllon's own angular script. Darzek moved over to the desk and pondered the three poems that filled the screen.

> The night was cloudless
> and shimmering with moon shadows
>
> > I reached for its beauty
> > and Death's talons clutched my hand.

A keeper of secrets
knows my death date

> She sculpts my future
> with sinewy hands
> intertwining happiness and longevity

but while she speaks
the whip is pointed
and I feel unseen vibrations.

Vibrant Death
> unwanted
> uninvited
scrupulously keeps the appointment
that no one made.

The screen went blank. Darzek searched the residence thoroughly, but he found no clues—not even the evidence of a hasty departure.

He returned to his own residence and filed an official request. A few minutes later he had a visitor: Kom Rmmon, now flustered with excitement because he had just received a direct command from Supreme. To a governmental bureaucrat on Primores, this was the equivalent of a message from God. He faced Darzek with consternation, and his naturally bluish complexion had taken on a purplish tint.

Darzek got him seated. He said sternly, "It is the command of Supreme and of Supreme's First Councilor, myself, that you answer. Where is the director of your department?"

Kom Rmmon gazed at Darzek woodenly.

"Answer! You cannot refuse a command from Supreme and from Supreme's First Councilor. Where is the director?"

"Not here," Kom Rmmon muttered.

"We know that he is not here. Where is he?"

"I can't speak here. Come."

He dashed to the entrance hall, punched a destination on Darzek's transmitter, and stepped through. Darzek paused to look at the setting before he followed him, frowning perplexedly.

He emerged in a public park. Kom Rmmon already was twenty strides from Darzek and hurrying away. Darzek matched his pace and followed him.

The world of Primores was beautiful as only an artificial world could be, crafted to perfection in each of its parts and with each small perfection skillfully fitted into the harmonious whole. At one time it had been an airless world, and the tinted domes that enclosed each of its public parks were a reminder of that sterile antiquity. Now the world's rainbow atmosphere provided a shimmering halo above the domes. Kom Rmmon wound his way through the lush, multicolored vegetation until he reached the edge of the park. Only then did he look back, and when he had assured himself that Darzek was following, he opened a door in the base of the dome and stepped through.

Darzek stepped through after him and followed, maintaining the twenty-pace distance.

The transmitter, which permitted whole world populations to move instantly between the blind oases that were windowless buildings and homes and enclosed parks, had transformed many worlds to unseen wastelands; but on Primores, the carefully kept landscape outside the dome was as park-like as that within. Kom Rmmon marched straight ahead for a hundred meters or more, finally coming to a stop at a low building that looked like a massive block of concrete.

He punched an indentification code, opened a heavy door, and stood waiting for Darzek, who had turned to look back at the park. There was no suggestion of a path worn through the closely cropped vegetation. Whatever the structure was used for, it was not used frequently.

Darzek entered, and Kom Rmmon followed and closed the door firmly behind them and secured it. They were in a small, tastefully furnished conference room.

Kom Rmmon dropped into a chair with an attitude of immense relief. "Now we can talk without being overheard," he said.

Darzek looked at him incredulously. "Who could have overheard us in the residence of the First Councilor?" he demanded.

"Supreme," Kom Rmmon said.

Darzek backed up to a chair and sat down heavily. He continued to stare at Kom Rmmon. "The director is engaged in an activity that must be kept secret from Supreme?"

"Yes."

"And—this room was built solely to have a place for conferences where Supreme can't listen?"

"Yes. The director supervised the construction himself. Supreme is everywhere else." Kom Rmmon shuddered.

This probably was true. Supreme's infinity of tentacles stretched into every building, every public and private place, every fissure of the planet. Supreme *was* Primores, a world-sized computer with its surface utilized for the governmental workers who were in fact its servants.

Darzek had never given a thought to the possibility that Supreme might be listening and making a record of his every chance remark. Even if he had, he doubted that he would have cared. "Is the director on the world of Kamm?" he asked.

"Yes."

"What is there about the world of Kamm that must be kept secret from Supreme?"

"There's a pazul."

"What's a pazul?" Darzek asked.

"A death ray."

Mentally Darzek twiddled his thumbs. The concept of a death ray conveyed no special menace to him. Among the strictly controlled products of a galaxy's science and technology were devices that could serve as frightful instruments of death. As far as he knew the legendary death ray was not among them, but he doubted that its presence could have added much to their destructive potential.

Then, with a start, he saw the problem as Rok Wllon had seen it.

Such products from member worlds of the Synthesis were not a menace because they could be controlled. But if the world of Kamm, an Uncertified World and a non-member of the Synthesis, had in fact produced a pazul, the implications were terrifying. No wonder Supreme had listed it as a potential trouble spot! Its science and technology must be enormously advanced, especially in their more destructive aspects. Darzek said as much.

Kom Rmmon remarked gloomily, "It has a vegetable technology."

Darzek stared at him. "Nonsense!"

"But it does. It has some very unusual tree-like plants. One—our agents call it the sponge tree—has a flabby bark and a soft, pithy interior, but when the core is aged and dried properly, and treated, it becomes enormously hard and durable. It provides the basis for a technology without metal. They use metals only for coining money."

"But they do have metals. I was wondering how they could evolve electrical circuitry with a wood technology."

Kom Rmmon's gloom deepened. "They haven't discovered electricity."

Darzek said gravely, "If they can produce a death ray with a wood instrument that uses neither metal nor electricity, they're an astonishingly talented species. I'll believe it when I see it."

"Our agents have seen it," Kom Rmmon said.

"Were they able to photograph it, or make drawings of it?"

"It's a pazul!" Kom Rmmon protested. "The agents who have seen it are dead!"

Darzek leaned forward. The hilarious notion of a wood pazul had suddenly become unfunny. "The Synthesis has lost agents on Kamm?"

"Nine."

Darzek winced. "*Nine?* What makes you think a pazul killed them?"

"Because nothing killed them. There was no cause of death, but they died."

"Some worlds have strange diseases," Darzek said. "The victim of one might seem to have died without cause."

"We've had agents on Kamm for more than a hundred years. We know the diseases. A pazul caused those deaths."

Darzek remained unconvinced, but at least he finally had an inkling of what was bothering Rok Wllon. The Department of Uncertified Worlds occasionally lost an agent, through accident or disease, but one in a hundred years would have been a reasonable average. If nine had died within a short time, there assuredly was something wrong on the world of Kamm.

"Tell me about Kamm," he said.

"It's the Silent Planet," Kom Rmmon whispered.

"What's so horrifying about that? Surely there's no natural law that requires a world's life forms to develop and retain a sense of hearing. Obviously the Kammian life forms have managed to survive and evolve without one, and even to create a civilization. What is there about Kamm that has to be kept secret from Supreme?"

"The pazul."

"Does Kamm have space travel, or anything approaching it?"

"No. Its technology is at level three."

Darzek felt increasingly perplexed. Kamm's technology ranked slightly below that of Earth during the Middle Ages. He asked slowly, "Why should Supreme care if an Uncertified World without space travel has a pazul? At worst, the people of Kamm can only destroy themselves. The Synthesis never intervenes in the internal affairs of such a world."

Kom Rmmon's blue-tinted expression was anguished. "There's a Mandate."

"Ah! What is it?"

"An Uncertified World with a pazul must be destroyed."

Darzek pursed his lips for a silent whistle. Supreme's Mandates dated from a distant past long since forgotten except by Supreme. Obviously in some crisis at the dawn of the galactic government's history a pazul had been flaunted, and Supreme's designers had provided the computer with an automatic response. Supreme learned new facts with appalling ease, but it had difficulty in unlearning old solutions; and it possessed a stubborn craftiness in its fondness for supporting old solutions with new facts. Darzek had attempted unsuccessfully on more than one occasion to reform Supreme's thinking.

Normally the only harm done was measured in inefficiency. Supreme could not be changed, but with patience, bureaucrats could be taught when to ignore a computer and what information to conceal from it.

But a Mandate was a procedure Supreme could carry out itself. It was programmed to react to certain situations with automatic orders to whomever or whatever was best placed to accomplish the Mandate. Once Supreme had positive proof of a pazul on Kamm, it would use whatever means were at hand and destroy the planet.

No wonder Rok Wllon had built an eavesdrop-proof conference room! The Director of the Department of Uncertified Worlds maintained a love-hate attitude toward his charges. He deplored their depraved conduct, their stunted moral senses, their barbarian institutions; but let an outsider utter a word of criticism, and Rok Wllon girded himself for the defense. If a Mandate required the destruction of one of his worlds, he would seek to prevent it with any legal means at hand.

But he would be incapable of resorting to an illegal means, however unjust the Mandate. He would keep a rumor, an assumption, a speculation from Supreme—but on a discretionary basis only while he investigated it thoroughly. Once he found proof, he would feel duty-bound to report it. No doubt this dilemma had brought about his peculiar conduct. He was obligated to search for proof, and he feared that he would find it.

Darzek said, "I come from an Uncertified World. My planet has developed atomic weapons, and probably laser beams that could kill at enormous distances, or microwaves that would cook a victim's liver before he became aware of it, or instruments to produce far worse atrocities that I couldn't even guess at. What's to prevent Supreme from deciding that my world has a pazul and proceeding to destroy it?"

"The death ray does not burn or cook or explode. It simply stops life."

It sounded like a non-answer to Darzek, but obviously Kom Rmmon did not know a better one. "What do the Kammian poems have to do with this?" he asked.

"They are evidence of a death cult on Kamm. Because of the pazul, the director thought."

"And the director went to Kamm to investigate in person. What has he learned?"

"I don't know."

"When did you hear from him last?"

"We haven't heard from him since he left Slonfus."

"Why haven't you asked your agents on Kamm about him?"

"They know nothing about him. They didn't know he was coming. He didn't want them to know."

"Had he been to Kamm before?"

"Yes. He went there several times to help look for the missing agents."

Rok Wllon was a veteran of service on many worlds, and he knew how to handle himself in any situation. But if he had been on Kamm for more than a cycle without sending back a single message, it was time someone in the Department of Uncertified Worlds faced up to the fact that the nine missing agents had become ten.

There was no point in alarming Kom Rmmon further. Darzek said, "If a world with a level three technology has a pazul, obviously it came from another world. The problem is to figure out who brought it there and why."

Kom Rmmon blurted, "Impossible!"

Contact of any kind with an Uncertified World was forbidden. The law was strict, the punishment severe, and as far as Darzek knew, there'd never been a violation; but it seemed silly to accept the existence of a death ray on a world with a level three, vegetable technology without even suspecting that it could have come from somewhere else.

A star map of the Kamm sector was displayed on the wall. Darzek went to look at it and quickly assured himself that a technologically advanced Synthesis world was the only possible source for the alleged pazul. Kamm's sector was sparsely populated and completely devoid of member worlds; and no inhabited non-member world in the sector had a technology rating remotely suggestive of a capability for interstellar travel. The question, then, was which member world of the Galactic Synthesis was responsible for the pazul on Kamm, and Darzek had his own method for checking that.

But even when he found out, the solution of the Kamm problem was certain to require more resourcefulness and initiative than could be expected of a bureaucrat. He said to Kom Rmmon, "What would I have to do in order to go to Kamm?"

Back in his own office, Darzek composed himself for an exceptionally tricky interview. He had to find out what Supreme knew about Kamm. Specifically, he had to find out why Supreme had listed Kamm as a potential trouble spot. Did Supreme already suspect the existence of a pazul on Kamm?

Darzek first requested reports on several worlds from Supreme's crisis list. Kamm was the only Uncertified World on the list, and the information Supreme supplied was a précis of reports filed by Synthesis agents over the years. It concerned geography, geology, sociology, religion, technology, politics, culture—a thorough summary, and it took Darzek more than an hour to read it.

For another hour he simply sat and thought—the outwitting of a world-sized computer was not a venture to be undertaken casually—and then he composed a request for Supreme. He cited the reference number of Supreme's listing of Potential Trouble Sources, added a heading, "World Listed in Error," and then he wrote, "Kamm. There is no justification for this listing in the information supplied. Please explain."

Supreme responded instantly: The reference number, Darzek's sub-heading, "World Listed in Error," and then a comment. "Kamm: Deleted because no justification for this listing appears in the information available."

Darzek studied that for a long time. Supreme's thought processes were forever a mystery, but he knew that Kamm wouldn't have been listed as a Potential Trouble Source without an apparently good reason. Somewhere in Supreme's infinite maze of cross references was the hint of a crisis on Kamm; but obviously Supreme could not produce that particular cross reference again unless someone posed the pertinent problem or asked the right question.

After a time Darzek gave up and went to see E-Wusk. The old trader sat amid the swirling turmoil of his business office, surrounded by clerks and seemingly carrying on a dozen transactions simultaneously. What Darzek had to say was too private for any office, even with the clerks banished to adjoining rooms, so he carried the protesting E-Wusk off to the structure Rok Wllon had fashioned. Kom Rmmon accompanied them to open the conference room, and then he left them there.

Darzek told E-Wusk what he had learned from Kom Rmmon.

"I've never heard of a pazul," E-Wusk protested.

"Probably they don't turn up very often in interstellar trade," Darzek said. "I'm not even sure what one is. I wish I knew what Supreme thinks one is, but I agree with Rok Wllon that this isn't the most propitious moment for mentioning pazuls to Supreme. Supreme has been known to draw conclusions from the questions we ask. Do you know of any way to override a Mandate?"

"No."

"Nor do I. Have you ever heard of a Mandate with such a severe obligatory penalty?"

"No."

"Nor have I. Now answer this. If it should prove true that the world of Kamm has an unlikely genius who has somehow managed to produce something Supreme considers a pazul, how is Supreme going to carry out the Mandate?"

E-Wusk opened his oversized mouth and then said nothing. He sat perplexedly elongating and then contracting one of his limbs.

"Precisely," Darzek said. "In the days when that Mandate was formulated, the Galactic Synthesis no doubt had a well-armed space navy that was subject to Supreme's orders. But that's ancient history. Today we have space law and order and no navy. No armed force of any kind. Weapons capable of destroying a world have been suppressed. So how is Supreme going to carry out that Mandate?"

"It couldn't," E-Wusk said.

"Would you guarantee that?"

E-Wusk thought for a moment. "No. We don't know what Supreme is capable of, and there's no way to find out except—"

"Which would be much too late. I've already learned never to underestimate Supreme. Next question. In my opinion, empiricism has limits that don't include pazuls. What could a world like Kamm have to offer that would justify the risk of contact for aliens?

E-Wusk did not hesitate. "Nothing."

"Here's the report on Kamm. Here are the star charts. Let's assume that there has to be something. Tell me what it is and who might want it."

E-Wusk took more than an hour. He studied the report diligently. He studied the star charts. Then he said again, "Nothing. Some of these woods sound interesting, but why pay shipping costs to import a substitute for metal when you already have metal? And there are plenty of interesting woods available legally and at less distance. Kamm is perched out in the center of a sector of Uncertified Worlds where it would have very little trade even if it could be traded with legally. There'd be few trade routes through this sector even if all of the worlds were Synthesis members. No, my friend. If the pazul came from an alien world, you can take it from me that it wasn't used to buy anything."

"That's what I thought, but I wanted your opinion."

"You have it." E-Wusk heaved a sigh. "Do you suppose there really is a pazul?"

"Undoubtedly there's something strange there, and it took the agents by surprise. And we know how the loss of nine agents would affect Rok Wllon. He'd feel personally responsible. He came to that council meeting intending to ask our advice, and we ridiculed him."

"He should have known better than to sing a song to the council," E-Wusk said.

"He thought we would see the same sinister meaning in those words that he did. Either that, or he hoped we'd convince him it wasn't there."

"But this is terrible!" E-Wusk exclaimed. "A member of the Council of Supreme! Missing on an Uncertified World! We can't permit that!"

"It's already happened."

E-Wusk subsided into his tangle of limbs. "Are you going to call a special meeting of the council?"

"No. This isn't a matter to be settled by debate, and I agree with Rok Wllon that the word *pazul* shouldn't be mentioned where Supreme is likely to overhear it. Not unless someone can figure out for certain how Supreme would handle that Mandate."

"Is there anything else I can do for you?"

"One of Rok Wllon's major character defects is that he doesn't tell anyone what he's doing," Darzek said. "I'm telling you. I'm going to Kamm. I'm going to try to find Rok Wllon. I'm going to try to find out what happened to those nine missing agents. I'm going to see exactly what this wood, non-electrical device is that the Department of Uncertified Worlds calls a pazul. While I'm doing all that, I'll send back reports—for your eyes only. They aren't to be discussed with anyone, not even the other councilors, except in this room and under a pledge of secrecy. I don't want Supreme suddenly deciding to destroy Kamm while I'm there working to solve this thing."

He got to his feet. "You're First Councilor in my absence. I have this advice for you. The best way to run an efficient council—especially a Council of Supreme—is to hold meetings as infrequently as possible."

E-Wusk said emotionally, "If nine agents are missing, and now Rok Wllon is missing—take care, Gul Darr!"

"I always do," Darzek said, "except when it interferes with my work. Now I have to turn myself over to the Department of Uncertified Worlds, and I hate to think what it's going to do to me."

CHAPTER 4

The question had been debated before: Did the potential reward from illegal trade justify the risk? Both the law and economics said no. Darzek refused to believe that an entire galaxy of superior intelligences would not produce an occasional crafty individual who could glimpse an illegal fast buck invisible to others and devise a safe way to grab it.

He had arranged a simple precautionary check of his own by having automatic space monitors set throughout the galaxy. Their usefulness in tracing malfunctioning space ships more than justified the expense. Now Darzek could settle the question of illegal trade with Kamm by asking a patrol to tap the monitors in that sector, and he did so.

Then he placed himself at the mercy of the Department of Uncertified Worlds, and twenty minutes after his arrival he was furiously angry at Kom Rmmon, the department, and the world of Kamm. Not even the anesthesia that accompanied his surgery completely quieted him.

Kom Rmmon had waxed enthusiastically over the alleged similarities between Kammians and humans. Darzek received the distinct impression that he could switch species by changing his clothes.

Now he discovered that a few unsubtle differences required drastic modifications in his appearance, and that no one could perform as a Synthesis agent anywhere without extensive training. He entered surgery in an exceedingly angry mood, and he was still angry when he came out of it.

He glared at his bandaged hands and feet, and then he examined his bandaged head in a mirror. "If you don't take good care of my ears," he told the surgeon, "when I return, I'll make you eat them."

The surgeon, a multistalked Padulupe who consumed only liquids, blanched.

There were two methods by which an agent of the Galactic Synthesis was enabled to pass as a native on an Uncertified World. One involved an elaborate disguise—a synthetic epidermis made to duplicate the external characteristics of the native life form and at the same time accommodate the alien agent within it. The other method was to take an agent whose physical appearance was similar to that of the native life form and to erase or modify any conflicting features with surgery.

The Kammians were startlingly human in appearance, but they had no ears, and they did have six fingers on each hand and six toes on each foot. They also had genital organs entirely different in appearance, function, and position from those of humans, but Darzek insisted on his inalienable right to draw the line somewhere.

His ears were removed and placed in deep freeze to await his return. Flesh was drawn smoothly over the aural openings, but his inner ears were not tampered with. He retained enough hearing ability to have the advantage of an extra sense on a world where the natives were deaf; but not so much that he would give himself away by reacting to sounds a native would ignore.

His hands and feet were widened to accommodate an additional finger or toe, and control of these was contrived for him through a process of nerve splitting that seemed miraculous to Darzek but was considered commonplace by his surgeon.

And there were other changes. The surgeon, working from projections of Kammian natives, made numerous minor alterations the way a portrait painter might make final finishing touches: a slight elongation of the eyes, a minute widening of the nostrils, the corners of the mouth turned up, the blond, naturally curly hair darkened and straightened, the color of his irises altered from blue to brown, all mammalian traces excised from his chest. Darzek had to learn to chew with a slight sideways motion, to spit out of the side of his mouth, and to control his tongue. Since the Kammians had no speech, their tongues were much less mobile than those of humans. Sticking out one's tongue on Kamm was more than a breach of propriety; it was a violation of the physiologically impossible.

Darzek knew that Kamm was called the Silent Planet, but he had not contemplated the implications of life on a world where no life form could hear. He was completely unprepared when Kom Rmmon showed him projections of Kammian natives fluttering their twelve fingers with unbelievable rapidity. When finally he had been convinced that the finger movements actually constituted speech, he considered calling the project off.

"Any sensible life form would have learned to read lips," he complained.

Kom Rmmon pointed out that reading the lips of an alien life form speaking an utterly alien language was likely to be as difficult as learning to read a finger language, and Darzek sat back resignedly and watched the projection. His crash educational program was just beginning.

"But keep it to the absolute essentials," he warned Kom Rmmon sternly. "I haven't time for a graduate degree in Kammian culture."

Long before his training was completed, he had a report from the space monitors that ringed the sector in which Kamm was located. These recorded a spectrum of information about every ship that passed within light-years, and this information had been compared with logs of ships known to have been in the sector. There were no unknowns. Every ship entering that sector of space was in fact a governmental ship on a governmental mission. No alien civilization had brought a pazul to Kamm.

Darzek read the report twice. "So," he mused, "the Kammians did it themselves. The problem now is to find out what it is."

The Department of Uncertified Worlds maintained an underground base on the largest of Kamm's five diminutive moons. The base provided storage and laboratory facilities for the use of Kammian agents. Jan Darzek saw it only briefly. He stepped through a transmitter frame on the Department of Uncertified Worlds supply ship and stepped out of a receiver frame in the moon base. Then he skipped aside; a moment later, supply cartons cascaded after him, and an automatic conveyor moved them away.

Darzek wandered about the base and was not surprised to find it deserted. Agents would visit it only on brief errands. Their work had to be done on the planet, and there never were enough of them to do it properly.

He decided not to wait for chance to provide him with an escort. The moon surface transmitter had a dozen destination settings, but only six were listed as bases on the island of Storoz, the center of activity for Synthesis agents. One of those had been crossed off. Darzek punched the setting for Storoz Base 1, the acceptance light flashed, and he asked himself what he had to lose and stepped through to the world of Kamm.

He emerged in a musty-smelling, totally dark room. He shouted; there was no response. He took two steps, and his hands encountered a damp dirt wall. Again a shout brought no response. He turned and fumbled in the opposite direction, and there his hands found a crude stairway fashioned of board steps with dirt packed under them. He climbed them and eventually figured out the trap door at the top. It was double, consisting of a sliding lower door and an upper door that was hinged and opened upward. He stepped through into a dim stone cellar. The transmitter room, a hole dug under it, constituted a secret subbasement.

He found another flight of stairs, this time solidly built of stone. He climbed them and opened the door at the top. He was in a dark hallway, but at the end of it, through a half-open door, he saw a glimmer of light.

Kamm's multiple moons provided just enough illumination for Darzek to glimpse a magnificent sitting room, exquisitely paneled and ornamented with a coffered ceiling. Some of the furnishings were familiar to him from projections he had studied—the mushroom-like stools, the elaborately carved chests of drawers, the half-circle sofa of which the other half was perpendicular and formed the back. He felt his way from object to object, scrutinizing them in the dim light. Some were strange, but he quickly identified one as a sort of loom and guessed that another functioned as a spinning wheel. The thick, marvelously resilient hand-woven carpet, if made available in quantity, would have ruined Earth's oriental rug business.

Darzek called out again and got no answer. He continued to fumble about. Finally he chanced onto what seemed to be a candle holder complete with candle, but he had nothing to light it with.

Windows of the other rooms did not catch the moonlight, and they were, all of them, dark. Darzek seated himself on the half-circle sofa and wondered what he should do. Obviously the agents who operated from this base were out. There was little that he could accomplish before morning, so he decided to go to bed. He didn't feel tired, but the sooner he got his time cycle co-ordinated with that of Kamm, the better.

He fumbled his way up the narrow stairway to the upper story. The moonlight touched one bedroom sufficiently to delineate the bed—a monstrosity that looked somewhat like a giant mushroom with an oversized stem and a flattened top. Darzek thought it symbolic of the problem of Kamm, which thus far he had seen neither head nor tail of. He went to bed and slept restlessly.

On his first morning on the world of Kamm, Darzek was awakened by an execution that took place immediately below his window. The shrieks of torment brought him to the window in a bound. He opened the sash, folded the shutter aside, and looked out.

Dawn was only the faintest figment of the new day's imagination, and all of the moons had set. Looking down on the dim street, which Kammians called a lane, Darzek saw a solitary cart passing, and each of its two wheels was uttering screams of anguish.

Darzek closed shutter and sash and returned to his bed, and before his eyes closed another cart passed by. And another. By the time dawn touched his window, a seemingly endless procession of carts was passing, with one following on the tailgate of another, and Darzek had managed to deduce that this Synthesis headquarters was located on one of the principal lanes, which the Kammians called surlanes, leading to the market place, and that this same excruciating cacophony would take place every market day.

He also had grasped the fact that deafness is synonymous with silence only for the deaf. This world of Kamm, this infamous Silent Planet, was in fact the most revoltingly noisy place he had ever experienced. No New York City traffic jam, even in the days when New York City had traffic, could rival a convoy of Kammian carts on the way to market. The Kammian squeaking wheel never got the grease, because no one heard the squeaking; and the incredibly tough, ridiculously named sponge wood seemed to last forever without lubrication. Every cart and wagon on the entire world of Kamm continuously uttered the pathetic shrieks of a wracked body being dragged to perpetual damnation. The world's ugly beasts of burden, the nabrula, snorted and hissed and moaned and bleated, splendidly oblivious to the fact that neither they, nor their fellow nabrula, nor any other creature native to the planet, could hear them. The Kammians themselves, for all their disconcertingly human appearance, did the same. They hummed and hacked and bellowed and wheezed constantly. Their very digestive noises provided a running counterpoint to every Kammian encounter. There could be no social constraint about noises—any kind of noises—when no one was able to hear them.

When it seemed pointless to remain in bed longer, Darzek began a daylight exploration of the house. He found no signs of recent occupancy. In the kitchen, an unvented stove that looked like a charcoal burner had not been used since being cleaned. In the pantry were bins of native foods and vegetables, none of which looked edible to him; but some of the bins were empty. The perishables had been removed.

He finally found a loaf of stale bread, and when he'd hacked the petrified crust away with a wood knife of surprising sharpness, the interior was quite fresh. It wafted a potent, perfume-like scent, and its taste was spicy and somewhat bitter. He dipped chunks of it into a highly scented, honey-like syrup and washed them down with a delightfully potent cider.

Then he returned to the vantage point of his bedroom window. He watched the passing traffic, and scrutinized the drivers and the occasional pedestrian, until the squinting windows and unbalanced façade of the imposing house across the lane began to irritate him.

He was becoming increasingly disgusted. There was a job to be done, time was critically important, and he couldn't make a move until one of the resident agents returned and showed him what to do. He didn't even know where he was.

Finally he said to himself, "You've got to learn to function on this world. Maybe the most effective way to learn is to walk out of the house and do it."

Major professions and occupations on Kamm had their own distinctive clothing, and Darzek already had noted that the house's occupant was a perfumer, a maker and vendor of perfumes—not only from the clothing, but from the jars and bottles and flasks of liquid scent that cluttered table and bureau tops in every room.

"So I'll be a perfumer," Darzek told himself agreeably. The clothing fit him approximately well, which on the world of Kamm was well enough. He donned a one-piece undersuit with long legs and arms—the climate of Storoz was uniformly cool throughout the year. Leg and foot wrappings served as stockings. There were wide-legged trousers that came to a flapping end just below the knees, cloth-topped high boots with jointed wood soles, a waist-length tunic, a long apron that gave him the feeling of wearing a dress, and, finally, the perfumer's trade-marks: the black and white striped cape and the imposing tall black and white striped hat.

Darzek scrutinized himself in one of the ornately framed mirrors that adorned each bedroom and pronounced the effect adequate. In a drawer he found a ceramic box with an ingeniously hinged lid—a money box. It was half filled with triangular coins of various alloys, each minted with peculiar glyph marks and the image of Kamm's hideous death symbol, the Winged Beast. Darzek helped himself liberally, distributing coins through the several pockets of his cape, his apron, and his trousers. He felt uncomfortable without some suggestion of a weapon, so he picked up a small wood knife in the kitchen. It was as sharp as a razor, and when he tested the blade, he found he could not break it.

He went to the front door, hesitated, decided to investigate the back yard first. Some thirty meters behind the house stood a square building of colored stone resembling that of the house. A narrow walk connected the two; on either side, filling the yard and flowing into neighboring yards, were unbroken waves of flowers.

In the outbuilding Darzek found a perfume factory. Strong-smelling leaves and roots and berries and flowers were hung up or spread out to dry. There were enormous ceramic kettles and crocks, some of them covered and filled with pungent liquids. There was elaborate distilling apparatus and a row of unvented stone fireplaces.

A few perfunctory glances satisfied Darzek. Beyond the perfume factory was a low, flat-topped building that his nose told him must be a stable, even though it had not been used recently. It was empty. A ramp leading up to the roof puzzled him until he looked next door and saw a pair of nabrula, the ugly Kammian beasts of burden, looking down at him. They got their air and exercise on their stable roof and thus avoided tromping their owner's flower-filled yard.

Darzek returned to the house. Again he paused at the front door, and then he stepped through it and turned for a careful look at the front façade of the building. A moment later, walking in the same direction as the now thinning line of vehicles, he set off for the mart.

But he felt alertly cautious, rather than bold. He was accustomed to wandering about on strange worlds, but those worlds were accustomed to the presence of gawking, blundering aliens, of strange aspect, customs, and mannerisms. The world of Kamm did not know of the existence of aliens. If he gawked and blundered, he would be considered a gawking and blundering native and treated as such. Perhaps gawking and blundering had contributed to the loss of those nine or ten Synthesis agents.

He reminded himself not to gawk, and to keep his wits about him so he wouldn't blunder.

But even a seasoned traveler like Darzek found it difficult not to gape about him on his first glimpse of a spectacularly beautiful world. It was hideously noisy; in direct compensation, as though the deaf Kammians had deliberately set about developing their remaining senses, it was vividly, dramatically, extraordinarily colorful.

And it was just as vividly, dramatically, and extraordinarily scented.

The very cobblestones underfoot had been selected for their colors, and they had been laid out by an artist. The varying shades of pink had been sorted and matched and arranged in a fabric of color that formed a magnificent mosaic, a textured pattern that was unending, that caught the eye and carried it as far as any winding section of the lane permitted, with striking visual motifs that received endlessly varied repetitions.

And where each narrow sublane appeared on either side—the city was not laid out in squares, and the lanes came and went haphazardly —colors flowed into colors, for each lane had its own individual shades and hues and patterns.

The stone dwellings were constructed in equally vivid patterns. They were two or three stories tall, set close on the lane with narrow yards at the sides and a vast expanse of yard in the rear—inevitably terminated by a low, flat-roofed nabrula stable.

The yards were filled with flowers, and floral ornaments and displays were seen everywhere. Vines with strikingly colored leaves entwined over lintels, providing splashes of contrast against the softer shades of the stones. Flowers filled windows and lined balconies. The yards were flower gardens without apparent formal planning; but colors shaded into colors and blossoms into strikingly hued foliage.

And on the fronts of the dwellings, placed with artful care, were baskets and ceramic containers of growing and cut flowers.

Kamm, the Silent Planet: World of color and of scent.

Each flower garden wafted such potent blendings of perfume that Darzek thought the owners arranged the plants as much for their scents as for their colors. And in the entranceway of each house, an alcove in which the door was set, hung a large ceramic beehive of a contraption, fashioned with artist's care and fired with splendid multicolored glazes. It was an incense burner. Each poured out its own highly individual scent: pungent, spicy, sweet, or bitter; or it burned a blended, delicate orchestration of scents. Did each householder have his own aromatic insignia? Or was the scent perhaps a greeting or a signal to the passer-by: welcome, stop in any time. Or—busy today, come back tomorrow. Darzek pondered the labyrinthine twists and turns of the alien mentality and was awed.

There was a scattering of pedestrians in sight, all of them headed in the same direction as Darzek. For a time Darzek observed the couple walking in front of him, probably a husband and wife. In the fashion of Kammian females, each plait of the wife's enormously long hair had been dyed a different color. These were piled into a towering headdress, where they were woven into vividly contrasting patterns. This edifice was a suitable companion piece for the tall, patterned hat of her husband; the two structures attained approximately the same altitude.

The female wore a tunic and flopping trousers matching those of her husband, but hers were in variegated color patterns where his were the solid colors of his profession. Her trousers were longer, extending to her ankles, and she seemed to be wearing low-topped shoes instead of boots. Her attire looked more masculine than her husband's because she wore no artisan's apron.

Darzek assiduously studied the male for a time—his gait; his mannerisms; the way he carried his hands when he walked; his chivalrous posture in politely bending over his wife's flickering fingers when she spoke to him, as though every syllable had monumental importance to him and he wanted her to know it.

The lane veered again, and its rows of residences ended at a broad boulevard. It continued on the opposite side as a lane of artisan's shops. He could see the mart beyond, with its makeshift avenues of tents, booths, wagons, carts. Darzek turned and strolled along the boulevard. Here the buildings were enormous—office warehouses, he speculated, for shipping and importing companies; through the mingled aromas that impinged on him from all sides, he had caught the tang of sea air.

He crossed to the stretch of park that lay in the middle of the boulevard. Stone paths crisscrossed it; rocks of striking shape or color were piled up in seemingly haphazard fashion, but these were used as seats by resting pedestrians. Around them grew lush plants and shrubs of such peculiar form and coloration that Darzek guessed them to be exotic imports. Vendors were selling food and beverages.

Darzek found himself a seat on a large rock and watched the passersby. Almost at once he made an important discovery. When two males of the same craft or profession met, they exchanged signals that varied with the occupation and sometimes were extremely complicated. For one purple-patterned pair, an uplifted palm. For a pair with green and black, a hand gripping the wrist. For one with pink and white, a bent elbow. The only exception occurred when one male was carrying something. Then both exchanged shrugs.

Darzek continued to watch. Eventually he saw two perfumers exchange their own mystic salute: Index finger of right hand held against the nose. Darzek got to his feet and walked on.

A moment later he was confidently exchanging the finger-against-nose signal with a fellow perfumer. He crossed to the far side of the boulevard and strolled down one of the narrow lanes of artisan shops, marveling at the variety and quality of workmanship—carvings, furniture, jewelry, knickknacks, every kind of item he could think of and not a few whose function he could not imagine, all fashioned exquisitely out of wood. There were lovely ceramics in dazzling colors, masterfully woven rugs and cloths, varieties of baskets and containers that looked like wickerwork. Occasionally he saw a representation of the hideous Winged Beast, the mythical symbol of Kamm's death religion, in plaques, ornaments, or jewelry. He was surprised to see it so seldom. It seemed to play a much more minor part in Kammian thought than Rok Wllon had believed.

He had seen both men and women carrying thin sided ceramic pots with gaping mouths, a sort of shopping bag into which they stuffed their purchases. He also had observed that the Kammian with his hands occupied was excused from the amenities of greetings or casual conversation.

"When in doubt," he told himself, "keep your hands shut."

He stopped at a ceramics shop and bought a pot. He found it astonishingly light. As he moved on down the street he added a few casual purchases that he thought he couldn't go wrong on—a bundle of scented candles, a chunk of exquisitely scented soap, a pie-shaped loaf of bread that seemed as strongly perfumed as the soap and was handed to him wrapped in a thin, crinkly substance he was unable to identify. With these credentials as a shopper and householder, and relieved of any obligation to make conversation, he blithely strolled on.

Now he was able to study the Kammians at close range. They were a sturdy race. The females, once he became accustomed to their outlandish hairdos, were handsome with a well-built rustic appeal. The flowing garments hinted at sensational Earth-type figures, which of course was an impossibility. The Kammians gave birth to live, dependent young, but they were not mammals. The males were stocky and robust.

Then he made a shattering discovery.

The Kammians were as fascinated with him as he was with them. Each person he passed turned and looked after him perplexedly.

Dumfoundedly he walked on, staring straight ahead of him in frozen bewilderment. He was dressed flawlessly, he was acting his role perfectly, he looked and behaved like the complete Kammian. And in this mundane little lane, with its throngs of coming and going shoppers, he stood out like an alien thumb.

CHAPTER 5

An instant later he realized what was wrong. The passers-by who turned to look after him were *sniffing* perplexedly.

Then he remembered the startling array of perfumes at the Synthesis headquarters. They were not there because the agent who occupied the house acted the role of a perfumer. They were there because he acted the role of a Kammian.

Kom Rmmon had mentioned that scent dominated Kammian psychology even more than color and touch. Everything was scented—candles, soap, bread, cider, cloth, everything. And every adult Kammian had personal perfumes for varying personal moods. Such scents were not the pungent aromas of incense one encountered at the doors of dwellings, but a subtle blending of fragrances that suggested something of the body rather than a concoction applied to it.

To meet a Kammian without a personal perfume was unheard of, and Darzek wore no perfume. No wonder passers-by turned and sniffed perplexedly!

Darzek's instant reaction would have been to buy himself some perfume and splash it on. Before he could act, he received another jolting revelation. The garments he wore identified him as a perfume maker. A Kammian without perfume was a freak, but a professional perfumer without perfume was unthinkable! He stood out in that crowded lane like a nude at a formal banquet, and there was nothing he could do about it. An unperfumed perfumer buying from a competitor would attract the attention of everyone in sight.

He stopped at the next soapmaker's shop and bought two large chunks of the most pungently scented soap in stock. At a neighboring shop he bought a bundle of foully reeking leaves, though he had no notion of what they were used for. He had the immediate satisfaction of being ignored by those he met.

A few moments later, the question of a personal scent for Darzek became irrelevant. He had reached the mart, where many vendors worked from carts or wagons, and each vehicle had been hauled to the mart by one or more of the ungainly nabrula. Each nabrulk possessed its own sulfurous odor and in addition was polluting the mart atmosphere with piles of incongruously small, noisome pellets.

This supplied Darzek with another puzzle concerning alien psychology. So acute was the Kammian sense of smell, so subtly attuned to the delicacies of scent, that it instantly detected a passer-by without perfume; and yet it could tolerate the stench of nabrula manure. He wondered if the Kammians were able to sniff selectively, to tune out the familiar odors that displeased them, just as a musician on Earth could sit surrounded by a trashy music he despised and not hear a note of it.

At the center of the mart, towering above the vendors, were the dual symbols of the religions of Storoz. Erected atop a slender pole was a soaring image of the hideous Winged Beast. Nearby stood the lofty, pyramidal Mound of the Sun. Darzek postponed studying them until he reached a closer vantage point. He strolled along the rows of carts and tents and booths, marveling again at the variety of goods and produce offered for sale and enjoying himself immensely. Kammians were enthusiastic and voluble hagglers. Fingers fluttered at dazzling speeds as vendor and customer shouted at each other in silent, simultaneous outbursts.

There also were artists present, sculpting relief plaques from life or painting and selling abstracts with dazzling color combinations. And there was an occasional poet, reciting an epic of ancient grandeur to a small audience that sometimes parted with a lead coin or two in response but more often turned away in boredom.

Darzek reached the end of the row of vendors, and abruptly he found himself looking into a long, narrow amphitheater. Its sloping sides were thronged with spectators. At the bottom, facing each other on foot, some ten meters apart, were two armed gladiators, one with a red cloak and the other with purple.

They were massive individuals, with long mustaches to match their beefy builds. Their armor was of leather: Each wore a knee-length tunic of a peculiar leather mail, a leather helmet, and leather leg guards and gloves. Strapped to the left arm was a leather shield. The right hand held a whip, its long lash coiled peculiarly and poised for action. The left hand carried another whip with a number of short lashes attached—the Kammian version of the cat-o'-nine-tails, except that there were more than nine and the lashes were not knotted.

The red gladiator took a step forward. Suddenly the purple opponent's long lash snapped. Red caught the vicious stroke on his shield and snapped a return stroke that the other side-stepped. They maneuvered, cautiously edging sideways, feinting whip strokes.

Darzek quickly found the spectacle boring. He turned his attention to the Kammians, who were tense with excitement. Doubtlessly they sensed a strategy of maneuver, of psychological intimidation, that was beyond his perception. He saw only a couple of costumed buffoons waving whips at each other.

Then the sudden intake of breath by the hundreds of spectators produced an audible effect, uncanny in the continuing silence that had been punctuated only by whip cracks. Darzek turned quickly. Purple had aimed a low stroke that coiled about red's leg. He jerked the whip. Red struggled frantically to keep his balance—and failed. As he toppled, purple raced toward him with hand whip ready to flail—but red, from a prone position, snapped off a stroke with the long lash. It cut like a lightning flash, and Darzek never saw the flickering end of it.

Neither did purple. Rashly charging in for the kill, his shield poorly positioned, he was struck full in the face. Blood spurted from a horrible mutilation. A ribbon of flesh hung from his face, and his eye had vanished. He reeled backward, defenseless, his entire body contorted with shock and pain, as red regained his feet and sprang toward him with hand whip poised. An official suddenly darted between them waving a banner.

Darzek turned to the spectators. Everywhere he looked, he saw fluttering fingers. For a moment he was too shaken to read them.

Then he understood. All hands were spelling out, over and over, *Blood! Blood! Blood!*

As Darzek turned away, the loser was being helped from the field. The winner stood in the center of the amphitheater, proudly holding the banner of victory aloft, and the audience was tossing coins to him.

Such were the knights of Kamm.

Such were the Kammians. Darzek had been condescendingly viewing this healthy, sturdy, well-balanced, creative people as almost human. Now he saw them as entirely too human, and their whip had to be one of the most infamous creations of any intelligence. The deadly sjambok of Africa seemed a toy by comparison.

He turned for a final glance at the arena. The next entrants were mounted. One knight sat at either end of the amphitheater on a pawing nabrulk, waiting while the official picked up the winning knight's money.

Still shaken by the bloody combat he had seen, Darzek returned to the cluttered mart and took a diagonal lane that led directly to the religious monuments. There he stood for a moment, looking from the colorful pyramid to the grim black symbol on the pole. They were light and darkness, or good and evil, or life and death—a dualism probably present in every religious consciousness; a conundrum posed on every world that had given birth to intelligent life. It seemed predictable to Darzek that this bright, peaceful, essentially good people, who could attend a gladiatorial combat and chant—with fluttering fingers—*Blood!*, should wage a bitter struggle among themselves as to whether they should worship life or death.

The Mound of the Sun was a monument to life—a life pyramid. It was not a cold edifice of tooled or polished stone, but a warm memorial to the living, vibrant with the color and beauty of growing plants and flowers. Paths meandered about it, in gradual ascents, and colored rocks sparkled amid the greenery. The Kammians left their market purchases in orderly rows about its base to climb it, whether a short distance or all the way to the tiny park-like area on its truncated apex, and to sit and meditate the beauties and mysteries of life or perhaps just to admire the view.

The companion monument was stark by comparison—a stereotyped representation of the fabled Winged Beast in a gigantic wood carving: wings outspread, the long, vicious fangs that filled the tapering snout bared, talons poised threateningly, and the whole painted a gleaming black. It towered almost twenty meters above the market on its slender pole. At its base stood two young males in black clothing and black capes—lackeys of the Winged Beast, or apprentice priests, or student soldiers.

In contrast to the relaxed crowds on the Mound of the Sun, few people came near the stark symbol of death. Those who did had a furtive air, as though they were paying off a blackmailer. They fumbled among their purchases and then approached the monument timorously. One of the apprentice priests handed out slender pointed sticks that looked like enormous toothpicks. On these the faithful impaled their offerings—pieces of meat, or bread, or cake, or other edibles. Bowing reverently with a queer, sidewise genuflection, they stepped into the black circle formed at the base of the pole by a mosaic of ebony-colored stones. They inserted the offering stick into one of the multitude of holes bored into the pole for that purpose. Then they backed away, hands raised pleadingly, eyes on the menacing Beast, until they reached their possessions.

They scurried off like one who has had a death sentence repealed.

Light and darkness; life and death.

Darzek set down his shopping pot and climbed the life pyramid all the way to the top. Looking over at the soaring Winged Beast, he pondered the sinister darkness in a people's soul that could call forth such a symbol, and he wondered what the missing Synthesis agents could have told him about that darkness.

The city lay to the south. From Darzek's vantage point he watched plodding nabrula pulling carts and wagons along the lanes; saw the scattered forums, the neighborhood markets, where women and children did their daily shopping or drew water from wells; saw the racks of wood curing behind the craft establishments; saw the hand-woven rugs airing; saw a thin haze of pollution rising from soap and candlemakers' factories. He reflected again that the idea of a pazul being developed in such a society was preposterous.

He moved around the pyramid and looked down on the harbor, where clumsy but colorful rectangular-sailed ships were maneuvering to their dockage. He asked himself whether even the most eccentric genius would waste time on death rays, or even conceive of such a thing, with the need for technological improvements everywhere evident. He muttered aloud, "Preposterous!" Then he winced and looked about him; but the female and three children seated nearby had of course heard nothing. They were looking out to sea—the wife and children of a sailor, perhaps, come to watch the absent one's ship return to port. The two daughters were amusing little replicas of their mother, their hair dyed and put up in identical patterns. The son wore a green sailor's garb. It was a charming family group, touchingly awaiting a re-union, and Darzek watched it with pleasure before turning away. A pazul? Preposterous!

At least he now knew where he was. The harbor faced north, and there was only one such port on the island: Northpor, one of the five Free Cities that were the property of the powerful Sailor's League.

He circled back for another look at the city before descending. He suddenly had become worried about finding his way home, and he wanted to trace his route. He took one look at the street pattern and froze.

He had thought all he needed to do was find a pink lane.

But all of the surlanes, the main traffic arteries, were paved with pink stone.

Wearily Darzek made his way down the pyramid. He was hungry and tired. His arms ached from carrying the shopping pot. He was ready to go home, wherever or whatever home was. He picked up his pot and walked away, trying to visualize the house he would have to find.

Hands seized him and threw him to the ground. His pot shattered; the contents went sprawling. Looking up, he saw one of the black-caped assistant priests positioned over him with a multiple-thonged hand whip upraised.

Darzek launched himself at the priest's legs and sent him toppling backward. The same instant the priest crashed to the pavement, Darzek was on his feet. He leaped aside as the second black-cape's whip came down. One lash struck his arm, sliced through the tunic, left a line of oozing blood. Stung by the pain, enraged at the unexpected, cowardly attack, Darzek seized the young priest, picked him up bodily, and hurled him at his fellow, who had just regained his feet and was advancing menacingly with whip upraised. Both crashed to the ground, and neither moved.

Darzek looked about him, hand pressed to his bleeding arm. He stood in the black circle at the base of the soaring Winged Beast, and he was surrounded by black-caped, whip-armed priests. They advanced on him slowly, in a tightening circle. He saw no way through it, so he stood still and waited.

Then one priest stepped out of the circle and approached him. Darzek acted before he could raise his whip. He charged, dove, knocked the priest backward. The two of them crashed through the circle, taking another pair of priests with them. The three priests landed heavily, with Darzek atop the one he had charged. He sprang to his feet at once and darted away.

He did not look back until he had reached the first row of vendors; but the priests were not following him. They stood quietly in a group, and a male in sailor's garb, wearing the high hat of a captain, was facing them.

Darzek did not wait for the denouement. He quickly lost himself in the crowd of shoppers. A moment later he encountered the sign of a manipulator, a doctor of external medicine. (A doctor of internal medicine was called a purger.) He went in and for a copper coin had his wound dressed. The doctor applied a fragrant herbal liquid to the bandage and tied it expertly. He asked no question about the source of the wound, which was just as well—Darzek hadn't been able to think of an answer. He preferred not to admit that he had absently—and stupidly—walked through the holy circle of the Winged Beast, and a priest had whipped him.

He bought another pot and filled it with strongly scented merchandise. Then he left the mart, walking up one of the narrow lanes of artisans to the boulevard, where he seated himself in the park, bought a goblet of cider from a vendor, and in addition treated himself to a strange sort of sandwich which was a small loaf of pie-shaped bread with the meat filling intermixed and baked with the dough. It made a satisfying meal for him and gave him some fortification for the trek home.

He walked along the boulevard, studying the pink cobblestoned surlanes that connected with it. He had no difficulty in picking out the one he had traveled that morning. He followed it for more than a kilometer, and suddenly it took a sharp zig he did not remember and widened into a flower bedecked oval he knew he had not seen before.

He turned back immediately, found the boulevard again, and picked another surlane. This time he was certain he had the right one, but he walked all the way to the city gates without recognizing the house he was seeking.

At dusk he was back at the boulevard again. He selected another lane and walked it until the darkness became total and he no longer could distinguish the color patterns of the houses.

Not until then did he admit that he was hopelessly lost.

CHAPTER 6

It was midnight, with all of Kamm's moons high in the sky, when Darzek found the warehouse. He knew that he could not go on much longer, that he had to find a place to rest. The crowning irony was that by Kammian standards he was rich. The coins he had picked up so casually amounted to a small fortune; and yet he had no notion of how to find an inn or even a flophouse. He did not even know whether Kamm had such things.

He needed a place to rest, but he also had to contrive a new disguise that he could wear with confidence. After the fiasco in the mart, every black-caped priest in Northpor would be on the lookout for the perfumer who had profaned the holy circle. He had to find the uniform of a different occupation, preferably one that he could perform; and as far as he knew, on the entire world of Kamm there wasn't any.

Peering through a window, he saw, in the warehouse's dimly moonlit interior, a bin filled with something that might have been clothing. The building's door was multiply hinged and secured with a crude wood lock. Reminding himself that noise didn't matter, Darzek pounded the tough wood with a rock and failed to dent it. Then he remembered his knife, and he quickly picked it.

He opened one of the hinged sections and slipped silently into the building. For a dozen steps he tiptoed. Then he stomped a foot and said aloud, sternly, "You don't have to, dammit! You can fall over things and slam doors and break everything in the place, and no one can hear you!"

The habits of a lifetime did not respond to logic. He continued to tiptoe.

He went directly to the bin; but the contents proved to be large sacks of a coarsely woven material. These would have provided him with a bed, but he knew that anyone finding a professional craftsman, a perfumer, asleep in such a place would have his curiosity aroused in more ways than Darzek was prepared to satisfy.

Darzek felt his way from bin to bin, still walking quietly; but the other bins were empty or contained only more sacks. Despairingly he turned to leave.

A faint noise overhead caused him to look up. A large trap door in the ceiling was open. So was a vent in the roof directly above it. A stream of moonlight clearly delineated the face peering down at him.

It was a child, a female whose Earth age might have been nine or ten. Her appearance starkly contrasted with those of the children Darzek had seen in the mart that day. Her hair was its natural, rather grubby color, arranged in a matted tangle instead of a piled hairdo. She was skinny and obviously undernourished, and she had an unwashed, unhealthy look about her. She wore only an undergarment, something like a baggy slip of coarse cloth.

She leaned forward, and her fingers moved. *What are you looking for?*

He hesitated. Then, feeling that he had nothing to lose, he raised his hands and answered. *Clothes.*

The dark, serious eyes regarded him steadily. Then her fingers spoke again. *Come up.*

Before Darzek could reply, a rope ladder dropped through the opening. He regarded it uncertainly for a moment; but he still had nothing to lose, so he climbed up.

The child had disappeared when he reached the top. The upper floor had rows of giant crocks down the center and along the walls were enormous bins filled with grain. Darzek looked about for the child.

She stepped from behind a crock at the far end of the building and gestured to him. She had raised a section of the flooring, and she was fumbling in a sack like those he'd seen on the lower level. It was her secret hiding place, and from it she was pulling garments and arranging them into sets.

Whose clothing is it? Darzek asked, holding his fingers under her nose as he spoke because the light there was dim. He didn't want the child to get into trouble.

My father's, she answered.

Darzek held his fingers under her nose again. *Where's your father?*

The Winged Beast took him.

He examined one of the sets of clothing. It was work apparel, dull brown in color, and it seemed clean and smelled fresh, but there was no hat or cape or apron.

He asked, *What was your father's work?*

Sweep, she answered.

Earlier that night he had seen crews of males in the distance, sweeping nabrula manure from the lanes by torchlight. By sheer accident he had found clothing for the one job on Kamm he could perform.

The child disappeared the moment he began to undress. He stripped to his undergarment. Then he removed all of the coins from his perfumer's clothing and fashioned a money belt from a leg wrapping he found with her father's clothing. He concealed most of the coins around his waist. Then he dressed himself.

When he finished, he saw the child standing on a crock at the other end of the building, looking out of a high window. He wondered how she lived and whether anyone looked after her. When she saw him walking toward her, she scrambled down and hurried to meet him. He held up his discarded perfumer's clothing. *Can this be sold?*

She fingered it as carefully as a tailor, examining with a scowl the cut left by the whip, holding the cape up to the light to inspect its lining. *Yes,* she answered.

Will you accept it in payment for your father's clothing?

She smiled and hunched her shoulder affirmatively.

Where do you live?

She gestured. *Here.*

She was a street urchin. He should have been aware that even such a prosperous and beautiful city as Northpor would have its slums, its poor, and its destitute, who lived where they could and scrounged for survival. Perhaps her father had been employed in some way by the warehouse's owner, and she knew her way in and out and simply continued to live there, in hiding.

They smiled at each other. Her youthful features gave Darzek a new insight into feminine beauty on Kamm: large eyes and perfect features; and, without the towering hairdo and ornate clothing, a delightful, unspoiled freshness.

Her smile illuminated even such drab surroundings as these.

He asked her, *Is there a safe place to sleep?*

She led him to the side of one of the bins and removed a panel. The bin's bottom was slanted steeply to facilitate the flow of grain, leaving a vacant, triangular space between its bottom and the warehouse floor. Sacks were piled there. Darzek crawled into the inviting opening as far as he could and stretched out on the coarse material. He was completely exhausted. He turned to look back; she had replaced the panel. "The time to worry about tomorrow is when it happens," he told himself. He fell asleep at once.

When he awoke, he could see light through cracks in the end panel. He turned over and stretched. Pain stabbed at his wounded arm, which was throbbing alarmingly. He crawled toward the light and carefully removed his bandage. His entire arm was swollen, but there seemed to be no sign of infection. Awkwardly he replaced the bandage, and then he sat back to meditate his hunger and think what he should do.

His career as a sweep would have to be postponed until he could move his arm effectively. He closed his eyes and reviewed again his blundering attempt to locate the Synthesis headquarters. He had not bothered to learn the cumbersome written language of Storoz. Only a special class of scribes had acquired that knowledge, so it had seemed unlikely that Darzek's ignorance would embarrass him; but evidently the average citizen had sufficient mastery of the strange glyphs to recognize street signs and his own house number. Darzek had thought he would have no problem in recognizing the glyph above the lintel on the Synthesis headquarters, but on his return, all such designs looked alike to him. He'd thought he couldn't mistake the pastel-shaded stone of the house and its distinctive pattern, but he'd found a hundred buildings on each lane that looked identical.

Perhaps the beehive-like incense burner would provide him with the clue he needed. The one at the Synthesis headquarters had not been in use, and he had puzzled over its function before setting out. As soon as night came, he should be able to walk about in his sweep clothing and look for a burned-out incense burner.

"Unless," he told himself ruefully, "they let all of them go out at night."

The panel opened and the girl looked in. She handed something to him.

It was a sandwich of bread and meat, such as he had eaten the day before. He accepted it with a smile. She ducked back out of sight and returned to offer him a crude wood mug filled with cool cider.

Again she vanished, and this time she returned with a sandwich and mug for herself. She sat down on the pile of sacks and kept her eyes on him while they ate in silence. When they finished, she placed the mugs and the crinkly wrappings from the sandwiches outside the opening. Then she sat back and continued to watch Darzek.

He slipped his sleeve down and showed her the awkwardly tied bandage. She immediately moved to his side, removed the bandage, studied the wound for a moment, and then replaced the bandage, tying it gently but firmly.

She resumed her place, once again keeping her eyes on him. He wondered if she had sold the perfumer's clothing to buy their food, and if she would be offended if he offered her money. Finally he handed her some coins and told her, *For our next meal.*

She smiled at him.

There was much that he wanted to ask her, but he would have to shape his questions so as not to arouse her suspicions. He decided to begin by stating the obvious. He could not remember the fingering for "stranger," so he said, *I am a non-citizen.*

She made no comment.

He asked, *How would I get work as a sweep?*

Go at night and see if they need anyone, her hands replied.

Do they often need anyone?

No.

Probably it was a universal law. There always were more unskilled applicants than there were jobs. *Is there any other work I could get?* he asked.

I'll look, she said.

She left, taking the mugs and wrappings with her, and she replaced the panel. Darzek waited until the sounds of her departure had faded, and then he eased the panel aside and cautiously looked out. He had heard no activity in or about the building, and he quickly discovered that it was deserted.

He climbed onto a crock and looked out of a high window. In his meanderings the night before he had lost his sense of direction. Now he saw how far he'd wandered from the center of the city. Only the Winged Beast and the top of the life pyramid were visible above the buildings to mark the site of the distant mart. His hiding place was one of a cluster of warehouses located along the shore. In the opposite direction he could see the city wall and rolling country beyond, marked off in small land holdings.

Several ships were tied up at the docks, and workers swarmed about them. Stevedores, carts, wagons, and a type of two-wheeled barrow were involved in the unloadings, but no part of the cargoes seemed destined for the empty bins or crocks in this warehouse. He contined to move from window to window, studying his surroundings and exercising his sore arm.

Now he regretted discarding the perfumer's clothing. He didn't know whether he dared move about freely and purchase necessities for himself as an unemployed sweep. He had a temporary refuge, but he was dependent on the child for food and drink. His position actually seemed worse than it had been the previous night. He paced about the enormous room, continuing to exercise his arm, and the day slowly waned to dusk.

Then the child returned. She said nothing at all to him, since her hands were full. She brought a sandwich for each of them, and she made a second trip up the rope ladder with the refilled mugs. This time they sat on the overturned bottom of a broken crock to eat. Again she kept her eyes on Darzek.

When they had finished, she gathered up the sandwich wrappings and the mugs and carefully wrapped them in a piece of sacking that she slung over her shoulder. Then her hands formed a word. *Come.*

Once again Darzek decided he had nothing to lose. He followed her.

They descended a simple wood ladder in the far corner of the building and crawled through a window casement into a shed attached to the warehouse. She removed a piece of the shed's wall, which provided an exit hidden behind a row of crocks. Darzek followed her through the narrow opening. She replaced the wall after them and hurried ahead to guide him.

Night was coming on quickly as they moved along the docks. The stevedores had finished their day's work and left; candles glimmered in the ships' cabins, and a few sailors were returning to their ships from forays on the mart, their arms laden with purchases.

They followed the docks to the far end of the harbor, where the shore curved sharply outward to form one of the two protective arms that almost enclosed the Bay of Northpor. There the haphazard array of warehouses gave way to majestic logs stored in carefully sited, crisscrossed piles. The storage area was checkerboarded with wagon paths, and they followed one of them. At the far side they came to a road that led directly to a gate in the city wall just beyond. Parked beside the road was a caravan, an enormous wagon with a wood building perched awkwardly on its box. Gathered around it, in the light of a cluster of flares, were the dregs of Northpor—the poor, the halt, the diseased. They were applying for work.

Darzek moved close enough to the flares so they could see to talk. He asked the child, *What sort of work?*

Forest, she answered.

Is it good work?

Her face brightened. *Yes. Good.*

Did your father do that kind of work?

Once. Before he was hurt.

Obviously the scruffy applicants thought it good work. They seemed pathetically eager.

But the employers weren't hiring just anyone. There were two doctors present, a purger and a manipulator, and both had to approve an applicant before the three males in dusky green work clothing would look at him. Those the doctors accepted were waved to a log that lay on the ground near the caravan. They had to pick it up and walk the length of the caravan and back with it. Few of the applicants got past the doctors, and few of those who did were able to pass the strength test.

Where is the forest? Darzek asked the child.

She pointed southward. Then her hands answered, *A night and a day.*

Riding? Darzek asked.

She gazed at him blankly. Probably she had never thought of distances in terms of riding.

It was much too far. He had to get back to the city and start a systematic search for the Synthesis headquarters and get on with his mission.

She was watching him hopefully. She seemed as pathetically eager for him as the other applicants were for themselves. He said to her, *Thank you for your help, but I must find a job in the city.*

Tears filled her eyes, and she turned away. Darzek gazed after her perplexedly, wondering why his lack of interest in a forest job could possibly matter to her. He turned away himself, intending to get back to the city and resume his search for the Synthesis headquarters. As he did so, light glowed softly in the dark interior of the caravan.

It glowed again, gained in intensity, remained half bright for a moment, and then slowly faded. One of the green-clad males in charge, evidently a scribe, came to the caravan door carrying a box.

Darzek moved in a wide circle and approached the caravan from the far side. There was a kind of running board along the wagon, and he stepped on it and pulled himself up. He edged along it to an uncurtained window and peered inside.

The interior was dark, and he could make out nothing at all.

He continued to cling to the side of the caravan. He had no notion of what he had seen, but he felt certain that it had no business happening on a world with a level three technology. His muscles soon protested his unnatural position, and his wounded arm began to throb furiously, but he held his position and waited.

Then the scribe returned. He went to the far end of the caravan, away from the door, and seated himself.

Abruptly the light glowed and brightened. It seemed blazing in that restricted space.

Darzek dropped to the ground before it faded. He almost landed on the child, who had trailed after him. He circled around to the other side of the caravan and took his place in line.

The child continued to follow him. Darzek turned to her. *What was your father's name?*

Lazk, she answered.

Then my name is Lazk. What's your name?

Sajjo.

They exchanged smiles.

Minutes later, Darzek had been hired. The officials, on the lookout for the healthiest specimens available, saw him at once and brought him forward out of turn. The doctors passed him with no more than a cursory thumping. The test log was heavy, but he had no difficulty with it. The scribe entered his name, Lazk, and handed him a wood chit. Another official administered a strangely worded oath of fealty to the Duke Lonorlk, who, Darzek gathered, owned the forest.

The scribe had one more question for him. *Family?* he asked.

The child was still trailing after Darzek, her face now wreathed with elation. Darzek suddenly understood: she had adopted him. The thought pleased him. She added to his protective coloration. No one would suspect the humble, hard-working head of a family; and if he could trust her—and he thought he could—she would be invaluable in teaching him about Kamm.

One child, he said.

Other families were gathering. At midnight the hiring had been completed, and the successful candidates, with their wives and children, set out for the forest, following after the lumbering caravan and the half dozen nabrula that pulled it in tandem.

The road ran just outside the city wall. After a time it began to climb, and soon they were able to look over the vast expanse of the city, dark except for several distant blazes of torches where sweeps were at work. The lucky families moved along jubilantly in the screeching wake of the caravan's ungreased wheels. Husbands and wives took turns carrying the smaller children. The older children cavorted about excitedly.

Darzek's recently adopted daughter walked at his side with sober maturity, disdaining the antics of the other children. But whenever a faint gleam of light from torches carried ahead of the caravan touched her face, he read rapture there, and something else.

The something else disturbed him; he had never been worshiped before.

Then one of the nabrula slipped its harness, and the driver brought the tandem to a halt. In the sudden silence, Darzek heard, somewhere far off in the city, the electrifying shout of a word: "Primores!" Then another: "Synthesis!" And another: "Galaxy!"

He resisted the impulse to run toward the shouts. Then he had to restrain himself a second time, to keep from kicking himself.

On a world of the deaf, when he could safely let his colleagues know where he was at any time by shouting, only a half-wit would allow himself to get lost. Throughout Darzek's agonizing search, he could have found the Synthesis headquarters at any time just by using his voice.

But now he had no need for his fellow agents. His position was secure, and he'd taken his own giant step toward solving at least one of the mysteries of Kamm.

Kom Rmmon had told him that Kamm's crude technology had not even discovered electricity.

But in this caravan he followed there was, unmistakably, an electric light.

CHAPTER 7

Darzek began work with two substantial advantages over the other new employees. He was healthy, and he'd never been malnourished. On the first day out, he was appointed crew chief. On the fourth day, he became village leader. Two days later he was superintending workers from three villages, and it had been made clear to him that his future in the work force of the Duke Lonorlk was very bright indeed.

He quickly learned why a temporary forest job seemed so desirable to the dregs of the Northpor unemployed. It was the food. On their long night and day march they received regular hot meals, from waiting caravans, and when they finally staggered into their work camp another hot meal was waiting for them.

And they continued to be fed sumptuously. Wives and children, including Sajjo, gained weight and bloomed.

Each family was assigned a caravan on wheels, somewhat smaller than the office that had accompanied them from Northpor. These were arranged in work villages of twelve to fifteen units, and they were moved every few days so the work crews could live close to their cuts.

Their first work had nothing to do with forestry. As soon as they received their housing assignments, all families were ordered to wash their clothing, all the bedding the caravan contained, and themselves, and to scrub their caravans thoroughly. While the families started that chore, using hot water the duke's foresters hauled in for them, the males were put to work digging latrines.

This concern for diet and sanitation astonished Darzek. Either the Duke Lonorlk had a social conscience far in advance of his time, or he had somehow grasped the fact that unhealthy, hungry laborers were unproductive laborers.

When they finished their cleaning chores, Darzek suggested a walk to Sajjo. His mind was on the caravan with the electric light, which had moved on into the forest with workers who were to be assigned to other villages.

Sajjo gazed at him with something remarkably akin to terror. *The Beasts!* her hands exclaimed.

Darzek looked about him at the peaceful forest. The maz trees that crowded the small clearing around their caravans were tall and stately, albeit strange-looking because the paper-like white bark gave them a nude look. Except when a wagon came through, the place was blissfully still. Their neighbors, whether awed by the imposing forest or uneasy away from their city cobblestones, remained close to their caravans. The few who were still in sight seemed to be waiting for their bedding to dry so they could retire. The others probably had gone to bed without bedding, which was a luxury few of them were familiar with. They were, all of them, utterly exhausted after the interminable walk.

Darzek was feeling exhausted himself. He would have liked to question Sajjo about the Beasts, but it was becoming too dark to talk. The luminous night creatures were streaking the forest with light, but they seemed to avoid the clearing.

Obviously both the electric light and the mystery about the Beasts would have to wait. *To bed, then,* Darzek's hands announced. Their own bedding was still damp, so they went back to their caravan and retired without it.

The forest held one inviolable rule: no fires of any kind, anywhere. Though Darzek never tested it, he got the impression that maz tree sap was as dangerously flammable as petroleum; but no fires were needed. Females and children were organized in shifts to work in a community kitchen, a mammoth stone building that served all of the work villages. It was built over a geyser that supplied hot water for bathing and laundry as well as heat for cooking. Each morning and each evening a wagon brought food and hot water from the community kitchen to all of the work villages.

The males of each village were organized into crews of four or five. Darzek was amused when he first saw the cutting tools supplied—wood saws and axes. But they proved better balanced and more efficient than any steel tools he could remember using. The prize item was an enormous saw shaped in a half circle. Even after seeing it in action he thought it wouldn't work, but a crew of sawyers manipulating it back and forth about a gigantic tree could cut through three quarters of its girth with incredible speed to reach the one-quarter notch that the ax workers were cutting simultaneously to direct the fall.

The techniques of forestry and conservation amazed Darzek as much as the concern for diet and sanitation. Only the most mature trees were harvested, and they were cut in a planned sequence so that each fallen tree made way for the fall of the next.

Darzek's rapid promotions pleased him and elated Sajjo, but several aspects of his position were less than satisfactory. For one, his relations with his fellow workers and his superiors puzzled him. His fellow workers were respectful enough, and in casual contacts they seemed friendly, but they avoided him as much as possible. He attributed that to jealousy over his rapid promotions. But his superiors also avoided him, though they obviously thought highly of him.

None of that bothered him as much as his failure to get near one of the office caravans that contained an electric light.

He began to take walks in the evening, in the direction of one of the caravans—with Sajjo tagging along with extreme reluctance simply because she followed him everywhere. These occasioned talk and curiosity among their neighbors; the Kammians feared the night, and one who did not was thought to be in league with the Winged Beast itself.

So Darzek had to give that up. Nor did he have any better success in approaching one of the caravans during the day. With each successive promotion he became better known, and his visit to an area where he had no proper business was likely to be noted and talked about. Fretfully he began counting the days he was wasting.

His only source of diversion was Sajjo. His promotions automatically conferred status on her, and in a comparatively short time she advanced from zero to the titular head female of the village. Females three times her age deferred to her, and she was excused from kitchen duties. The other females, who themselves had been waifs before they became wives of drudges, delighted in honoring her. When a peddler came through, they pooled a few work chits and bought hair dyes, but when they attempted to color and arrange Sajjo's hair to reflect her new station in life, she rebelled. Her release from kitchen duties merely meant that she had more time to follow Darzek about. Now she did so even when he was at work, looking on solemnly from the distance, never in the way, but always present.

During the brief periods when Darzek was home during daylight, when he and Sajjo could see well enough to talk, he attempted to learn as much as he could about Kamm and its people.

About the Beasts, he said to her one evening.

He sensed the barrier instantly. She not only feared the Beasts; she feared any mention of them. This had to be connected somehow with the compulsive fear of the night and its creatures that seized all the Kammians when darkness fell. On the long march to the forest, his fellow workers and their families had kept to the center of the lane and shuddered visibly when a luminous night creature fluttered near. And when the procession halted for rest and food, they preferred the hard lane to a soft place in the grass nearby. Here in the forest, nothing but a work order would keep anyone out after sunset, and that unfortunate worker hurried home at a run the moment he was released. Only Darzek's superiors seemed not to mind the dark—perhaps because their work took them out in it frequently.

Are these night creatures somehow related to the Winged Beast? Darzek asked Sajjo.

They light the way for it, she answered.

So the night creatures were considered harbingers of death.

These questions so disturbed her that he changed the subject. In subsequent talks he made her recite everything of note she could remember about her life—which did not take long, since it made an uneventful tale of squalor. Then he set her to telling him all of the folklore she could remember.

And still he was unable to devise an excuse for getting near one of the office caravans.

It was his fifteenth day in the forest, at dusk, when Darzek stood at a crosslane waiting for his superior to pick up the daily work report that Darzek had chalked on a piece of bark: trees felled, felled trees trimmed and ready for sectioning, standing trees with ground cleared for the morrow's felling. A worker of Darzek's background was not expected to be able to write numbers—probably none of his superiors could write them, either, except the scribes—so a series of marks on bark constituted his daily report.

The superior was late. When he did arrive, he was in a hurry. His fingers flipped a message at Darzek, and he rode away, urging his nabrulk to greater speed.

Darzek turned stoically and trudged along the lane. He had caught only a part of the message, and he intended to interpret it in his own way. He would take the day's count to the office himself.

Eager as he was, he plodded. He was tired. A supervisor's work was exhausting, for he had to lend a hand in everything his workers undertook and run from crew to crew. It would have looked suspicious if Darzek had seemed to welcome this chore of a ten-kilometer round trip at the end of the day, so he plodded.

It was already dark when he reached the office caravan. He opened the door, mounted the steps, and entered the dark interior.

There was no one there.

He felt his way the length of the room and found the strange apparatus on the scribe's worktable. He could see nothing at all, but he remembered a lever that the scribe had pushed down at intervals to produce the light. Darzek found it and pushed it down.

The feeble gleam that resulted seemed blinding in that dark room. Darzek stared in fascination while the glow lasted. Then he looked about uneasily. The light surely would have been visible from a distance, but he had seen no one near the caravan, and he heard no one coming. He pushed the lever again and again, each time studying the contraption until the light faded.

Finally, unwilling to risk being caught there, he returned to the entrance and seated himself outside the door. When he heard footsteps approaching, he slumped comfortably and feigned sleep, and the scribe fell over him.

The scribe led him inside the caravan and to the worktable, where he worked the electric light himself. He was grinning at Darzek; the duke's officials took no offense when their employees worked hard enough to exhaust themselves. While the scribe kept the light going, he examined Darzek's report, asked a few questions about the day's work, and gave Darzek a commendatory back of the hand pat on his forearm.

Darzek left for home, and while he walked, he mulled over the electric light and its generator.

It was a crude mechanical device that could have been built by any bright high school student on Earth. The lever applied tension to a leaf spring of highly resilient wood. The spring, through a simple system of wood gears, turned a generator that furnished the electricity that lit the light. Darzek detected nothing in the mechanism that he had not already encountered in Kamm's technology. Wood springs and gears were common. Any glass blower could have produced the bulb, once he had been given the idea. The filament probably was a loop of the indestructible sponge wood. Only the use of metals was new. Kamm was supposed to employ metal only in coins.

But coins had been the source of metal in the generator! One of the strip contacts actually had the dim image of a Winged Beast still visible —incontrovertible evidence that the builder had hammered it out of a copper coin! The magnetism was provided by rough pieces of lodestone.

Darzek found his disappointment crushing. He had wasted fifteen days and probably caused the Synthesis agents an agony of worry, and all he had accomplished was to track down a mechanical contraption that any Kammian handyman could have built with a few instructions. It made an extremely poor light. A candle would have been more efficient and much more convenient, but the highly flammable maz wood prohibited the use of fire in the forest. The choice was between a poor electric light and none.

"In short," Darzek told himself, savoring his disappointment, "that electric light is a rudimentary mechanical device that conforms with Kamm's known technology in every particular."

Then he halted abruptly. The device conformed with Kamm's technology in every particular; any Kammian handyman could have built such a generator and light if he knew how—*but there was no possible way for him to know how.* That crude device was in fact a fiendishly ingenious adaptation of fantastically complex principles. Something decidedly was wrong in the forest of the Duke Lonorlk.

Moving on, Darzek felt much better about his wasted fifteen days. The inventive genius who had contrived that generator certainly knew enough about electricity to contrive any number of other things. Perhaps even a pazul.

A moment later he became aware that he was being followed. He turned; Sajjo hurried to catch up with him. She took his hand and skipped along at his side. She must have followed him all the way to the caravan, and if the night creatures, now flitting about them in hordes, were frightening her, she gave no sign of it.

The workers received a half-day holiday every ten days. This holiday also was their payday. Officials distributed coins, and there were peddlers who came out from Northpor to help commemorate the occasion. With the second such payday, the workers had accumulated enough money to make substantial purchases. Wives and children appeared in stylish outfits, and the workers themselves began to discard their patchwork clothing in favor of practical, long-wearing outfits of dusky green.

On that second holiday, Darzek went for a relaxing walk through the forest with Sajjo. She bounded along at his side, ecstatic in her new dress, trousers, and shoes. He had exchanged his own sweep's costume for the green of the forester, and as he strolled along he reflected that they must make a handsome couple.

Sajjo now did her own hair styling. Her first efforts had produced the impression of a gigantic bird's nest of unknown species, but with a little practice she had become quite artistic. Her days were radiantly happy now; she kept the little caravan impeccable, and she had come to enjoy, in her quaintly quiet way, her status as the head of the superintendent's household. Whenever she could she continued to follow Darzek about with a devotion that was sometimes embarrassing—especially when he wanted to visit the latrine.

But their forest outing had a purpose. A couple of days before, he had found an old piece of canvas-like cloth rotting on the forest floor. He put Sajjo to cleaning it, and when she finished there was an undamaged piece large enough to make an awning for their caravan home. He had performed the necessary measurements, and now he wanted to cut a couple of poles to support the awning.

He was cautious enough to ask permission. His superiors were surprised and wanted to know why. When he had explained, they were still surprised, but they matter-of-factly gave permission to cut strip saplings—strip being a bastard kind of wood that now and again got spored in the forest and crowded out the valuable maz trees. Workers were encouraged to make their caravans home-like.

Darzek found two strip saplings of the necessary size, cut them, and let Sajjo help him strip them and trim them to the proper length. With each of them carrying one, they started back through the forest toward their village.

Suddenly Sajjo froze. She literally halted in midstride, with one foot a few centimeters off the ground, and at the same instant she held up a hand to stop Darzek. He regarded her with puzzlement, and then he stared in the direction where her eyes were riveted.

A knight, clothed in the pale blue colors of the Duke Lonorlk, was crouched in the undergrowth, arm back, whip coiled for action, gaze fixed on a small forest pool. His clothing matched the forest vegetation so well that Darzek had trouble picking out his silhouette a second time even though he knew the knight was there.

Darzek remained motionless; Sajjo gradually let her foot sink to the ground, but she seemed scarcely to be breathing.

Suddenly, on the far side of the pool, one of Darzek's workers strode into sight. His wife followed a short distance behind him, carrying their infant child. Mother and child had been wan and sickly when they arrived in the forest. Now both had bloomed and gained weight, and she and her husband were like young lovers, going everywhere hand in hand and laughing much and saying little.

As the worker strode forward, a large, spotted, long-legged forest creature leaped up, took half a dozen bounding strides, and disappeared into the forest on the far side of the clearing. The knight, who perhaps had been waiting in ambush for hours, leaped up at the same moment and snapped his whip—futilely, for it did no more than cut a red furrow on the beast's flank as it disappeared.

The knight swiftly recoiled his whip and turned on the frightened worker, mustaches bristling furiously. Before Darzek could move, the whip snapped a second time and the worker fell, his throat cut deeply. He gasped and choked for an instant and died. The knight coiled his whip again and turned on the woman and child.

But this time Darzek was ready. As the knight drew back his whip, Darzek charged. The butt end of the sapling struck the knight squarely at the base of his skull. The whip fluttered ineffectually as the knight crashed to the ground. He lay there, motionless.

Another whip sang past Darzek's ear. He whirled; he had not seen the second knight, but Sajjo had. As the knight aimed his whip she had charged into him, burying her pole in his stomach. While he lay on the ground, gasping, Darzek leaped to him and coolly smashed his skull.

He stepped back and turned to the woman, who was paralyzed with terror. *Go home,* his fingers told her. *Go back to your caravan at once. You left your husband walking in the forest. You saw nothing.*

She rushed away with her child. Her face was frozen in emotional shock, but at least she seemed to comprehend.

Darzek bent over the first knight. He was dead. Quickly he dragged the second knight to his side and cut a short piece from one of his saplings. This he placed in the dead worker's hand. Then he motioned to Sajjo, and the two of them calmly strolled away.

She emulated both his stride and manner instantly, and he observed her self-control with a father's pride. In spite of the horrifying scene she had witnessed, she walked along with him as though nothing had happened.

He found another strip sapling and cut and trimmed it. He hid the one from which he had cut the piece he'd left with the dead worker. Then they quietly finished their walk. And, when they reached their caravan, they worked together to erect the awning.

Darzek never learned how the duke's officials interpreted the evidence of that tragedy by the forest pool. Most likely—since there was no science of detection on Kamm—they had not known how to begin. They found two dead knights and a dead worker. They certainly knew the habits of knights well enough to reason that the worker had interfered with a hunt. One of the knights had killed the worker; somehow the worker had freakishly managed to kill both knights, and that completed the equation.

Except for the worker's wife.

Late that afternoon they took Darzek to identify the dead worker.

Then they turned his wife out of her caravan. Darzek, seeing this happen, went out himself and invited her into his own living quarters.

It is not permitted, an official said stiffly.

I am a worker without a wife, Darzek said. *Am I not permitted to have one of my own choice?*

Of course. But the wife of a worker who has slain a knight is not permitted to remain. If you choose her as your wife, you must leave with her.

Darzek thought for a moment. It was time he left the forest anyway, and he was still feeling outraged at what he had witnessed. *I could not in good conscience permit a female with a small child to try to return to Northpor alone. I will leave with her.*

The officials shrugged and walked away.

Darzek told Sajjo to pack their belongings, with enough food for the walk to Northpor. He told the widow they would leave together.

A short time later two other officials, Darzek's immediate superiors, called on him. Darzek was a valued employee. They attempted to reason with him. He already had risen high in the duke's service. He certainly would rise much higher. Why should he sacrifice his career over a secondhand wife of a treasonous worker? They would ask the duke himself to select a wife for Darzek from among his own servants.

The worker was my friend, Darzek said. *He was not treasonous. He worked hard and served the duke well. He and his wife were happy. I will not abandon his wife.*

They shrugged in turn and went away. Darzek looked after them uneasily. He had no idea whether such dedication to principle would be respected or viewed as an act of treason on his part. It seemed wise to leave at once.

Sajjo had made a neat bundle of their belongings, which consisted only of extra clothing they had bought. She had packed food into a small crock and added another crock of cider. The widow, also, was ready to leave.

But Sajjo had disappeared.

It was already dusk, and night descended quickly in the depths of the maz forest. Darzek frantically looked around the village and asked his neighbors; no one had seen her.

He waited in an agony of indecision: Had she suffered a belated reaction to the horrors of murder? Had she simply run off rather than leave the forest?

Suddenly he saw her, moving furtively among the trees. She carried a bulky sack flung over her back. Darzek grabbed his own belongings, motioned to the widow to follow, and hurried off. He did not pause to redistribute their possessions until they finally reached the surlane to Northpor.

Then he took the widow's child, a bright, gurgling male baby named Badje, and grabbed as much as he could carry with his free hand. Sajjo insisted on keeping her sack, which obviously was heavy. The widow carried her own possessions and the food, and they started off along the surlane. Since the widow and Sajjo were both in splendid health, Darzek hoped they could reach the city early the next morning. If they did not, he intended to hide out during the day and finish the journey the following night.

As they walked, he listened as intently as his impaired hearing permitted, and a short time later he heard what he had expected: the muddled rhythm of approaching nabrula hoofs.

He rushed his group into hiding at the laneside, and an instant later six knights galloped past, looking from side to side and obviously searching for something. They took to the laneside again when he heard them returning.

For the remainder of the night he continued to listen for approaching nabrula and alertly watch for potential hiding places; and he remarked to himself that a society where the nobility sought revenge on innocent wives and children of commoners was disgustingly reminiscent of too much of Earth's history.

It was almost morning when he finally became curious about Sajjo's precious burden. She was reluctant to show it to him, but finally she submitted with a shy smile.

He opened the sack; it was the electrical generator from the office caravan.

She had seen his interest in it the night he was hired in Northpor, and she had followed him the night he had inspected it. When she knew they had to leave, she had stolen it for him.

He burst into laughter, seized her, and kissed her. This was a daughter after any Synthesis agent's heart.

Now he could not wait to get to the Synthesis headquarters. His arrival there would electrify the agents in more ways than one.

CHAPTER 8

The second night after Darzek's return to Northpor, he drove with Sajjo as far as the mart. It was his first outing with a newly acquired nabrulk and cart, and he preferred to learn how to handle the beast when the city's lanes were empty.

They clunked and screeched along the now invisible mosaics of the colored cobblestones, and their cart was the only thing that moved except for the crews of sweeps, whose torch-lit progress could be glimpsed from time to time.

The mart—the colorful, vibrant center of commerce and entertainment—was dead. Carts, wagons, nabrula were gone. Tents and booths were closed. All was deserted.

Like the workers and their families in the forest villages, the citizens of Northpor retreated to their dwellings at night. It was the most salient feature of Kammian psychology and the one most difficult for the outsider to comprehend. The Kammians avoided the night. In the rural areas they could be said to have abandoned it to those luminous and pheromonal insect- or reptile-like creatures that shunned the day.

But the night creatures were rarely seen in cities. City dwellers so despised them that they took pains to leave nothing about for the creatures to eat. Even nabrula droppings were scrupulously swept up each evening and placed in covered crocks. Further, any potential lairs or hiding places for such creatures were ruthlessly sought out by day and their occupants slaughtered. The only locale in the entire city of Northpor where the night creatures went unmolested was the mart.

Darzek had not been aware of this. He happened upon their luminous display unexpectedly, and he halted the cart to watch it. The night creatures lived in the soil and amid the stones of the life pyramid. And they fed at the shrine of death.

All of the bits and particles and chunks and pieces of food impaled on the pole during the day as offerings to the Winged Beast were consumed by these nocturnal creatures, who descended on the black shrine like a scintillating plague of thieves. They lighted the mart with their darting luminescence, making bold patterns of colored light as they battled for the Winged Beast's scraps. There were dozens of species and dozens of color and flight patterns.

And not all of them were luminescent. Darzek got a whiff of a particularly vile scent and caught his breath.

He turned to watch Sajjo. She, at least, seemed to be adaptable. She had overcome her fear of darkness enough to follow him about in the forest.

But she was not watching the night creatures. She was watching him. He started the nabrulk with a flick of the reins.

Darzek and his family had entered Northpor at dawn, along with the stream of carts and wagons headed for the mart. He planned to go directly to the Kammian version of an inn. Both Sajjo and the widow, Wesru, knew where several inns were located, though of course they had no personal experience of them. Once he'd found accommodations, Darzek intended to systematically search for the Synthesis headquarters, shouting his way through the lanes of Northpor. And he would take Sajjo along, to keep him from getting lost or wandering in circles.

But he found the Synthesis headquarters himself, without shouting, on his way into the city. He found it by recognizing the house opposite, which he had scrutinized more carefully than he realized while looking out of the window at the traffic on the morning of his arrival. In his earlier, frantic search, it had not occurred to him to look for the house across the lane.

Once he had found it, he had no difficulty in identifying the headquarters house. He turned and marched up to the front door, with Sajjo and Wesru following him wonderingly. During a lull in the traffic noises, he knocked vigorously and shouted, "Anyone home?"

There was no response. He tried the door; it was locked. He knew that he had left it unlocked.

He handed the baby to Wesru. *Wait here,* he said.

He moved around to the back of the house, tiptoeing through the flowers and noticing as he did so that they were beginning to look scraggly. Weeds were springing up among them.

The rear door also was locked. Darzek quickly picked the lock and entered the house, shouting again, "Anyone home?"

The remains of his breakfast lay on the bench where he had trimmed the hard crust from the bread he ate. The remainder of the loaf was still there, now covered with mold. He passed quickly through the house, from the upstairs rooms to the concealed trap doors in the basement and the transmitter frame below.

He'd found the right house, but there was no sign that anyone had been here since he left. Dust lay thickly everywhere.

He went to the front door, tripped the ponderous lock, and opened it. *Come in,* he told Wesru and Sajjo. *Welcome home.*

While they waited, their wonderment had changed to uneasiness. Now their uneasiness was transformed to astonishment. The immediate problem was food, and Darzek dispatched Wesru and Sajjo to the nearest neighborhood forum to buy as much as they could carry. While they were gone, Darzek functioned as baby-sitter and tried to convince himself that he'd made progress since he last sat in this kitchen. "But in what direction?" he demanded, and he had no answer.

By the time they had finished a hasty breakfast, all of them were reeling with weariness. Darzek got the others comfortably ensconced in an upstairs bedroom, hoping that the luxury of the place wouldn't keep them awake.

He had no time for sleep himself. There was something very peculiar about the agent situation on Kamm, and the more he thought about it, the more uneasy it made him.

He went directly to the subbasement, closing the trap doors after him. His first stop was the moon base. There was no one there. Neither could he find any certain indication that anyone had been there recently. The floor of the supply room was jammed with cartons brought in by the automatic conveyor. Several cartons had been opened, seemingly at random, but Darzek could not say whether this had been done since his own arrival on Kamm.

He spent some minutes contemplating the complexities of the communications center. Any kind of an SOS message about missing agents would eventually reach Supreme, so probably it was just as well that he didn't know how to send one.

He returned to the base transmitter and visited in turn each of the other four Synthesis headquarters on Storoz. He quickly determined that these were located in the other four Free Cities controlled by the Sailor's League: Midpor, Eastpor, Southpor, and Westpor. All were houses in comfortable neighborhoods. All were deserted. Only one building showed signs of recent use. There was fresh food in the headquarters in Southpor, the rooms had been dusted recently, and the flower-crammed yard had received cursory attention. At the other three houses, the yards were weed-cluttered, food lay molding or rotting in the pantries, and nothing had rippled the interior dust for weeks.

In the Southpor headquarters, Darzek left a message written in the Galactic script: "I'm in Northpor. Lazk."

Next he did a quick tour of Synthesis headquarters on the two continents. He found them as deserted as those on Storoz, but the evidence there was of planned departures. No perishables had been left behind, and arrangements seemed to have been made about upkeep. Lawns and gardens were in good shape.

He returned to the moon base again and tackled the base file. It was a simplified code computer, but he still had to work out the code. Eventually he succeeded in dialing the personnel records, and he read them with care. Nine agents had been lost on Kamm. (There was of course no mention of Rok Wllon, who had arrived secretly.) As Darzek suspected, all of the remaining agents had been transferred to Storoz, probably to search for the missing nine. At the date of final entry, there had been ten agents on Storoz, organized into two teams.

Now there were none. The missing nine, plus Rok Wllon, had become a missing twenty, and he was the only Synthesis agent at large. There could be no more impulsive forays into maz forests, whatever the attraction. He would have to weigh each action with care, plan it meticulously—and make certain that each room he entered had more than one exit.

He returned to Northpor. He saw no reason why he should not make that headquarters his own. Kom Rmmon had assured him that the Free Cities were the safest places on Kamm.

But he had to start behaving like a normal Kammian, and at once. This was a perfumer's house. Probably the Synthesis agents had acquired it from a perfumer and adopted his trade. If the perfume factory remained idle much longer, the neighbors might get curious—and curious neighbors were a leading cause of problems for agents anywhere. Further, Darzek needed a trade that would give him status at home and a lawful excuse to travel, and he had to be proficient enough to pass as a native.

When Sajjo awoke, Darzek led her out to the perfume factory. As they stood looking at the enormous stock of dried and drying leaves and roots and berries and seeds and flowers, he asked her, *Do you know how to make perfume?*

She dropped a shoulder negatively.

Do you know anyone who does?

I know one who helps a perfumer sometimes, she answered.

Is it far? Would it take you long to find him?

She gestured negatively.

Go get him, Darzek said.

Sajjo dashed away.

Darzek returned to the house. Wesru had a pot of a savory-smelling stew simmering, and she was bustling about giving the house a long overdue dusting and cleaning. Darzek slipped away to the sub-basement, where he had hidden the stolen electrical generator. He sat there in darkness, occasionally pressing the lever and watching the crude bulb glow and fade.

"Twenty missing agents," he told himself, "and at least some of them must be alive somewhere and desperately in need of help, and what are you doing?"

If the generator illuminated any part of the answer Darzek needed, he was too blind to see it.

It was almost evening when Sajjo reappeared, this time with a Kammian youth of about twenty trailing after her. Except for his height, he looked very much as Sajjo had looked when Darzek first saw her—pale, thin, and extremely ragged. Sajjo introduced him—Hadkez.

He didn't know me, she said proudly, encompassing in a gesture her grand clothing and her hairdo.

Darzek sat the two of them down to Wesru's stew, and Hadkez ate enormously. Only after they had finished did Darzek ask him, *Do you know how to make perfume?*

Some kinds, he answered.

Would you like to live here and help us make perfume?

His affirmative was ecstatic.

When can you move in?

He had nothing to move, and he was there. Darzek assigned a second-floor bedroom to him. Wesru took the adjoining room with Badje; there also was an unused spare pantry that could be converted into a nursery off the kitchen so she could keep an eye on the child during the day, while she worked. The role of housekeeper delighted her.

Sajjo found a bedroom for herself on the third floor, a small room with white furnishings. Darzek, going up later to see how she liked it, found her looking out of the window just as he'd seen her in the warehouse when she'd had to stand on a crock to reach a high window; but her face no longer had the same remote, lost expression. Now she belonged to something, though she hadn't yet comprehended what it was.

Neither had Darzek, but he had learned that establishing a solid Kammian identity for himself was going to require more work and planning than he had expected. He took the one downstairs bedroom for himself, so his comings and goings would be less likely to arouse curiosity; and before he retired he went to the subbasement and again pondered the mystery of the electrical generator.

In the morning Darzek went out with Sajjo and Hadkez and bought a cart and nabrulk. Hadkez proudly drove it home and made the beast comfortable in the flat-roofed stable.

Then he went to work making one of the perfumes he was familiar with, soaking a mixture of dried leaves and roots and then beginning the tedious distillation process that would extract the oils.

While Hadkez worked, Darzek considered the amount of labor involved in looking after a nabrulk, tending the garden, and running errands. He asked Sajjo if she had another friend, and she dashed off and returned with Sjelk, who looked like a younger brother of Hadkez—which he was. Sjelk immediately went to work on the flower garden.

Darzek returned to the perfume factory to watch Hadkez. So tedious did the process of distillation prove to be that he worked far into the night at it, and Darzek and Sajjo made their excursion to the mart without him.

It was on the following day, while they were bottling their first perfume—which to Darzek smelled very attractive indeed—that Darzek learned about wholesale perfumers. Most vendors of perfume had a few special scents that they prepared themselves, but in order to offer the variety that the people of Kamm required, they patronized wholesalers.

Darzek immediately ordered out the nabrulk and cart, and they drove to the wholesaler Hadkez had worked for and returned home with twenty crocks of perfumes. These they could bottle as needed; and they could make enough perfume of their own to give the impression that the factory was functioning.

The next day Darzek obtained a market permit for Lazk, perfumer, and rented a permanent booth. Hadkez and Sjelk, outfitted in new perfumers' costumes, delightedly took to selling perfumes in the mart, and Sajjo helped out as much as she could. Wesru was instructed in keeping the process of distillation going while Hadkez was away.

Overnight Darzek had created a prospering business. The stock of coins he'd found in the house was getting perilously low, but already there was income from the mart; and when he belatedly thought about it, he gave the other Synthesis headquarters a thorough search and discovered more hordes of coins in each.

The other headquarters were still deserted. No one had been in the house in Southpor since he left his note there, and it now seemed certain to Darzek that there were twenty missing Synthesis agents on Kamm.

For the moment there was nothing he could do about that. He first had to establish himself solidly as a Kammian; *then* he could think about tracing the missing agents.

Already the other vendors and exhibitors at the mart greeted him as a colleague. To the populace, as he made his well-perfumed way about the mart in his distinctive perfumer's cape and hat, he was a member of one of the most respected professions. He found that he did not need a personal perfume for himself. A perfumer, handling scents throughout his working day, as well as distilling and bottling them, always carried with him a potently blended aroma of his profession.

For several days he delighted in wandering about the mart; in pondering why one keeper of secrets, or fortuneteller, had a line of waiting customers and another was ignored; or why the patients of one purger or manipulator emerged wearing expressions of contentment while the patients of another staggered out looking ill.

He continued to marvel at the way the deaf people of Kamm assiduously cultivated their remaining sensations: sight, smell, touch, and —now that he had experienced some of the gourmet foods available at the mart—taste. The major professions on Kamm were paint, dye, and perfume making, and the weaving of special fabrics with tactile qualities. The Kammian passion for color was everywhere flamboyantly evident. Wherever Kammians lived or worked or simply passed by, one smelled perfumes and incense. And weavers hung up strips of cloth so that passers-by could pause and stroke them, and they did so with eyes closed, as though they were receiving erotic stimulation from the sensations the various textures provided.

There were in fact Temples of Sensation at the mart—tents offering brief excursions into the forbidden limits of sight, touch, and smell. Giggling couples entered them self-consciously and emerged an hour or two later, complacently perspiring. But no Synthesis agent, no alien, would dare to venture into a place where his reactions, if not his anatomy, were so likely to advertise his alienness.

Darzek soon decided that his fascination with the Kammians was getting him nowhere. He left the perfume business to Hadkez, and he submerged himself in moon base records, searching for information about the world of Kamm that would supplement his abbreviated training. He devoted an entire day to the study of Kammian history.

The island of Storoz was a sizable land form located midway between the two major continents of Kamm. Northpor was one of the five Free Cities located there, the five being seaports owned and governed by the Sailor's League, a political power to be reckoned with on Kamm. The League also owned Free Cities on each of the continents.

The measure of freedom in a Free City was considerable. Away from those conclaves, Storoz was made up of a dozen provinces, eleven ruled by dukes. The twelfth, located in the interior mountains that ran down the center of the island like a deformed backbone, was a theocracy. In all of these provinces, a decadent aristocracy or an entrenched priesthood maintained despotic control over a terrorized peasantry, and strangers were subject to arrest and torture or death at the whim of any passing knight—as Darzek knew full well.

Under the circumstances, it did not seem unusual that an occasional agent would be lost; but the Synthesis lost no agents on Kamm for more than a hundred years. During that period of time its training methods for service on the planet were perfected and its agents amply demonstrated their ability to take care of themselves.

The sudden loss of nine—or ten, or twenty—agents suggested the unexpected introduction of a new element. The Department of Uncertified Worlds thought it knew what that new element was: a pazul.

Darzek turned to the history of the Sailor's League. The island of Storoz was the original home of Kamm's sailors. They were ideally situated to prey on shipping passing between the two Kammian continents, and Storoz fostered a sturdy race of pirates long before there was any written history of Kamm. The pirates were so efficient that they drove other shipping from the seas; so they switched from piracy to commerce and made an absolute monopoly of intercontinental transport. They were and remained such admirable sailors that the name for Storoz in one native language was, "Land of intrepid men who master ocean storms."

For centuries the sailors had been refugees from the feudal system run by the oppressive Dukes of Storoz, and it still was possible for a bright peasant youth to escape to a career at sea—and ultimate wealth —but at this late date apprentice sailors usually were sons of sailors, most of whom maintained homes in one of the Free Cities.

The Sailor's League operated all of its ships on a unique profit-sharing system whereby even an apprentice sailor did very well for himself. Much of that wealth was invested in beautifying the Free Cities, and all of the impressive larger homes there belonged to sailors. The exquisite taste responsible for the loveliness of Northpor was typical of Kammians, but not of Kamm. It occurred only where the citizens could afford it. The one conspicuous exception was the great ducal city and seaport of OO. Most of the dukes were notoriously parsimonious— where beauty or anything else was concerned.

And it was the dukes that interested Darzek. Facinating as the sailors were, with their skills, and their ships, and their cities, and their wealth, he saw no clue to the fate of the missing agents in any of those. His mission lay in the opposite direction.

Ten ducal provinces, separated by sketchy or ill-defined boundaries, extended from the sea to the mountains all around the oblong island. The eleventh was the Province of OO, the smallest province, which was completely surrounded by that of the Duke Kiledj. The mountainous

Central Province was ruled by the head of the ancient Death Religion of the Winged Beast, and he was designated Protector of the Faith. His barren province was in fact the wealthiest, because of its mines. His black knights were not only priests, but also miners and smelters and coiners—they made coins for the entire world of Kamm. What they did with their wealth was not known.

It seemed to Darzek that very little was known about any of the dukes. He read through the list of their names: Merzkion, Fermarz, Lonorlk, Kiledj, Rilornz, Suklozk, Borkioz, Pabinzk, Tonorj, Dunjinz, OO. None of them meant anything to him except the Duke Lonorlk, whose employee he had been.

He turned off the file and sat gazing at the blank screen. He'd found no clue whatsoever as to where the missing agents had gone or what they were trying to do.

He still did not have a starting point.

He returned to Northpor, and for a time he sat in the basement, working the lever that kept his stolen generator operating. This, too, should have provided a clue, but it continued to elude him.

He climbed the stairs and joined Wesru in the kitchen, and she smilingly placed a bowl of spiced vegetables before him with an enormous chunk of boiled meat floating in it. The baby Badje was happily playing in his nursery with toys Sajjo had brought from the mart. Sajjo came in herself a moment later, with excited tales of the day's business, and Wesru filled a bowl for her.

Darzek suddenly realized that both of them were watching him anxiously.

His preoccupation had seemed alarming to them. He smiled, and they smiled back at him and began to eat.

Suddenly a voice exploded in the hallway behind him. "What in the name of the seven gods of Perquali is this?"

Darzek turned. A female of Kamm, with a monstrously piled hairdo, and a male, ostensibly a peddler, stood staring at them from the hallway.

Darzek asked conversationally, "How about the nine bastard gods of Wikwipolu?"

The two continued to stare. Then they burst into laughter.

CHAPTER 9

They were Riklo and Wenz, novice agents who had been on Kamm only a couple of months longer than Darzek. They had arrived at a moment of crisis over the missing agents, when the team leaders had other things to worry about, so they were plunked down in the safest corner of Storoz—the Free City of Southpor, which was surrounded by the province of the senile Duke Borkioz—and told to behave themselves and learn what they could, and eventually someone would get around to training them properly.

They'd been working as a team, peddler and keeper of secrets, in the Southpor mart and on the circuit of wayside forums through the Duke Borkioz's province. But eventually they'd become curious about what the other agents were doing, so they visited the moon base and the headquarters on Storoz and on the two continents, and all of them were deserted except one. Someone had eaten food recently in the Northpor headquarters. That night they'd shouted in the streets, without any response, so they'd gone back to Southpor, resumed their traveling, and tried to think of what they should do next. It was after another circuit of the province that they'd found Darzek's note.

Darzek's Kammian family had gone to bed. The three agents were conferring in the sitting room, and Wenz was keeping the place lighted by operating the electrical generator, which fascinated him. It was Riklo who tersely recounted their history, and now she had a complaint.

She and Wenz were graduates of the Department of Uncertified Worlds Academy—which Darzek hadn't known existed—and they'd thoroughly mastered the principles of sound operation on Uncertified Worlds, and Darzek was flagrantly violating all of them.

"Close contacts with natives," Riklo announced, "are strictly forbidden."

Darzek, who had based a career on his talent for ignoring stupid regulations, regarded her with interest. He already had begun to wonder what sort of alien life form that attractive Kammian female cocoon concealed. "Nonsense," he said. "Who looks after the flower garden, and cleans the house, and takes care of the nabrula for you in Southpor?"

"Nobody," Riklo said indignantly. "We do those things ourselves."

"And look at the time you waste acting as your own servants. No wonder the agents on Kamm have accomplished so little! And here's another point. Houses empty for long periods of time arouse curiosity. If there were servants in residence, or a native family with children to run errands and make friends with neighbor children, the place would look normal. Agents who keep strictly to themselves are going to attract suspicion a lot more quickly than those who share their residence with natives."

"There's no possible way to tell which natives can be trusted," Riklo said stubbornly. "The risk is too great."

"There's another point," Darzek said. "Look at that electric generator. No one knows how long the Duke Lonorlk has been using electric lights in his forests to avoid the danger of fire, and the Synthesis would never have known it if my adopted daughter hadn't taken me to apply for a job. The more close contacts we have with natives, the more effective our work will be. A few agents simply can't keep track of what happens on an entire world."

"You keep changing the subject," Riklo announced indignantly. "What about the danger from those close native contacts?"

"There isn't any. I took some hungry people, and gave them jobs they can take pride in, and an excellent place to live, and all the food they want. There isn't much they wouldn't do for me in return. Let's talk about the missing agents."

They knew Rok Wllon—he had visited the academy while they were there. But they had no inkling that he was on Kamm. None of the agents they'd talked with had mentioned it.

"He came here to look for the missing agents," Darzek said. "Did you happen to hear anyone mention where they disappeared?"

"In the provinces," Riklo said. "Three in Merzkion, four in OO, and two in Fermarz."

"Then he went to OO, since more of them vanished there. So I'm going to OO."

"That would be suicidal," Riklo said. "OO is such a dangerous place that the Storoz team closed its headquarters there."

"Nonsense. Why?"

Riklo said scornfully, "Don't you know *anything* about Storoz and its history?"

"Just what I found in the moon base file," Darzek said cheerfully. "I may not have been looking in the right place. Tell me about Storoz and its history."

At some point in the island's remote antiquity, the kingship had rotated among the dukes. Then one duke made himself king permanently, with the great port of OO as his capital city. The other dukes
were reduced to the status of provincial administrators.

The king occupied a dual position: political leader and head of the
island's religion, with the title, Protector-King; he was ruler of the land
and protector of the faith. But the kings became increasingly oppressive, and finally one took the ridiculous step of forbidding the dukes
the right to make their own cider, and they revolted, deposed and mur-
dered the king, and established their independence.

The king's son survived, but he was reduced to the status of a mere
duke, ruling the lands that the former king had held personally. As a
result, the dukedom at OO was the smallest on Storoz, but it also was
one of the wealthiest, containing the island's largest and most prosperous city as well as its best agricultural land.

"Then the present Duke of OO is a direct descendant of the last
King of Storoz," Darzek mused.

"True," Riklo said. "But so are all the other dukes, because of complicated intermarriages among the nobility. In fact, so is the Protector.
He's the brother of the present Duke of OO."

Darzek leaned forward alertly. "That's suggestive. Which of the present dukes have dreams of restoring the monarchy with themselves as
Protector-King?"

"Probably all of them do. And the Protector, too."

"Of course they do. Aristocracy and priests are the same all over the
galaxy. Which brings us to religion. The Mound of the Sun and the
Winged Beast. They're in direct contention. Who's winning?"

Before the revolution, the Winged Beast had been the symbol of the
official Storozian religion. Afterward, the dukes had resented the control exercised over their subjects by the priestly knights of the Winged
Beast, so they threw out the knights and fostered a rival, informal
religion. It caught on, and the Winged Beast was worshiped in secret if
at all. But within the past few years, the present Protector had gained
some concessions: the return of the Winged Beast symbol to market
places and forums and the freedom of the citizens to worship it if they
chose. In addition, a few knights and lackeys of the Winged Beast had
been admitted into each province and into the Free Cities as religious
guides. The old religion was making a comeback.

"But they have to behave themselves," Riklo said.

"I know," Darzek answered. He had just learned that morning, from
Sajjo, that the knights and lackeys of the Winged Beast had been ex-
pelled from Northpor for forty days by the Sailor's League for attacking

an unidentified free citizen, a perfumer, who had absently walked through their holy circle.

"The exception is OO," Riklo said. "The Protector's brother has re-established the old faith as the province's official religion. There are enormous numbers of knights and lackeys of the Winged Beast in OO. They combine their role of religious leadership with that of an official police force. That's what made the place so dangerous. It was the first province where we began to lose agents. After the fourth vanished there, the headquarters was closed. There hasn't been an agent there since. It'd be suicidal to go to OO. It'd also be silly. Why would Rok Wllon be looking for agents who vanished months ago? Why wouldn't he look for the ones who vanished most recently?"

Darzek was studying a map. "You have a point. Where did they vanish most recently? Merzkion or Fermarz?"

"I don't know. Visiting either place would be suicidal. Both dukes have pazuls."

Darzek smiled. "Did your Primores headquarters tell you so?"

"At least one of the missing agents was seen dead as his body was carried away," Riklo said. "I talked with the agent who saw him. There's no mistaking a death caused by a pazul. Anyway—your training was miserably inadequate compared to ours, and we're novices. If we three start looking for twenty missing agents, there'll soon be twenty-three missing agents."

"In other words," Darzek said, "it isn't safe."

She glared at him.

"And in the meantime, those missing agents may be tortured—or worse." He was looking at the map again. "The best route would be Merzkion, Fermarz, and then OO. Merzkion first, since it's closest."

"I'll come with you," Wenz said. "I'd like to have a look inside the Duke Merzkion's castle. If he has a pazul, I want to see it."

Darzek regarded him with interest. "Do you know how to get in?"

"Of course."

"How?"

"Come outside, and I'll show you."

They went outside to the most shadowed corner at the rear of the house. While Darzek watched openmouthed, Wenz walked up the side of the building. No cat burglar on Earth could have approached such finesse. He deftly climbed a sheer wall and then climbed down again.

"I'll climb up to the highest turret and pry open a window," Wenz said. "That ought to be the last place they'd expect anyone to break in. I'll dress like a lackey—that's the lowest order of the duke's servants. If I get into trouble, I'll go out the nearest window and hide on the roof. I can spend a week there, if necessary, and search the place from top to bottom."

"And if he gets into trouble, there'll be no one to support him," Riklo said bitterly.

"I wouldn't want any support," Wenz said. "Going alone, I'll have no one to worry about but myself. But I won't get into trouble. Who'd suspect a lackey on the top floor of the castle? If the Duke Merzkion has a pazul, I'll find it."

"I'm less concerned about the pazul than about who's locked in the duke's dungeon," Darzek said.

"I'll find that out, too," Wenz promised.

"Very well. We'll go together. Riklo can stay here or go back to Southpor."

She said, still sounding bitter, "As long as the two of you are going—"

"I wouldn't order any agent to do this," Darzek said. "When twenty disappear out of twenty, it isn't difficult to calculate the risk. We don't even have a simple weapon for self-defense. The Department of Un-certified Worlds is run by nincompoops."

Riklo held up an amulet she was wearing on a thong about her neck —a carving of the hideous Winged Beast. "These were in the last supply shipment," she said. "There's also a carton of stun rifles up there. Primores is finally conceding that we have a problem."

Darzek rushed the preparations. Riklo and Wenz had to return to Southpor to dispose of their nabrula, and he had to acquire another cart and a tandem of nabrula equal to rough rural travel. Certain work had to be performed—in the way of devising hiding places in the cart for their alien equipment—that the agents had to do themselves.

Finally the cart was packed and they were ready to set out—and then Darzek had to suffer a tempestuous and tearful parting from Sajjo, who seemed fiercely jealous of Riklo. They moved south through the province of the Duke Lonorlk, traveling slowly in the manner of itiner-ant tradesmen, pausing occasionally in a tiny peasant village in the hope of attracting a customer or two, and stopping each night at a wayside forum.

These foul little parks were the rural marts. The peasants came each evening to see what the day's travel had tossed up there and to shop a little and gossip with neighbors—and to perform religious rites if they chose, for each forum featured a shabby Winged Beast on a pole and a diminutive hump that served as a Mound of the Sun.

Since the forums belonged to no one, no one cleared away the moun-tains of nabrula dung, and a night in that environment, surrounded by the stench of manure and the reek of the night creatures that came to feed on it, was almost more than Darzek could stand. He meditated again on the Kammians' strange ability to smell selectively.

On the ninth day out of Northpor, they crossed an unmarked boundary into the province of the Duke Merzkion. The same day they encountered their first sponge forest. The spongy bark of these trees grew in tough layers like a thin parchment with porous material interleaved. Darzek recognized the parchment. It was used as wrappings for bread and other merchandise at the Northpor mart. The soft core of this tree, when dried and cured, was the basic building material of Kamm, and it could be processed to a toughness difficult to believe in a non-metal.

On the tenth day they were following a lane that took them obliquely past the Duke Merzkion's castle. They found a vantage point and studied the massive stone building with binoculars. The stones were a foreboding gray; the dukes had no money to squander on costly imported colored stone and no ships that could occasionally bring such luxuries back as ballast.

As they studied the castle, Wenz made his final plans. While he investigated the fortress, Darzek and Riklo would explore the countryside, looking for traces of the missing agents. Their carts, equipment, and nabrula had vanished along with them. Peasants may have appropriated these, or they may simply have been abandoned. Either way, traces should have survived.

When Wenz had accomplished as much as he thought he could, he would signal them to meet him at the rendezvous point.

He left them with a grin, looking rather silly in his lackey clothing. The tight-fitting blouse-like tunic and the ankle-length apron that completely concealed his flopping trousers gave him an appearance of someone's grandmother—except that not many grandmothers wore red, a highly appropriate personal color for the Duke Merzkion.

That night Wenz signaled on schedule from the highest window of one of the turrets. They answered him with a single flash of light, and then they moved off to begin their own search.

At dawn they were exploring the byways in the neighborhood of the castle, searching for abandoned camp sites. By midday they had found nothing at all, so they turned onto a principal surlane to take their search to the territory north of the castle.

And there the black knights overtook them on their way to a rendezvous with the dead Wenz, who had looked for the duke's pazul and found it.

Shrugging off Darzek's protests, Riklo carried Wenz's body all the way back to the cart. When they reached it, she proceeded with her own autopsy, trepanning the skull, removing the brain and the organs and nerves of sight, hearing, and smell. These she placed in a perfume jar, filled the jar with an essence that might serve as a passable preservative, and sealed it. She did the same with the lungs, with a length of intestine, with samples of tissue from various parts of the body.

While she worked, Darzek dug a grave. And when she was quite satisfied that she had enough samples for a careful study of the effects of a pazul, they buried Wenz.

The first light of dawn made little impression on the gloom of a sponge forest, but the night creatures knew what time it was. They were scurrying to their daytime lairs when Darzek and Riklo finally were able to wash up from their nighttime exertions. When they finished, they faced each other across the cart.

"Feeling squeamish again, Earthman?" Riklo asked hoarsely.

Darzek did not answer.

"He'd been dead almost a day—he must have died shortly after he signaled us." Riklo added defensively, "We couldn't take his body back. By the time we reached the lab it would have been too decayed to study. This way, we're certain to learn something about the effects of a pazul. At least his life won't have been completely wasted."

"His life won't be wasted," Darzek said. "Now we know where the pazul is. All we have to do is find out what it is."

She turned quickly. "You're going into the castle?"

"Of course. How else can we find out what it is?"

"You're going to walk into a castle you know nothing about, containing a pazul that looks like you don't know what, located you don't know where, and expect to come out alive? The pazul might be triggered to go off automatically. Wenz was the most alert and resourceful person I've ever known, and he didn't survive in that castle for an hour."

"That's all right," Darzek said. "I'll watch the duke and be careful not to step anywhere he doesn't."

Riklo faced him in silence for a moment. "What do you want me to do?" she asked finally.

"I want you to get these specimens back to the lab as quickly as possible and get them into a proper preservative. And I want you to write a complete report on everything that's happened and leave a copy in plain sight in the moon base. There's no guarantee that either of us will survive until help comes."

She said incredulously, "You're going alone?"

"Of course. And I'm going tonight."

"I'll come with you."

"No. Positively not. We're the last two agents on Kamm. One of us has got to hurry back and write that report. Too bad Rok Wllon isn't available to read it."

This proof that there actually was a pazul would have pleased Rok Wllon immensely. It was one of the few times Darzek could remember when the Director of the Department of Uncertified Worlds had been right.

By midday they were back at the scene of the previous day's altercation. While Darzek retrieved one of the dead knight's riding nabrula, which were still grazing in the forest, Riklo dug up clothing and equipment for him. Then they found themselves a secure clearing deep in the forest where Darzek could prepare for his foray.

He improvised a stunning set of mustaches for himself out of nabrula bristles, gave his hair a dark wash, and stained his face to produce the effect of the deep tan acquired by traveling knights. While he worked on himself, Riklo converted the blotched yellow nabrulk to a black- and purple-spotted creature of a different breed.

By midafternoon both of them had finished. Darzek was the complete knight of the Winged Beast, riding a steed that no one in the duke's castle could possibly recognize. He parted from Riklo where the surlane forked—he to head for the castle and she to turn north. They cached a change of clothing and a package of emergency supplies for him in a clearing near the fork. He would leave a message there when he completed his mission—just in case something happened to him before he made contact again—and he would adopt the identity of the lowest of peregrinating vendors, a wandering foot peddler, and travel only by night until he reached the neighboring province of Duke Fermarz. Riklo would rush to Northpor and take the specimens to the moon lab. Then she would travel to Fermarz by ship and meet Darzek there.

Darzek turned his nabrulk and lopped away, whip raised, mustaches fluttering defiantly, a formidable picture of aggressive confidence. He practiced the fierce expressions he'd seen knights use and felt ridiculous. Fortunately he met no one on the lane, and when he was able to glimpse a corner of the castle roof above the trees, he retired to the forest to rest. The nabrulk grazed contentedly on young sponge shoots, and Darzek stretched out on a pile of fallen bark, closed his eyes, and mulled over his tactics. Since he had a long wait, he even dozed a little.

Shortly after nightfall, at the grunz, the hour of the Kammian evening meal, he started his reckless gallop toward the castle. By the time he swerved into the steeply ascending branch of the lane that led to the castle gate, he was traveling with all the speed he could coax from the lumbering nabrulk. He brought the beast to a snorting halt with its bulging nose pressed against the gate in the outer wall.

His dramatic arrival went for naught. Even to his impaired hearing, the clattering hoofs of his nabrulk had sounded as though they could be heard for kilometers—but in this castle there were no ears. Disgustedly he uttered a shout and leaned over to pound on the gate before he thought to look around for some kind of signal pull.

He saw a dangling rope. He grabbed it and jerked. Somewhere in the distance it set something in motion; the return stroke snatched the rope from his fingers.

He looked about him. The lane branched off on either side, probably leading to side entrances. There could be no rear entrance because of the cliff. Darzek held the nabrulk's nose against the gate, snatched at the swinging rope, and pulled it again.

A panel covering a barred peephole in the gate opened. A moment later one of the massive sections began to swing aside. It stopped when the opening was wide enough to admit the nabrulk, but Darzek sat scornfully motionless and kept his mount from moving until the gate had been opened all the way. Then, without a glance on either side, he deigned to ride through.

The gate clumped shut behind him, and the dozen or so lackeys who had manipulated it chased after him through the castle grounds and overtook him before he reached the main entrance. In their grandmother costumes, they looked as ridiculous as Wenz had.

At the main entrance to the castle, other lackeys were waiting to raise the heavy, portcullis-like doorway. Darzek rode through it reflecting that Kammian history must have recorded some spectacular siege horrors to produce such a massive castle and a tradition of precautions still being faithfully adhered to even though no Duke of Storoz had been besieged for centuries. He had noticed how promptly the lackeys had closed the outer gate after admitting him; and he had noticed how the lackeys at the main entrance studied the landscape to see whether an army had accidentally slipped through the outer gate with him before they opened the castle to a solitary knight.

Darzek did not need an ultrasensitive Kammian nose to identify the ground level of the castle as its stable. He had hoped to arrogantly ride his nabrulk into the duke's presence, wherever he was, for the name of Darzek's game was bluff, the more insolent the better; but a single glance convinced him that he could coax the massive beast up the long ramp to the next level only by walking ahead of it and hauling on the reins, which would contribute very little to his necessary air of hauteur.

He looked about him. The corridor was lit by perfumed torches. The arched doorway off to his left led to the stables. The doorway on his right stood open, and he could see storage rooms beyond. Obviously his route lay upward.

He dismounted, tossed the reins to a lackey, tucked his whip under his arm. His hands spoke disdainfully. *Take me to the duke.*

One of the lackeys turned at once and headed for the broad ramp, and Darzek followed him. He was enormously relieved that it was not a staircase. Probably its width and gentle slope were planned so that carts could be hauled from one level of the castle to another, but the knights of Kamm could have preferred ramps for the same reason that Darzek did: so they could ascend or descend without stumbling over the outlandishly long, curved toes of their riding boots.

Long before Darzek reached the top of the ramp, he could hear the clatter of the banquet room. Noises produced by the unrefined guzzling of food blended with the racket of other revolting table manners that would have affected the appetites of fellow diners anywhere except in a land of the deaf. As the lackey started down the broad corridor past more flickering, perfumed torches, Darzek lengthened his stride to overtake and pass him. Through a wide archway at the end of the corridor, he could see diners seated at rough tables. None of them looked in his direction. They were totally occupied with the heaping platters of food. Darzek strode toward them.

As he approached the arch he began to run. He ran carefully—his planned dramatic entrance would be a farce if he stumbled over his toes. He burst through the arch at top speed, leaped, landed perfectly on the nearest table, scattering the platters. Miraculously he retained his balance. Two tables away, on a raised platform, sat the duke and his superior advisers, a solemn row of red-clad, gluttonous knights. Other knights, lackeys, servants, and retainers sat at the lower tables. Beyond the duke's party, the castle females were eating.

The duke's face went white with fear and surprise. Darzek, the glowering black knight of the Winged Beast, transfixed him with his most formidable stare.

The previous day, for some nefarious purpose known best to himself, the duke had sent out three of his own knights disguised as knights of the Winged Beast. Darzek guessed that he wanted their misdeeds blamed on the black knights rather than on his own. Now the duke found himself suddenly confronted by an apparently genuine knightly priest who arrived at an unheard of hour on an unknown mission that easily could have concerned the duke's own transgressions. Darzek had gambled that the duke would display a thunderingly guilty conscience the moment he appeared, and the effect was gratifying.

The silence that filled the room quickly became stifling. Not a single mouth ruffled that ominous hush by chewing. No hand reached for food, and what the hands already held remained frozen between platter and mouth. The plump little duke, whose mustaches were designed for a much larger face, had been caught on the upstroke of mastication. He opened his mouth and forgot to close it, and the mouthful of food rested revoltingly on his tongue.

Darzek paused long enough to make the most of the tense tableau, and then he aimed his fingers at the duke.

So this is the hospitality with which you greet distinguished emissaries. Shall I then transact my business with your underlings? No doubt I should find them better bred than you.

The duke's mouth remained open. The silence continued.

Very well, Darzek hands continued. *I'll return to the stables and confer with the nabrula. Both their manners and their intelligences should be an improvement over those of the food slops I see here.*

He turned. His leap carried him completely through the arch and out of the room. Again he miraculously managed to keep his balance. He landed and sprang sideways. Three long steps brought him to a narrow ascending ramp at the end of a short corridor. He darted up it.

Behind him, the monumental hush in the dining room continued. No one looked out to see where he had gone. He turned at the top of the ramp and all but collided with an elderly lackey. Darzek's fingers stabbed an order. *Take me to a vacant room.*

The lackey turned obediently. At the end of the corridor he opened a door. Darzek pointed his Winged Beast amulet and sent him toppling to the floor. He dragged him into the room and closed the door behind him.

He dashed to the window. His sense of direction had not failed him. He looked out onto the deep valley, with the duke's luminous garbage dump directly below.

Quickly he stripped off the knight's armor and clothing. He jettisoned everything: clothing armor, boots, even the mustache and whip. He wiped his head with a damp towel he had brought, leaving his hair several shades lighter. He altered his complexion in the same way before he tossed out the towel.

Then he turned his attention to the lackey. He stripped him and struggled into the uniform. He could barely get the tunic on; the trousers and apron, being loose-fitting, were less of a problem, but they fit Darzek with an unstylish tightness. The sandals, though a vast improvement on the absurd riding boots, were painfully small. When he finished, he surveyed himself in a mirror. He made a passable lackey, he thought, but only for the castle's dimmer corridors.

He dragged the unconscious lackey behind a mushroom-shaped bed and left him. He would be unconscious for hours, and by the time he awoke no one would believe him even if he had the courage to talk. Darzek left the room, closing the door behind him, and sedately, in his best lackey manner, he climbed a ramp to the next highest level. He was under no illusion about the security of his disguise, since Wenz had been caught in a lackey uniform two nights before, but it was the only one available.

As he headed for the next ascending ramp, he walked through stifling waves of perfume. Scent—from torches, from drapes, from wall hangings, from incense burners—scent was potently present throughout the castle, but on this floor it was overwhelming. On any other world he would have thought he'd located the castle's harem; but on Kamm, perfume was used by males more than by females. He moved among the powerful fragrances breathing through his mouth, and he took the first ascending ramp he came to with a feeling of deep relief.

When he reached the next floor, he was at the top of the castle except for the turrets. He paused to listen attentively, but no sounds of pursuit reverberated below him. Seemingly his bold ploy had worked to perfection.

He derived small satisfaction from that, because he had no idea of what he should do next. The source of the death ray might be smaller than a flashlight. Perhaps the duke carried it in his own pocket. Darzek did not know what to look for, or where, or how long he would be able to search before his ill-fitting lackey's uniform betrayed him.

But he knew that the pazul could be found. Wenz had found it. And he had found it high up in the castle. In the short time he'd been alive there, he could not have descended far.

Darzek found the spiraling ramp that pointed upward into one of the turrets. He climbed to the top and began to investigate its rooms as he descended. The ramp occupied the center of the tower, and at each level a room completely surrounded it. The effect, Darzek thought, was that of a square doughnut. These were storage rooms, packed with cabinets and chests of drawers and wardrobes, all filled with discarded clothing of various kinds and functions. Apparently the Duke Merzkion threw nothing away. Darzek gave the rooms a cursory search by moonlight, only occasionally risking a flash from his hand light. He doubted that the most alien mentality would conceal a pazul among discarded clothing.

In one room he happened onto a strange device. It looked vaguely like a rifle, but after examining it cautiously he decided that it was a broom. It had a long handle and a thickening base that was fitted with nabrula bristles. He picked it up and carried it with him. Somehow it seemed to give him the proper air of a lackey going about his business— even if neither he nor those he met knew what that business was.

He had searched rooms three quarters of the way down the spiraling ramp when a scurrying sound of feet reached him from below. He paused on the ramp and looked down. At that instant a knight led a crowd of lackeys into view. There were no torches lighting the turret ramp, but Darzek's form was visible in the dimness, and the knight saw him and ordered him down. As Darzek slowly descended, hobbling like an elderly lackey, the knight's fingers asked, *Have you seen a black knight?*

Darzek leaned his broom against the wall and answered with the mien of humble stupidity. *There are no knights here, sire, saving only your own honorable self.*

The knight did not wait for him to finish. He turned and hurried away, and the lackeys rushed after him. Darzek methodically finished searching that tower and moved on to the next.

And to the next. And it was in the third tower, as he mounted the spiral ramp to commence his search, that he stumbled over a body.

He knelt and flashed his light.

It was Riklo.

CHAPTER 10

Long after the momentary brightness had faded, Darzek's vision retained Riklo's image in all of its pathetic detail. She wore the clothing of a female attendant. A trickle of blood had flowed from one nostril. Her synthetic face looked normal, but her eyes, which were her own, had hemorrhaged.

As he bent over her, suddenly he caught the rhythm of shallow breathing. Then she moaned faintly.

She had found the pazul.

And she had survived—barely.

He picked her up and carried her down the spiraling ramp. His thought was to get her away from that exposed place, where they were at the mercy of the first passer-by.

But when he reached the main corridor, he hesitated. He had no idea where to take her. By dramatically fixing a knight of the Winged Beast in everyone's mind, he had made it possible for almost anyone else to pass unnoticed; but a lackey carrying a female attendant would certainly occasion comment, especially if the pair were headed toward an exit.

Suddenly she spoke. "Where are you taking me?"

He put her down and supported her until she regained sufficient control of herself to stand unaided. "I had some idea of getting you out of here," he said.

"What happened?"

"Don't you know?"

She closed her eyes and swayed dizzily. "Where are we?"

"The Duke Merzkion's castle. Don't ask me what you're doing here. I'm looking for a pazul, and you're supposed to be on your way to Northpor."

"Oh."

"I suppose you came to help me look. In any case, you found it. In this turret."

"Oh."

"Don't you remember?"

She thought for a moment. "I climbed the ramp. I was opening each door I passed and looking in, and I started to open a door, and that's all I remember."

She took a step and staggered, and he caught her before she fell. He started to pick her up again.

"I can walk," she said.

She shook free of him, took another step, and collapsed. He caught her just in time.

"Let me rest a moment," she pleaded.

"I will—just as soon as I find a safe place for you."

He picked her up again and quickly moved to the far end of the corridor, where he mounted the ramp into a turret he'd already explored. He entered one of the rooms, dumped the contents of a wardrobe onto the floor, and helped Riklo to stretch out on the pile of clothing.

"Where are you going?" she asked.

"I'm going to have a look at the pazul. Then I'm coming back here, and we'll decide how we're going to get out."

He closed the door to the room and hurried back down the ramp. In the main corridor he turned toward the central turret—but an army was there ahead of him, a file of knights and whip-armed lackeys that already had reached the turret and started up its ramp. Darzek faded back out of sight and watched. Two knights took up positions at the bottom of the ramp, and the lackeys arranged themselves just above. The turret was under guard. So was the pazul.

Darzek turned away. The time had come to settle for what they already had and get out while they could—if they could.

One of the knights had noticed Darzek and turned to watch him, so he affected the slow pace used by lackeys performing nominal duties and moved away from the turret where he had left Riklo. He turned into a side corridor, a short hallway with a single door on either side. He hesitated, opened one of the doors, entered. It was a group bedroom with a row of mushroom beds.

He lay down on one of them and carefully counted off five minutes. Then he left, walking slowly back the way he had come. The knight had lost interest in the limping lackey and turned his attention elsewhere, and Darzek was able to slip up the turret ramp unnoticed. He opened the door of the room where he had left Riklo—and found it empty.

He thought for a moment. He was certain she had not been captured, or the entire floor would have swarmed with officialdom and lackeys.

One of the casements was open slightly. Darzek went to it and leaned far out so he could look down the sheer wall of the castle. For a time he saw nothing at all. Then a drifting cloud suddenly released the light of two moons, and there she was. She and Wenz had been of different species, from different worlds, but she possessed a talent similar to his. She clung to the side of the building like the insect she may have been.

Darzek closed the window and turned away. She had imposed her own solution, leaving the way she came, and there was nothing more that he could do for her. His choices lay between looking for a place to sleep and finding his way out of the castle as quickly as possible. He decided to get out.

An ornate ceramic pot with a cover of wood stood on a low table. He aimed his hand light into it and found it filled almost to the top with polished stones of various colors and shapes. He picked up the pot and carried it with him.

He descended the ramp and limped along the corridor. Two knights and two lackeys now stood at the bottom of the ramp to the central turret, but they paid no attention to him. Eventually Darzek's descent down a main ramp took him out of their line of sight. He continued to descend, and he met no one until he reached the level where he had left the unconscious lackey.

There the ramp ended in chaos. Knights stood about, their fingers confusedly asking questions that no one answered. Four lackeys were carrying out Darzek's unconscious, nude victim. Other lackeys came and went. Darzek boldly entered into that revolving swarm and managed to emerge intact on the far side.

On the next level, a crowd of lackeys surrounded him. Some were conversing among themselves, something about a nabrulk, but Darzek could not follow their rapid speech without conspicuously staring at their hands. The traffic thinned out, and he found himself plodding along behind a knight in armor. Still carrying his ceramic pot, he followed on the heels of the knight's massively toed boots. The ruse worked perfectly. The knight never looked back, and everyone they met thought Darzek was an attendant carrying something for his master. No one considered him worthy of a second glance.

The knight strode past the banquet hall and took the main descending ramp. The reek of the stables drifted up to meet them, and Darzek started breathing through his mouth. The knight went directly to the vast, vaulted room that was the main stable. In the center of that room, the duke himself stood surrounded by knights and lackeys.

They were examining a nabrulk. The beast's yellow hide looked familiar, and Darzek risked a second glance at it and discerned a network of faded spots. It was the nabrulk he had ridden into the castle, and the creature was being cleaned. Riklo's dyes had not fooled the castle's nabrula keeper for long.

Off to one side, a group of knights in full regalia stood waiting, each with a lackey holding the reigns of his nabrulk. The knight Darzek had been following joined them.

Darzek turned back. Still carrying his pot, he left the stable and entered the doorway on the opposite side of the entrance corridor. Beyond the storage rooms he found a ramp leading downward. A torch flared at the bottom. He descended quickly. Minutes later he was on his way back up. The duke's dungeon was a shoddy, cramped place, and the only prisoners were dazed peasants. The guards, if there were any, had left their posts for the excitement on the upper levels.

Darzek returned to the stable. The knights were still there, talking among themselves. Darzek edged close to them and found a position behind a pillar. Obviously the knights were going somewhere. Before they could go, someone would have to raise a portcullis and open a gate. He set his pot down and waited alertly.

Finally the little duke turned his back on the nabrulk and waddled over to the knights. A knight signaled, and the heavy portcullis was hauled up. This was not the door Darzek had entered, but a much wider one, through which four knights could ride abreast.

Lackeys hurried up with nabrula, and the knights swung into their saddles and went through the opening in ranks of four. A crowd of lackeys surged through after them.

Darzek went with the lackeys. At the outer wall the knights halted, their nabrula stomping and wheezing restlessly, while the lackeys arranged themselves along a massive gate. Darzek selected his own position with care. They heaved and pushed, and when the gate finally stood open, Darzek was stationed at its outer end. When the lackeys scurried to either side to get out of the way of the knights, Darzek simply moved around the end of the gate. And when, after the knights had ridden away, the lackeys closed the gate, Darzek was left outside.

He was not missed. He waited in the shadow of the wall until the knights had passed beyond his hearing and the portcullis had crashed down. Then he dashed to the safety of the sponge forest and limped off through the waves of light and scent emitted by Kamm's night creatures, with his stolen lackey sandals severely cutting his feet.

Avoiding the road, Darzek went directly to the forest clearing where his supplies were cached. There he found the perfumer's cart, the three nabrula, and Riklo, who was already lost in a restless, feverish sleep in the cart.

He watched her for a time, deeply concerned. Then he decided that sleep probably was better for her than anything he could think of doing. He stretched out beside her, and the two of them slept long into daylight. Darzek was awakened once, by the rumble of nabrula hoofs on the nearby lane. He sleepily muttered for them to go away, and they did.

Finally he stirred himself, slipping cautiously from the cart to allow the restlessly feverish Riklo to continue her sleep. He ate some dried meat, washing it down with pungent Kammian cider, and then he seated himself on a nearby sponge log to meditate.

When Riklo awoke, still feverish, he tried unsuccessfully to feed her. Finally he decided that she herself was the best judge of what her alien physiology required. He returned to his log, and after a time she joined him there.

"Feel like talking?" he asked her.

"No. But I suppose we'd better."

"I'll talk and you listen. Interrupt me when you feel like it. Just for a start, let's consider a problem in Kammian psychology. You're the Duke Merzkion. You have a pazul, an invincible death ray. Naturally this is the most valuable thing you own, so for safekeeping you put it in a room at the top of your castle and contrive a booby trap so the thing will kill anyone opening the door. Why?"

She did not answer.

"It's a mystery to me," Darzek went on meditatively. "But maybe it's self-evident that this is the best way to protect a pazul. Let it protect itself. I assume there'd be a way to turn the thing on or off from outside the room. But consider this next step. There's a mysterious stranger loose in your castle, and you suspect that he has designs on your pazul. Do you sit back, chuckling quietly to yourself, and wait for the pazul to kill him—as it did in fact kill another mysterious stranger a couple of nights earlier? You do not. You rush an armed guard to the spot. Is the guard supposed to protect the pazul, which doesn't need any protection?"

Again Riklo did not answer.

"Obviously the guard was there to guard something. If it wasn't the pazul, which didn't need it, was there something else of value in that tower? And if there was something else of value there, why wasn't the pazul placed to guard that along with itself?"

Riklo said regretfully, "I should have looked when I had the chance."

"If you had, you'd be dead. Can you remember any more than you could last night?"

She could not. She remembered opening the door cautiously and peeking in. The next thing she knew, Darzek was carrying her.

"When the beam hit you, you staggered backward and collapsed," Darzek said. "In doing so, you closed the door. That saved your life. It also saved mine. If you hadn't got there first, I would have found the pazul a few minutes later, and I wouldn't have opened the door a crack and peeked into the room. I was ducking into those rooms quickly, as Wenz must have, to get out of sight. I would have walked into the full blast of it. Tell me this. If the Duke Merzkion has a pazul, why hasn't he marched off to conquer Storoz with it? He could, easily."

"He wouldn't dare," Riklo said. "The Sailor's League would retaliate if he touched the Free Cities. No ships would come to Storoz. The economy would be ruined."

"Would the Sailor's League retaliate if he limited his conquests to the provinces and didn't interfere with the Free Cities?"

"No," she said, after a moment's thought. "If he promised to respect the rights of the Free Cities and not interfere with trade, they wouldn't care who ruled the provinces."

"Then why hasn't he marched? With his pazul, he'd be invincible."

Riklo leaped to her feet. She staggered, regained her balance, and excitedly waved away Darzek's helping hand. "Merzkion isn't the only province where we've lost agents! Some of the other dukes must have pazuls!" She paused to reflect. "The Duke of OO, for one. And probably Fermarz. And there could be others. I'll go back tonight and look at the pazul through the window. There couldn't be any danger in that, since it's aimed at the door. I should have done it last night. Now that we know where it is, and what it does—"

"No," Darzek said firmly. "We don't know how it's aimed, and we don't know what it does. And no stranger is going to get into or near the Duke Merzkion's castle tonight or any other night for a long time. He'll have the grounds under guard and every approach watched. He's already searching the countryside. The sooner we leave here, the better. We have work to do. We've got to get Wenz's specimens to the lab. We've also got to devise a shield against that metal detector, or we won't be able to carry secret equipment. After that, I'm going to call on one of the other dukes. It's reason enough for not marching to war with your pazul if you know your neighbor has one."

They returned to Northpor as fast as their three nabrula could take them, traveling by night and hiding by day until they left the province of the Duke Merzkion. And Riklo was ill and feverish most of the way, lying weakly in the cart. Twice she hemorrhaged badly, from the nose, and several times she became disorientated and babbled to Darzek in a language he did not understand.

The moment they arrived in Northpor, he put her to bed in Wesru's capable care. He went directly to the moon base, where he transferred the Wenz specimens and then spent a futile hour searching for medicines and medical information that could be helpful to Riklo. The base file had no suggestions concerning pazul disease.

He was more successful with the metal detector. The file directed him to a special kit of protective films. A few tests told him which film to use, and he returned to Northpor and lined the secret compartments of the cart with it.

Sajjo and Hadkez burst in upon him to ecstatically recount their enormous success with the perfume sales. They hauled him off to the factory to sample three new scents Hadkez had developed, and Darzek gave Hadkez the task of restocking the cart for its next expedition. The news that Darzek was leaving again plunged Sajjo into gloom, and she dashed off to her own room.

That night Darzek took over the watch in Riklo's room. He armed himself with a pad of paper from the moon base. Between his ministrations to the feverish Riklo, he filled the pad, writing down everything that had happened since his arrival, and what he had learned, and what he thought it meant. He also described what he intended to do next, and why. The next morning, he took the pad back to the moon base and left it in a conspicuous place. And he appended a note for the Department of Uncertified Worlds Headquarters, expressing his opinion of departmental procedures where twenty agents could disappear without leaving a single memo that could be useful to those trying to find them.

Riklo was feeling much better. She'd suffered cruelly in the jolting cart, and a day of rest in a comfortable bed improved her condition drastically; but she was still weak, and her prognosis seemed so uncertain that both she and Darzek accepted without mentioning the fact that it would be a long time before she could travel.

"You're leaving at once?" she asked.

"I must," Darzek answered. "As long as there's a possibility that any of the missing agents are alive, I have to keep trying to find them."

"You're going to OO?"

"Perhaps. But first I'm going to call on the Duke Merzkion's neighbor, the Duke Fermarz. What do you know about him?"

"Very little. Most of the dukes seem like blurred copies of each other. When are you leaving?"

"As soon as I've made a few arrangements."

On the Northpor quay he spoke to a sea captain, who referred him to another captain; and Darzek quickly negotiated passage for himself, his cart, and his three nabrula to Fermarzpor, a small town that was the Duke Fermarz's only seaport. The ship would sail with the midnight tide. Darzek went home to make his final preparations.

He chose his supplies with care and packed them away in the secret compartments of his cart: binoculars, a kit of medical supplies, three extra Winged Beast amulets, a pair of stun rifles, a blade that looked like a machete, a rope equipped with a gun that shot it to a height of twenty meters, half a dozen hand lights, and a torch that produced enough heat to melt metal. As far as Darzek knew, there was no metal in Storoz except coins, but this time he intended to be prepared for anything.

He drove his cart aboard the ship, got the nabrula comfortably housed in a shed behind the long cabin, and went home for another farewell with his household. Sajjo was so disconsolate that she would not come down to say good-bye to him.

The following night, after an unusually fast run down the coast, Darzek harnessed his nabrula to his cart. The sailors unblocked the wheels, the captain—pleased with a passenger who paid in advance in coins, caused no difficulties, and could lift a mug of cider as well as a sailor—raised both hands in farewell, and Darzek drove his cart ashore at the port of Fermarzpor.

He also drove straight through the pleasant little town and some distance into the country before he found himself a resting place, so as to leave any inquisitive port officials far behind. He unharnessed the nabrula and tied them so they could graze. Then he reached back into the cart for the tarp and blankets he used for bedding—he preferred the ground to the hard boards of the cart bottom.

His hand encountered something that twisted and struggled. He snatched it away and ripped the canvas flaps open.

It was Sajjo.

He regarded her with mingled dismay and amusement, but because she'd been hidden in the cart since the previous night, he only asked, *Are you hungry?* The light was too dim for talking, but when he brought out food, she ate ravenously.

The light also was too dim for recriminations. After she had eaten, he waved her back to the comfortable cocoon she had fashioned for herself at the rear of the cart. He made up his own bed on the ground. They would talk in the morning.

Riklo and Darzek had traveled as husband and wife and as perfumer and keeper of secrets, or fortuneteller. But Sajjo needed no special role beyond that of a perfumer's daughter, and she assumed it ecstatically. They wended their tedious way from wayside forum to stinking wayside forum, with pleasant interludes of travel through a lovely countryside.

The Province of Fermarz seemed much more prosperous than that of

Merzkion. It was crisscrossed with small farm holdings and dotted with attractive little villages, some of which had their own artisans. But Darzek knew that the Duke Merzkion also had rich farm lands near the coast, and his enormous holdings in sponge forests were worth a very tidy income.

Sajjo shyly confessed on the first morning that it was Riklo who had suggested stowing away. *She said you needed help and someone to look after you.*

Darzek had hardly seen her during his abbreviated stay in Northpor. Now he observed that she was centimeters taller and that her business experience at the Northpor mart had given her a poise that made her seem years older. Her alert young mind had easily picked up the manners and tastes of her stylish mart customers. Now her hair was beautifully dyed and arranged flawlessly, and she wore the simple clothing designs appropriate to her age with an adult flair.

She immediately made herself invaluable, performing all of the housekeeping, cooking when there was time for it, and vending their perfumes, which permitted Darzek to wander about as much as he liked, talking with peasants or fellow vendors who had the inclination, and observing what he could.

But there was little enough to observe in a foul-smelling, unkempt forum, where the Mound of the Sun was eroding away and the carved Winged Beast had blown from its pole in the last storm. The peasants continued to worship as though the life pyramid reached its customary height and the Beast were still present. In the rural areas of Kamm, even change did not produce change, and it was a relief to Darzek when, at the end of the fourth day, they came to the castle of the Duke Fermarz.

It occupied the top of a tall, isolated hill, and at the base of the hill, on the side of easiest approach to the castle, a sizable town had grown. It was large enough to have a formal market square, and Darzek and Sajjo drove directly to it. They set up their display of perfume samples, and then Darzek strolled about for a look at the mart.

Perfumers, dyers, peddlers, all kinds of itinerant artisans and vendors came to such rural centers of commerce. They did a modest business for a time; and when the townspeople had inspected and sampled their wares, or satisfied a curiosity about what information a new keeper of secrets might have to offer, their trade fell off and they moved along to the next mart.

Sajjo had a modest rush of customers as soon as they opened for business. Darzek, returning from his circuit of the market place, found her so busy that he joined her, and the two of them dispensed perfumes until evening to a steady stream of townsfolk.

With the evening came two purple-caped knights to the mart, accompanied by a scribe. One knight took the names and professions of the day's arrivals, and while the scribe entered this information in his records, the other knight prowled about their carts and tents with something cupped in his hands. Fortunately, the new shielding worked.

Darzek thoughtfully watched the inspection party move on to the next newly arrived vendor. Then he turned to Sajjo, who had been thoroughly indifferent to the menace of the duke's knights.

These new perfumes of Hadkez must be good.

They are beautiful, Sajjo announced, using the Kammian term of highest approbation. *Ours are the favorite scents in the entire Northpor mart. The perfumer Hadkez worked for wanted him to come back, but he wouldn't.*

They must be beautiful, Darzek agreed. Privately he was less than enthused about this unexpected genius of Hadkez's for creating new scents. He preferred an anonymous mediocrity to popular success, which could bring more attention than he cared for.

He went to talk politely with his fellow vendors, who were closing for the night. He asked one or two questions of each, and when he returned to the cart he was in a thoughtful mood.

What's the matter? Sajjo asked.

Tell me why the Duke Fermarz would call in all of his knights and use them to guard his castle, Darzek said.

Sajjo gazed at him perplexedly.

Normally the knights are scattered all over the province, Darzek went on. *They have important peacekeeping, and judicial, and administrative duties. But now they do nothing but guard the castle. The lane up to the castle has a series of check points, where all traffic is stopped and searched, and the knights are maintaining guard posts all over the hill.*

The duke is afraid of something, Sajjo announced.

Right, Darzek agreed.

And since the Duke Fermarz's call for help seemed to have come only a couple of days after Darzek's invasion of the Duke Merzkion's castle, Darzek thought he knew what it was.

Like the Duke Merzkion, the Duke Fermarz was afraid someone would steal his pazul—or whatever the pazul was guarding. The Duke Merzkion must have sent word to him at once, by fast messenger: Someone tried to steal mine. Better guard yours well. And the Duke Fermarz called in all of his knights.

Trying to look into an alien mind, Darzek thought, was like peering through the window of a strange room furnished entirely with trick mirrors. In time, the windows that looked out on reality might become the most distorted of all.

Obviously the dukes did not think of their pazuls as offensive weapons. Otherwise, since the two dukes obviously were in league, why didn't they conquer Storoz together? But if they thought of their pazuls as defensive weapons, why did they place so little confidence in them?

He knew he had no chance at all of getting up the hill to the castle. He did not even consider it. At the same time, the Duke Fermarz was so obviously guarding something of immense value that Darzek was reluctant to leave.

They remained at the mart, and he helped Sajjo handle the rush of perfume trade and watched the formations of purple-caped knights get in each other's way moving about the ridiculously safeguarded castle hill.

CHAPTER 11

With the castle blocked off to him, Darzek fell back on his pastime of studying Kammian psychology. He had been attempting to comprehend the alien mentalities that surrounded him; suddenly, to his vast amusement, he discovered that these aliens were the same vendors and customers he had met on so many worlds.

The newly arrived vendors moved slowly up and down the rows of tents and carts, craftily weighing the virtues and liabilities of each vacant space. Those with foodstuffs to sell preferred positions near the entrance. Kammians who followed the old religion would see the looming Winged Beast as they entered the mart and buy something for a sacrifice; and many customers preferred to buy foodstuffs on their way out of the mart, so that their hands and arms would be unencumbered when they haggled over more expensive purchases. Vendors of dyes liked to set up near weavers, who sold quantities of undyed cloth. Perfumers liked a position where there were as few nabrula as possible, so that their scents could be enjoyed by prospective customers without olfactory distractions. All vendors preferred to crowd in with their competition rather than to set up by themselves in a remote part of the mart. A customer seeing display after display of similar merchandise might be moved eventually to stop and buy, and all the vendors benefited. A solitary display did not provide such motivation.

Having watched for several days this sly maneuvering for desirable sites, Darzek was intrigued to see one newly arrived cart make immediately for the most remote corner of the mart. The elderly driver got out agilely, unharnessed the single nabrulk, and led it to the back of the cart, where he tied it to a feed trough. A pull of a rope folded down a canvas-covered framework at the side of the cart, and a sizable tent had been erected almost instantaneously. While Darzek watched in amazement, the owner deftly pegged it down. A jerk of another rope unrolled a small banner. A moment later, having moved in a few furnishings, the owner was seated in the tent entrance, ready for business.

Darzek drifted closer, wondering whether the mechanical ingenuity that had produced the unfolding tent could also have fashioned other contrivances. An electrical generator, for example.

Then he saw something even more startling. While this new vendor was still moving into his tent, a passer-by noticed his banner, turned into the mart, and hurried toward him. Shoppers already in the mart were streaming in that direction. The vendor had scarcely seated himself before he had a waiting line.

Darzek moved close enough to scrutinize the banner.

It contained only a large line drawing of a face, and the face seemed to be a fair likeness of the old man who sat in the tent opening. There was no hint of who he was or what he did.

Darzek asked one of the waiting customers. *Bovranulz,* was the answer. It meant, "Old Blind One."

He was a clairvoyant, a fortuneteller, a keeper of secrets; and since the mere unfurling of his banner brought a rush of business, he had local fame and a following. Probably he had been traveling the same circuit for years and making a regular stop here.

His popularity did not interest Darzek. Any keeper of secrets who put on a good act and kept his gibberish vague enough so that all of his predictions seemed to come true could achieve popularity. Darzek wanted to know who had designed the Old Blind One's folding tent. He returned to his own cart, seated himself in its shade, and continued to watch.

That evening, the ducal inspection team of two knights and a scribe made its usual visit to record the day's arrivals. This time, instead of striding into the mart to curtly administer their inquisition, the three halted at the mart entrance. One of the knights signaled to the scribe, who remounted his nabrulk and clattered off up the ascending lane to the castle. The two knights quietly got in line with those waiting to consult Bovranulz.

A short time later the duke himself arrived, accompanied only by the scribe who had carried the message. And the duke, a lank, mournful-looking individual whose mustaches seemed always destined to droop, took his place in line and quietly awaited his turn.

Darzek went to Sajjo. *Did you ever hear of a keeper of secrets named Bovranulz?* he asked.

Of course, she answered. *Everyone knows of Bovranulz.*

Of course, Darzek agreed. *Obviously. Everyone knows of him. Do you know the names of any other keepers of secrets?*

She did not. Bovranulz was one of a kind. He was unique. Darzek left Sajjo to her customers, strolled over to the far corner of the mart, and got in line. To see Bovranulz.

Dusk was approaching. Normally the vendors would have closed for the night, but some of them remained open to importune Bovranulz's customers as they left the mart. The line moved slowly, shortening in front of Darzek and lengthening behind him.

As Darzek edged along with the patient crowd, he experienced a sensation he had not known before. A mystical feeling of oneness with the People of Kamm overwhelmed him. With it came a sharpened sense of urgency.

Ahead of Darzek was a tottering oldster who perhaps wanted to know if his rheumatism would ease. Behind Darzek was a young female carrying an infant—was the problem hers or the child's? There was the duke, quietly waiting his turn like any commoner. "We are all commoners before the forces of fate," Darzek mused. Next to the duke stood a female who on Earth would have been in her mid-teens. Her fingers twisted and intertwined nervously, and her need seemed far more compelling than that of His Highness.

The People of Kamm. The dukes were choosing up sides, a super-weapon was waiting to be used, and these, the innocent commoners, would pay the high price of ducal folly.

If Bovranulz had genuine powers, Darzek thought, he would speak of the horrors of destruction to a white-faced duke.

But when the duke finally had his turn, he strolled away peacefully, nodding to a subject who performed the Kammian genuflection to him, half bow, half curtsy. He seemed in a complacent mood—had the seer assured him that there was no plan afoot to raid his castle?

The line moved up.

The seer was seated in the recessed tent opening with a rug hung before him on a frame. The suppliant leaned over the rug, bringing his head close to that of the seer. The seer's hands were concealed by the rug and visible only to the suppliant. As darkness set in, the seer lit candles on either side of him to keep his hands visible, and the glow of candlelight suffused the aged face. It was a rudimentary but effective system of confidentiality, and it underscored the seer's role as keeper of secrets.

But Darzek was completely unable to figure out how the suppliant asked his questions.

The line moved up again. Finally Darzek was close enough to see what was happening, and his perplexity deepened. The suppliant merely leaned over the rug and studied the seer's concealed hands. He asked nothing at all; he merely read the answer. Then came the clink of a coin in a coin pot, the suppliant stepped aside, and the next in line took his place.

Finally it was Darzek's turn. Uncertainly he took two steps forward and leaned over the rug. Since he had no notion of what was expected of him, he did nothing at all. The deeply wrinkled face loomed close to his; the clouded, sightless eyes stared at him—stared through him, and Darzek gazed into the infinity of their nothingness.

Suddenly the fingers moved. Darzek looked down at them.

You have come far.

Darzek had to will himself to remain motionless. Then he decided he was being foolish—half the people in the mart, the vendors and their families, had come far. As the Kammians measured distance, this place was a long way from Northpor.

The sightless eyes continued to stare at Darzek. The fingers moved again.

I thank you for your concern for my people.

Again Darzek had to will himself to remain motionless.

Do not be alarmed. I am keeper of secrets. What do you wish to ask me?

He was a mind reader. Darzek did not believe in mind readers. He knew too many of their tricks—he even had performed mind-reading tricks himself—but he could not disbelieve what he was experiencing. He struggled to bring his thought into focus. Rok Wllon—

Your friend is alive.

"Where?" Darzek thought.

He travels.

Again Darzek thought the word, "Where?" This time he got no response.

Then his mind formed a question about the pazul. Again there was no reply, so he reshaped the thought and reshaped it again.

It is a frightening question, Bovranulz's fingers said finally, *but I do not understand it.*

Darzek dropped two coins into the pot and turned away.

Sajjo had closed their perfume display and was preparing their evening meal. Darzek lit a small torch and sat down beside her. *What do you know about Bovranulz?*

He is a keeper of secrets.

Does he speak truly?

She seemed astonished at the question. *Of course! He is a keeper of secrets!*

The first bold night creatures of evening were uncertainly venturing forth and then scurrying back into hiding. Sajjo glanced at them uneasily. Then, with a shy smile, she handed Darzek his bowl of stew and a chunk of heavy bread to dip into it. She served herself, and the two of them ate sitting side by side, with Sajjo occasionally glancing up at him and smiling. A purple lock of hair kept slipping from her hairdo; each time it happened she scowled and tried to tuck it back into place. Darzek marveled again at the way she had matured in the short time he had known her.

And she seemed as completely happy as any individual Darzek had ever known. It was not due to the sudden transformation from stark poverty to affluence. It was because she now belonged to someone. She had an adopted father at hand, and a warm family unit in Northpor to which they would return. Also, she was herself an important economic cog in that unit.

They finished eating, and she expertly cleaned bowls and stewing pot. When finally she turned to him, Darzek said, *Have you a question for the keeper of secrets?*

She gazed at him in astonishment. Only people with problems, with troubles, sought out a keeper of secrets. Obviously she had none.

Darzek gave her a coin. *Go to him. Think a question for him. Ask him if the Winged Beast really took your father.*

She took the coin and hurried away.

The torch burned out, and the night creatures became more daring. Darzek waited in the dark for a time, and then he lit another torch, thinking that Sajjo might be uneasy about returning to darkness. Also, he wanted to know how Bovranulz answered her.

Finally she came, hurrying from one patch of light to another where an occasional vendor was still eating an evening meal by torchlight. She plunked herself down beside him, her face aglow with happiness.

He said—the Winged Beast goes only where it is welcomed or feared. Her smile broadened. *My father never feared it.*

Did he tell you anything else? Darzek asked.

She looked away shyly. *My new father will triumph over the Winged Beast.*

That was kind of him, Darzek said and wondered what it meant. He sent Sajjo off to bed in the cart, and then he walked across the mart again toward the tent of Bovranulz.

The line was shorter now. Some of those waiting carried torches. The spectacle of Kammians, who feared the night, waiting in line with torches to see a keeper of secrets amused Darzek. He paused to talk with a peddler he had become acquainted with, and he asked, *Why don't they see him in the morning?*

The peddler seemed surprised. *Bovranulz leaves in the morning. He never stays but one night at the small marts.*

Darzek considered this, and then he got in line a second time. Suppliants continued to arrive, but there were fewer of them, and the line seemed to move faster.

Again Darzek took his place leaning over the rug and looking into the sightless eyes. He thought a series of questions about Rok Wllon.

He is alive, Bovranulz answered. *He travels.*

Darzek shaped a thought about Rok Wllon's health.

He survives, the fingers answered.

Darzek formed a question about the other missing Synthesis agents. After a long pause, Bovranulz answered, *Some live. I count three, but there may be more. They are captives. They are in a place under the ground.*

Darzek risked one more question. The seer had not understood his earlier thought about the pazul. Now he formed a mental picture of the probable devastation a pazul could wreak upon the innocent People of Kamm. He visualized a village street strewn with bodies, and then he focused in like a zoom camera on the agonies of a dying child.

The seer winced. Pain distorted his face. For a long moment he sat rigidly, head bowed, sightless eyes clenched shut, and then his fingers spoke. *The village of Karlanklo.*

"Where? When?" Darzek's mind demanded.

The Province Merzkion. The day the Mother Moon is full.

Darzek did a fumbling calculation. Four—or perhaps it was five—days hence. He would have to move quickly.

You will go, the fingers said, *but the picture has been drawn.*

Then, as Darzek hesitated—eager to be off but reluctant to leave while there was the possibility of another revelation—the fingers continued to speak. *We visit OO-Fair together, though we do not meet there. But much will be revealed to you in OO—including the danger that you carry with you.*

Darzek dropped his coins into the pot and turned away. He walked swiftly across the mart to his cart, where he maneuvered the nabrula into place one at a time and harnessed them. Sajjo had conscientiously put everything away except the cooking pot and its frame, and Darzek shoved those into the cart and got the nabrula moving.

A moment later Sajjo's head appeared. Darzek pointed a finger, and she obediently returned to her bed. At the intersection below the castle, he took the surlane north, and he drove leisurely, letting the nabrula follow a lane they could see better than he and plod along at their own pace. Long before he reached his destination, the test would become one of endurance rather than speed.

It made no sense to Darzek that the Duke Merzkion would destroy one of his own villages; but if he did, Darzek wanted to see his pazul in action.

Either way, this provided him with an excellent opportunity to test Bovranulz's revelations.

They traveled both day and night and reached the unmarked boundary between Fermarz and Merzkion on the third day. As they moved into Merzkion Province, Darzek began to ask peasants about the location of a village named Karlanklo, a phrase that meant, "village in the shadow of the half-hill." There were enough villages with similar names to keep him in perpetual confusion and uncertainty and give him the feeling of approaching a linguistic horizon where the meanings of all words merged. Every commoner they met had to be questioned; every village they saw had to be investigated—sometimes to the immense surprise of its occupants, who of course saw no reason to confuse their village of Barmarklo with the village of Karlanklo—which, as everyone knew, was located an uncertain number of travel units in the direction from which Darzek had just come.

They wandered on. The Duke Merzkion's castle appeared on the horizon, was next seen far off to their right, and finally could be glimpsed behind them. Its foreboding presence made Darzek cautious despite his haste, and this caution enabled him to avoid an entire company of knights by taking to the sponge forest at precisely the right moment.

The knights galloped past. Darzek pulled back onto the lane and followed after them slowly—anxious not to overtake them and equally anxious not to meet them on their return.

He was worried about Sajjo. He easily could have left her with the family of a friendly vendor in Fermarz, but instead he had brought her into a danger that could prove deadly. She could sense his growing anxiety, and now she sat quietly beside him, no longer fluttering her fingers in gay chatter about the things they were passing.

Then the lane curved out of the forest and along the crest of a hill, and the village was spread out across the valley from them: a tiny collection of stone houses crowded up against a truncated rise of ground that made the name inevitable and the place identifiable at a glance.

And they were too late. Death was there before them.

Males lay in the tiny fields that had so grudgingly yielded these peasants a livelihood. Males, females, and children lay in the one village street. As Darzek brought the cart to a halt and stared aghast at the carnage, a few pathetic moans drifted up to him—the more pathetic when Darzek reflected that he was the only living thing within earshot that could hear them.

It was not the pazul that had done this, but the company of the Duke Merzkion's knights on a rampage. Their vicious, cutting whips had sliced the bodies of these innocent villagers to the bone, severing veins and arteries, cutting through tissue and muscle and nerves. The victim of a severe lashing lay helpless until he bled to death—which mercifully did not take long.

The knights were still there, ransacking the humble dwellings on foot and searching in silent fury for any life that had escaped them.

Darzek backed the cart into a crosslane, a mere wagon track that led into the forest. As soon as they were out of sight of the surlane, he halted. He crawled into the cart, folded the hand-woven carpet out of the way, and took two stun rifles from a secret compartment. He set both rifles on full power.

Then, looking sternly at the wide-eyed Sajjo, he said, *Hide in the forest. Stay away from the cart—if the knights find you near it, they'll kill you. If I don't come back, wait until dark and take the surlane north. Travel only by night until you leave Merzkion. Understand?*

She gave him a grave affirmative.

Darzek left the forest and set off down the lane on foot. The knights were still intent on their looting, and he reached the middle of the village before anyone saw him.

The blood orgy had stirred all of the knights to frenzy. They were throwing things about, grunting in fury, kicking and lashing at bodies long dead. The first knight to glimpse Darzek through a window was in a short whip range. He came charging out at him, multithonged side arm poised, intent on the pleasure of lashing one more victim to death, and Darzek cut him down with a squeeze of his weapon's handle.

Before the knight's body had crashed to the ground, Darzek whirled, the weapon buzzed again, and he disposed of two knights who were charging at him from the rear. Then, as the houses erupted knights, Darzek backed up against a windowless façade and sprayed the street with both weapons. In a moment the entire company of knights was spread the length of the tiny village's lane.

Darzek went from house to house searching for anything that lived, knight or peasant. He found neither. He had deliberately set the rifles at killing power—that was neater than cutting their throats.

Darzek turned and trudged back along the lane. Halfway to the forest, he turned again and looked down on the village. The scene of carnage was precisely the one he had imagined for Bovranulz.

"The problem with a clairvoyant," Darzek told himself, "is the same as the problem one has with a computer—asking the right question, in the right way, and interpreting the answer. If I could learn to do all three, Bovranulz would be extremely useful."

Taking a last look at the village, he wondered if he should have intervened. Massacring one company of knights wouldn't improve conditions in the Duke Merzkion's province. It was much more likely to cause additional reprisals.

But Darzek had considered it a solemn obligation. In a pen near the village stood two large, yellow riding nabrula—now backed into a corner and quivering with terror at the reek of blood that permeated the village. They were the nabrula of the phony black knights Darzek and Riklo had disposed of. The peasants had found them and probably reported that fact themselves—they'd know they couldn't safely make use of stray riding nabrula—and the knights instantly concluded that the villagers had ambushed their brethren.

Darzek turned again and started toward the crosslane where he had hidden the cart. Just before he reached it, three knights came galloping out of the forest. They halted to ponder this strange tableau, where dead knights and peasants filled the village lane, nabrula wandered about disconsolately, and a perfumer in professional dress calmly strolled toward them carrying glittering objects.

They had missed the blood orgy, and they were wary, rather than vengeful. One of them started a charge and then turned back at once. The others continued to ponder the scene. Then, in a single movement, all turned and fled.

Darzek got off three shots at them, but the distance was too great to bring down the nabrula or do more than temporarily stun the knights. Two of them slumped in their saddles, but their nabrula, thoroughly frightened by the shocks that hit them, fled in terror.

"A pity," Darzek muttered. "Sometimes one should weigh the risks before paying off an obligation. This is going to make life hell for perfumers."

Sajjo was waiting for him at the edge of the forest, and he knew that she had seen everything. He made no explanation to her. They climbed into the cart, and he drove with the stun rifles on the seat beside him. He took the first branch lane they came to and followed it until they had put the duke's castle safely behind them. Then he pulled into the sponge forest, where they removed the perfumer's tent from the cart, turned it inside out, and painted the gaudy stripes of a peddler on it. Darzek also buried his perfumer's cape and hat.

Their success in Fermarz had drastically reduced their stock of perfume. Darzek dumped the rest of it and buried their bottles and crockery. Then they returned to the surlane. At the first intersection, he turned south.

Sajjo spoke for the first time since he had left her in the forest. *Where are we going?*

To OO, Darzek answered.

Sajjo grinned delightedly. OO had a fairyland reputation.

But Darzek had something else in mind. He had learned as much as he could in Merzkion and Fermarz. It was time to have a look at the province where so many agents had vanished—where the danger was so menacing that the Storoz team had closed its headquarters there.

They had been underway a day and a half before Darzek remembered Bovranulz's prediction: They would visit the OO-Fair together, though they would not meet there.

CHAPTER 12

Darzek and Sajjo entered the Province of OO as peddlers with nothing to peddle. Darzek had acquired the official peddler's clothing while passing through the Province of Kiledj, which surrounded OO; and he and Sajjo had been studying peddlers' wares at the forums and marts they had passed, comparing quality and prices. In OO they were able to buy directly from artisans. They concentrated on choice carvings and soon built up a respectable stock.

The Province of OO was both a summation of Storoz and its culmination. Everything Darzek had seen elsewhere in Storoz was present there in greater intensity. The soil looked richer, the farm land more productive and better cultivated, the villages tidier and more picturesque. Even the wayside forums had their nabrula manure hauled away daily for fertilizer. The province's crafts—practiced everywhere, for most villages had a lane of artisans—were the finest in Storoz and were eagerly in demand at all of the island's marts, as well as for export. Young artisans and artists of talent came to OO to learn and remained there to prosper.

By the time they reached the great city of OO, they were ready to peddle; and Sajjo was bursting with excitement at the new venture and dazzled at the charm and richness of the province. Her memory of the village of Karlanklo seemed to rest lightly on her. Darzek wondered if she had not been more perplexed than terrified at the carnage she witnessed only from a great distance.

The city of OO, the only major port on the island that was not governed by the Sailor's League, surpassed even the Free Cities in its magnificence. The lanes, narrow in other cities, were wide, sweeping avenues in OO. The most vividly hued stone had been employed for pavement and buildings, and the people of OO displayed the most dramatically colored and patterned garments and the most lavish hair styles. The variety of crafts and products was unrivaled.

Even the duke's castle was a palace with battlements. The brooding gray granite of the other dukes' strongholds here gave way to gleaming, resplendently hued marble.

It was midmorning when Darzek and Sajjo arrived, and much of the city's ten thousand population, as well as its throngs of visitors, seemed to be crowding the OO-Fair, a gigantic mart that—like the marts of most port cities—stretched along the harbor. They went directly to the fair themselves, registered, and set up their cart in its allotted space.

Darzek left the proud Sajjo in charge of their merchandise display and took their nabrula to the assigned stable. A sweep promptly cleaned their display area when he left, and another followed him all the way to the stable—evidence enough of the strict sanitation practiced in OO. Darzek, once away from the stable, breathed the pure, tangy sea air and thoroughly approved.

Above the booths and carts and wagons and tents of the fair's vendors rose the usual Mound of the Sun and hovering Winged Beast—the latter a monstrously large carving. Beyond them, Darzek could see the stubby, rectangular, vividly colored sails of the ships in the harbor and at the docks.

Darzek began a circuit of the fair, wondering in which of those hundreds of tents Bovranulz, the Old Blind One, would be revealing—and keeping—secrets. It would have amused Darzek to stand in line for an interview, since the old man had predicted they would not meet in OO; and there was much that Darzek wanted to ask him.

But there also was much that he had to find out for himself, and quickly. He needed to know at once whether the Duke of OO, too, was guarding something of immense value. Darzek's apparently aimless wandering about the fair was directed so as to give him a good view of the castle from several angles.

This was the province where the duke, the brother of the Winged Beast's Protector, was attempting to revive the old religion. The Mound of the Sun had not been dismantled, but even from a distance the atmosphere of neglect was evident. Black capes and hats could be seen everywhere. Whip-armed lackeys, with somber black uniforms to match their capes, moved about in pairs, eying everyone and everything suspiciously. Black knights, wearing lavish black uniforms trimmed with a lustrous velvet-like cloth instead of armor and sporting tall, black, short-toed boots with an image of the Winged Beast embossed upon each shank, patrolled in haughty solitude, and everyone made way for them.

Under the eyes of these priests of the Winged Beast, the people of OO—prosperous, superbly civilized, creative—moved about sullenly in an atmosphere whose repression was as noticeable as the humidity on a muggy summer day. They lived under a shadow, and Darzek, looking up at the hideous black symbol that soared above the fair, knew what had cast it.

The life pyramid, which offered a park-like atmosphere at other marts, was deserted in OO. Black-caped lackeys stood at each corner, and their fingers snapped sharp signals at anyone who seemed disposed to linger there or even look up at it. More lackeys surrounded the image of the Winged Beast, and they halted for questioning those passers-by whose obeisance they deemed less than suitably reverent. Darzek, remembering his experience with irate black-capes in Northpor—where they were subject to discipline by the Sailor's League if they let their tempers get out of hand—felt profoundly sympathetic.

The people of OO were frightened. Even the children were frightened. Darzek read mute terror in every gesture, in every hesitant purchase, in every pale face.

The tension was exacerbated by the unnatural silence of the place. Darzek had thought Kamm a noisy planet, but here the carts, except for that of an occasional late-arriving vendor, were parked in silence. The nabrula were banished to remote stables. The very uneasiness of the populace seemed to subdue its natural noises. The humming, the grunting, the snorts and coughs that elsewhere were spontaneous emittances of all Kammians, were not heard.

The people even walked silently, their wooden-soled shoes somehow negotiating the cobblestones without clomping. Females and vendors haggled with soundless gestures. Itinerant musicians, such as would have been a prominent feature of a fair on almost any other world, were replaced by shabby performers shaping whirling discs of color into exotic patterns for small groups that watched intently but did not applaud.

Kamm, the Silent Planet. For the first time that concept oppressed Darzek. Silence seemed to hang about him heavily as he watched the slow-moving crowds, watched the triangular-shaped coins fall noiselessly onto the vendors' padded trays, watched insect-like creatures buzzing in furious silence over a soggy pile of something that looked like sea mollusks. He repressed an urge to cry out; he knew the sound would drop from his lips unheard.

And everywhere were the priests of the Winged Beast, their blackness starkly delineated against the brightly appareled populace. One knight, elegant in his velvet-trimmed uniform, startled Darzek into alertness by walking slowly past and then whirling suddenly to stare at him. He walked on a short distance and again turned to regard Darzek suspiciously.

Darzek told himself sternly, "A peddler on fair day who stands around gaping and doesn't peddle is not behaving normally, and blackie spotted that with one glance. This may be a primitive planet, but its police aren't stupid. So move!"

He walked on, making a looping circle of half of the fair and studying the castle when he could. He saw no tent that remotely resembled that of Bovranulz. Finally he returned to his own cart, where Sajjo was displaying her stocks of carvings to a crowd of prospective customers. Darzek was about to join her when he noticed that the black knight was following him. Sajjo observed this at the same time. She glanced quickly from the knight to Darzek, and her eyes widened with fright; but she turned her attention to her customers and did not look in his direction again. "Sajjo," he thought, "is a better agent than most agents I have known." He sauntered on, intending to lose himself in the crowd.

"There should be nothing abnormal about my looking at the wares of my competitors," he told himself. "Other vendors are doing that."

But apparently something was abnormal. The knight continued to follow him.

Moving with the crowd, he started another circuit of the fair. The sun was high overhead, and pangs of hunger prodded him to what he hoped was a thoroughly normal action. He bought some meat-filled pastry, and after proper hesitation and a brief argument about the price, he had a mess of seaweed measured out for him. He despised this particular Kammian delicacy, but in order to masquerade as a native he had to eat—and apparently enjoy—native foods. Munching on his purchases as he went, he continued to drift with the crowd.

Belatedly he discovered that his particular crowd eddy was approaching the soaring image of the Winged Beast. He moved along with it, performing the required genuflection as enthusiastically as he could manage and even leaving some of his lunch impaled on an offering stick.

After he had safely passed beyond it, he turned and looked back at the massive carving. It had been shaped from a sponge core of amazing size—each of the vast wings was a single carving, as was the body. The figure was completely black except for the fangs that the long, tapering snout bared in its vicious snarl and the knife-like talons that terminated the four feet. These were painted yellow. It was a nightmarish fantasy of a beast of prey, and its heavy shadow did indeed seem symbolic of the mute, brilliantly colored terror that gripped the citizens of OO.

When next Darzek looked behind him, he saw that the black knight was still following. Uneasily he tried to move faster, pushing his way through the crowd. His peddler's cap probably served as a beacon, so he leaned forward, hoping to make it invisible behind the towering hairdos of a group of peasant females.

He dared another backward glance and saw that the knight had given up the chase and was standing respectfully at attention. At the same instant, the crowd began to draw back in alarm.

A gaudily gilted carriage—actually a wagon with an abbreviated caravan erected on it—moved slowly through the fair pulled by two teams of gold-ornamented nabrula. Behind the carriage staggered a Kammian male, his body nude to the waist and painted black. Behind him marched ranks of the black-caped apprentice priests, each solemnly swinging a short, multithonged whip.

Darzek followed the example of his neighbors in keeping his eyes humbly averted, but he risked an occasional, surreptitious glance. And as the carriage passed him, he photographed its occupants with one swift look. There was no mistaking the Duke of OO, who lounged in resplendent gold robes and kept his bloated face and disdainful grin focused straight ahead. It was the figure beside him that startled Darzek into raising his head and staring at the carriage. This huge, rough-looking individual wore the gold clothing of a ducal retainer with a hood covering his head. By fortuitous circumstance a shift of position made the hood gap at the moment Darzek looked, and he saw clearly the one physical attribute that could not possibly belong to a native of the world of Kamm: The duke's companion had an ear.

The young priests strapped their victim to the post supporting the Winged Beast, and their ranks filed past him in an orderly manner, each priest giving his back one stroke. They did not even swing their whips hard, but the first lashes of those vicious thongs cut the back to ribbons and subsequent strokes began to peel off long strips of flesh. The blood gushed. The man wreathed in silent agony.

Darzek had to nerve himself to watch. He decided that the half-hearted style of whipping was done deliberately—it kept the victim alive and prolonged his torment.

The duke and his companion watched impassively. The citizens began to edge away. They applauded blood at a knightly gladiatorial contest, but they turned their backs on an act of torture. Soon the crowd had thinned out noticeably, and Darzek could see throngs of people moving along the lanes leading back into the city, headed for home.

As the crowd dispersed, Darzek suddenly realized that he was becoming increasingly vulnerable. The knight had seen him again and was moving toward him purposely. His hands, still too distant to speak clearly, seemed to be signaling something. Darzek's mind had been totally occupied with the astonishing anatomy of the duke's companion. Now it occurred to him that he'd have to move quickly if he expected to pass that vital information along to anyone. Other black knights and lackeys were closing in on the market place, questioning the citizens, questioning the vendors, and acting formidably suspicious of everyone. Darzek turned away and lengthened his stride.

Suddenly a whip snapped past his head. A citizen directly ahead of him staggered and spun around, clutching his arm. A dull red stain instantly obliterated the green and yellow pattern of his sleeve.

Darzek began to run even before his mind completely grasped what was happening. The whip snapped past him again, and a male's purple hat sailed to the ground at Darzek's feet. Beyond him, a child looked up bewilderedly with a bloody face. Darzek's mind thundered angrily about the vermin who would use a whip in a crowd, but he ran on without breaking his stride.

By the time he reached the last row of vendor's carts, he had outdistanced the pursuit. Both knights and lackeys, running laboriously in their ornamental footgear, floundered far behind him. The whips continued to snap, even though Darzek was far out of range, sending the vendors to cover inside and under their carts. Darzek hurdled a low stone wall and found himself on the wide pavement that ran along the docks—empty except for a scattering of huge, weather-worn warehouses. It was a dead end; there was no hiding place.

Darzek did not hesitate. He ducked into the sheltering shadow of a warehouse, crossed the pavement in three leaping strides, darted along a dock, and took a soaring leap to the deck of a ship. He quickly crept behind the stubby cabin.

It was a namafj boat, a boat that fished for the commonest sea food on Kamm, and it smelled as though last week's cargo was still aboard. The stench was overwhelming. "Better a stinking boat than a place of honor strapped under the Winged Beast," Darzek told himself.

He opened a door. Clothing hung on pegs. Quickly he ripped off his own clothing and pulled on what came to hand: rough trousers, a long smock with ties, a sailor's green cape and hat. He transferred his belongings and took a moment to check the setting on his Winged Beast amulet. Then he grabbed at the handle of a tool and decided it was a broom. He hid his peddler's clothing under a pile of cushions and stepped back onto the deck. The clothing stank as badly as the ship, but Darzek reminded himself that at this moment social acceptability wasn't his objective.

The docks swarmed with black-capes. For the moment they were ignoring the ships, so Darzek ignored them. Deliberately he turned his back on the docks and began to sweep the deck—which needed it badly. When they came, as they certainly would, his only chance for escape lay in his assuming the guise of indignant innocence. He concentrated on that, and by the time the first black-cape landed on the deck with a thud, Darzek had talked himself into the mood of a furious sailor whose status and League were being insulted.

He whirled, jammed the broom handle into the black-caped lackey's stomach, and then brought the other end down on his head. As the lackey reeled backward, Darzek flung the broom down. *Off! How dare you board without permission? Off!*

He knew nothing about the authority of a priest over a ship in the OO harbor; but fortunately this novice priest seemed to know even less. He backed away.

Where is the peddler? his hands signaled.

Darzek glared at him insultingly and made his hands speak as though to a child. *A seagoing peddler?*

He took a menacing step toward the priest, who backed up and asked, almost politely, *Have you seen a peddler?*

Over there, Darzek said, gesturing toward the fair, *I saw a thousand. Here there are none.*

The priest stood looking at him uncertainly.

This outrage will be reported, Darzek's fingers snapped. *Off!*

The priest turned, made the leap back to the dock, and joined his fellows. Darzek picked up his broom and resumed sweeping. When he tired of that, he entered the cabin, arranged some cushions, and lay down. He thought he might as well rest while he could. He was likely to need the energy before the day was over.

Also, he needed to think.

The Duke of OO's companion had been an alien from outer space. This could only mean that an Uncertified World—a non-member world—had developed interstellar travel without the knowledge of the Galactic Synthesis.

"The true measure of intelligence," Darzek muttered, "is one's ability to adapt to the impossible. I know this is absolutely impossible, but I saw it, and I'm going to believe it. I know that creature did not come from a member world of the Synthesis. Therefore a non-member world has somehow achieved interstellar travel right under the collective noses of agents of Rok Wllon's Department of Uncertified Worlds without anyone noticing. Rok Wllon will have conniptions when he hears about it, and I sincerely hope we'll both survive long enough so I can have the pleasure of telling him."

The presence of an alien in the carriage of the Duke of OO gave Darzek an instant solution to half of his problems. It was all the explanation he needed for the strange metal detector, and for the pazul—whatever that might be—and even for the electrical generator, though why an alien would go to the trouble of disguising it in the technology of Kamm would probably remain a mystery.

For all of five minutes Darzek felt elated. Then he began to consider the new problems raised by the presence of the one-eared alien, and for the next hour he felt increasingly depressed. What could aliens possibly want on the world of Kamm? And why would they be passing out pazuls to the decrepit nobility of this small island?

When finally he looked out at the docks again, the black-capes were still prowling there. Watching them through a half-open square port, he wondered what had gone wrong. The knight had taken one glance at him and instantly turned in pursuit. As far as he knew he had done nothing, committed no action that had not been readily accepted elsewhere, but in some way he had betrayed himself.

It would be safer to stay where he was until dark; except that the members of the crew might return at any moment, and he couldn't predict how that complication would work out. Also, he was deeply concerned about Sajjo.

"Sailors," he told himself, "do go ashore occasionally. Why shouldn't I?"

He left the cabin, pretended to fuss about the deck until the patrolling black-capes were as far from the ship as they were likely to get, and then he leaped ashore and strode boldly along the harbor. He passed a black-caped lackey without a glance; the young priest seemed to pay no attention to him. Darzek exchanged the traditional crossed thumbs greeting with a passing sailor and turned into the fairgrounds through a break in the stone wall.

The duke's free entertainment had ruined the day's business. Many vendors had closed, but a few of them were still trying to salvage something from the sparse crowd that remained. Darzek threaded his way among the rows, looking for his own cart. He saw it and started toward it; and then he whirled and pretended to interest himself in an innocuous pile of wood ornaments amid a cluttered peddler's display.

Black-capes swarmed about the cart. Stealing an occasional sidelong glance, Darzek saw them bring up his tandem of nabrula, kick the beasts into position, harness them, and lead the cart away. There was no sign of Sajjo.

He turned his back on the pleading peddler and walked toward the harbor. There, ten meters from a stony-faced, black-caped lackey, he sat down and dangled his feet over the edge of a dock.

Something had to be done, and at once. And he hadn't the faintest notion of what it could be.

CHAPTER 13

Twice Darzek got to his feet. Each time sober reflection convinced him, before he had taken a step, that his best course was to wait for darkness. He could not rescue Sajjo without first finding out where they had taken her. If he, already a fugitive, drew attention to himself by making inquiries in that seething fair, the black-capes would instantly invite him to join her.

And his tiny amulet stun weapon could not cope with the army of priests that continued to rampage through the fair and around the docks. He should have no trouble in learning where the black-capes took their prisoners, and in darkness he could even invade the duke's castle, if that were necessary.

He sat down again, and dangled his feet, and tried to figure out what had gone wrong so suddenly. One glance, and a knight had taken after him. The seizure of his cart was even more unaccountable. On the other hand, two black-caped lackeys were at that moment standing watch within thirty strides of him, and neither showed the slightest suspicion of this idle sailor. Had the priests been warned about a peddler and his daughter? And who could have given such a warning?

All of Darzek's special equipment was with the cart. He doubted that the black-capes would discover the secret compartments, but for the moment it was lost to him. He had only his amulet.

Out in the harbor a ship was approaching, clumsily tacking toward the docks. Darzek watched it idly for a few minutes, and then he returned his thoughts to the question of what to do about Sajjo. When he glanced up again, the ship was drifting some eight or ten meters from the dock, and the captain, standing atop the low cabin, was pointing insults at Darzek with flickering fingers.

Look away, you sniveling dirt digger! On your feet, you depraved offspring of a hornless nabrulk! Look away!

Startled, Darzek scrambled to his feet. A deck hand swung an arm deftly, and a thick rope shot at Darzek. He ducked out of the way, stumbled, fell on his back on the muddy cobblestones. The heavy rope landed across his chest with a thud, and he lay there for a moment, temporarily stunned. Two passing sailors seized the rope and hauled lustily. They were joined by others, and the ship was slowly drawn toward the dock.

Darzek got to his feet confusedly and started to walk away. The ship's captain took a long leap from the top of the cabin to the dock, seized Darzek's shoulders, and spun him around. He towered over Darzek, brawny, red-faced, unusually large for a Kammian, and his hands shook with anger as he flashed insults under Darzek's nose.

Dirt digger! Sniveling dirt digger! When does a sailor refuse to look away? Don't think I won't report this! I'll have you back digging before your ship sails! He gave Darzek a searching scrutiny. *I've never seen you before. You're too old to be an apprentice. Who's your master?* Darzek made no response. *Let's see your chip,* the captain demanded.

Darzek's only recourse was to bluff. He drew himself up and demanded, *Who do you think you are?*

It was the wrong question. The captain reared back in rage. *Who do I think I am? Why, you sniveling dirt digger, I'll show you!*

His hands clamped on Darzek's throat. Sailors were gathering around them, and Darzek saw a black-cape edging closer. As he struggled dizzily, fighting for breath, he knew that only his amulet could save him—his hands were clutching it—and to use it would be fatal.

Suddenly the captain's hands relaxed. He backed away and stood looking past Darzek respectfully. Darzek, rubbing his throat, felt a hand on his shoulder. As he turned he gripped his amulet again, expecting to find himself face to face with a black knight; but it was another sea captain who confronted him, an older man, obviously a veteran of distinction, for he wore a special, multiply tiered captain's hat.

For a moment he scrutinized Darzek. Then, without a word, he motioned Darzek to follow him and turned away. As Darzek set out after him his one thought was to escape, and he looked about vainly for a hiding place. Then two black-capes halted and saluted when this captain approached them, and Darzek decided that the situation had complexities that might work to his advantage.

The captain led Darzek to the far end of the harbor and aboard a large ship. Without a word he opened a door, stepped aside to let Darzek enter the cabin, and then followed him. Then he barred the door. Compared with Darzek's previous ship, this one was designed for luxury cruises. The furnishings were opulent. The captain pulled out a polished, elaborately carved chair for Darzek, arranged another for himself across a polished, elaborately carved table, and from a tall jug poured cider into two tumblers. He pushed one at Darzek.

Then, before Darzek could lift the tumbler, the captain's hands spoke. *I'm Captain Wanulzk. What is your name?*

He was slim, almost fragile-looking, and as small for a Kammian as the other captain had been oversized, but Darzek sensed the toughness his slight frame concealed. His bronzed face was calm and confident, his dark eyes alert and penetrating. It was, Darzek thought, searching his recollections of Kammians he had known, an honest face. This captain was intelligent, rather than cunning. He would outmaneuver an enemy, but he would not deceive him.

Needing time to think, Darzek raised the tumbler and sipped. It was a sailor's cider—the sip burned his throat.

Obviously this captain was a personage. Sailors and black-capes alike respected his importance. He had saved Darzek from a tense situation that could have ended disastrously.

Darzek wanted to know why.

He sipped again. The captain kept his eyes on him, waiting, and finally he said, *I understand that your real name would have no meaning for me, but I must call you something. What name are you using?*

Darzek almost dropped the tumbler.

He set it down carefully and replied, *I am Lazk.* He was about to add, *A humble peddler,* when he remembered the stolen sailor's clothing he was wearing. At the moment there was no possible way he could account for himself, in any respect.

Lazk, the captain repeated. He jerked a shoulder with satisfaction. *My old friend Bovranulz told me about you, but of course he had no name for you.*

Darzek was too dumfounded to speak.

Bovranulz told me a peddler at the OO-Fair would be in desperate need of help and merit it. And though Bovranulz described you with care, the scrutiny of every peddler at the fair would not have identified you with certainty even if there had been time to do so. I had to wait until the trouble developed, and it was complicated by the cursed duke and his amusements. I saw the black-capes chase you, but by the time I reached the docks you'd disappeared. It wasn't until I saw a sailor behaving with shocking insubordination that I realized what had happened.

Darzek continued to examine the situation warily, determined that his desperate need for an ally should not trap him into a fatal error. He decided to tell the captain only what the black-capes already knew and see how he reacted.

My young daughter was taken by the black-capes, Darzek said.

The captain's right hand cupped an exclamation.

My cart, also, Darzek added. *And my three nabrula. Would it be possible to find out where they were taken? A poor peddler cannot easily replace a cart and nabrula, and a dearly loved daughter is beyond price. I don't even know what Sajjo could have done to offend them.*

The captain regarded him with evident amusement when he spoke of his cart and nabrula, but obviously he considered the daughter a serious matter. *Her name is Sajjo?* he asked. He got to his feet and left the room. When he returned, he again barred the door.

He sat down and leaned forward, and his hands spoke with intense seriousness. *I don't know where you come from or who sent you or why. But Bovranulz says you are unlike these other outsiders that pollute Storoz, that you are a friend of our people, and I have no choice but to believe him. Too many times my life has depended on him, and he has never failed me. So I believe, and I will do what he asks. He asks that I tell you what the League knows about Storoz.*

Darzek shaped a question. *The Sailor's League?*

Yes. Officially we have no interest in the internal affairs of Storoz. In actuality, most of us are Storozians. This island is more than a home to us—it is our birthright. Even if the dukes honor our Free City charters and leave us alone, we cannot ignore the iniquities they perpetrate in the provinces of our fathers and the cruelties they inflict on our relatives. Officially we have no interest, but we take a very active private interest. Through that private interest we have learned much. Do you know that the Duke of OO—a remote ancestor of the present duke— once was King of Storoz?

Darzek signaled an affirmative.

He was Ruler of Storoz and Protector of the Faith—which means that he ruled both in this world and the next. He controlled the government of his people and also their religion. He had another title that few now remember: Keeper of the Winged Beast. The kingship was hereditary, but there was an earlier tradition that the king in his arbitrariness forgot: the kingship once was held by different dukes in turn according to a system no one now remembers except the dukes themselves. The dukes deposed him; but then they could not agree on a plan for rotating the kingship again, so each duke became ruler of his own province, and the office of Protector was taken by the ruler of the mountain province, which always had been the Realm of the Winged Beast. All this you know?

Only a little of it. Please continue.

Do you know that the Protector is attempting to revive the kingship?

Darzek signaled a negative. *But it does not surprise me,* he added.

He is. The dukes are distrustful—even the Protector's own brother, the Duke of OO, is distrustful. Each would enjoy ruling all of Storoz, but none would enjoy being subservient to another duke. And because the Protector is the Duke of OO's brother, the others fear that the Protector is plotting to restore OO to the kingship. The Duke of OO fears that the Protector is plotting to take over the kingship himself and again combine the offices of Ruler of Storoz and Protector of the Faith.

The Protector swears that none of this is true. He is dedicated to the principles of the religion he protects, and he would cheerfully surrender his office to a legal king, chosen in the same time-tested and divine manner in which kings were selected in the past.

You said no one but the dukes remembered what that was, Darzek observed thoughtfully.

Probably no one has ever known except the dukes and the Protector. We know only that the kingship was held by different dukes in turn, and that is the system the Protector would restore. Now all of the dukes are currying favor with the Protector, and his favor has a price— the restoration of the old religion. For long years in Storoz, religion has been a matter of conscience. One worshiped the new or the old or none at all, as one chose. But now the old religion rules in OO. The cursed black-capes terrorize the people and force them through fear to worship the Winged Beast. You have seen it. Some of the other dukes are ready to do the same, as the price of the Protector's favor.

But you permit black-capes in the Free Cities, Darzek observed.

The captain scowled. *Of course. Freedom of choice still counts there, and it isn't freedom if one isn't free to worship the old as well as the new.* He paused for a moment, and then he continued, *There are these outsiders. I don't know who they are or what they seek. Do you know?*

No. I did not suspect their existence until I saw one in the duke's carriage today. Does the Duke Merzkion have outsiders as guests?

From time to time.

And—the Duke Fermarz?

From time to time. We don't know for certain, but we assume that all the dukes have had such visitors. A few have made them guests.

Darzek spoke slowly. *There are two questions: What they seek, and what they offer for it. Since there is talk of reviving the kingship, they may be offering to make their hosts king—in return for certain favors.*

And—the favors?

I can answer only that they would be bad for the people of Storoz and bad for people anywhere on this world. Eventually they'd be bad for the duke that granted them, but a duke who wants to be king does not think beyond the kingship.

That is our belief, the captain said.

If the outsiders have visited all of the dukes, they may be promising more than one duke that they'll help him become king.

It's even more complicated than that, the captain said gloomily. *There is more than one kind of outsider. In addition to yourself, that is.*

Darzek stared at him. Then he reflected that members of the different human races probably would have impressed the Kammians as being more than one kind of outsider, and different kinds didn't necessarily mean outsiders from more than one world. *How different?* he asked.

Their features are entirely different. I have seen them myself. One kind has a strange physical construction around the back of its head, from one side to the other. The other kind has a small, round opening on each side of its head, high up.

Darzek took a deep breath and wondered why he was accepting that shattering information so calmly. He asked, *Are these different kinds of visitors in contention with each other?*

The Duke of OO entertains only the one kind. The Duke Merzkion entertains only the other kind. Beyond that, we know for certain that one kind tried to turn a duke against the other kind.

To Darzek, this information was at least as devastating as a pazul. *Some of the dukes may be making promises to both kinds of visitors, hoping to gain the support of both,* he pointed out.

The captain gestured his agreement. His gloom had deepened. *They are scoundrels cheating one another, and the people of Storoz must pay the winner.*

Are there any good dukes? Darzek asked. *Dukes worthy of the honor of the kingship and able to use power for the benefit of all?*

Two. Two out of eleven—or twelve, if we count the Protector. Thus has the blood of our royalty rotted.

I know lands where two out of twelve would be something to be proud of, Darzek told him. *You said the dukes feared that the Protector was conspiring to bring the kingship to his brother, the Duke of OO. Is he?*

The ancient religion is harsh. Its dicta are cruel and merciless. The Protector believes that harshness and cruelty are purifying and should be applied relentlessly. He hopes to restore the ancient religion to its former high status and thereby revive the ancient glory of Storoz. He is dedicated. If there is an ancient religious canon for the selection of a king, I think he would apply it honestly—and unswervingly.

Then he's a fanatic, Darzek suggested. *And incorruptible.*

In matters of religion, we know of nothing to indicate that he is not. And since his brother, the Duke of OO, is dedicated to the pursuit of life's pleasures and the avoidance of its responsibilities, our feeling is that the Protector would not help him become king. He knows as well as we that this would be a catastrophe for the people of Storoz. But if the Duke of OO gains the kingship honestly, certainly the Protector will do nothing to prevent that.

Is there any chance that the dukes might agree to the restoration of the kingship?

There is. They may have agreed to it already.

Darzek leaned back, eyes closed, to consider the effect of this information on his own mission. The problem of a pazul on Kamm had been solved; at least, it had been transferred elsewhere, and the Department of Uncertified Worlds could deal with it on whatever world or worlds were responsible.

This left him two things to work for: The expulsion of the aliens along with all of their hardware, and the rescue of Rok Wllon and any of the missing Synthesis agents who had survived.

I must think deeply about all of this, Darzek told the captain. *My own mission is to protect your world and its people against the plots of outsiders, and to rescue friends whom the dukes have taken prisoner.*

It was the captain's turn to meditate. Finally he asked, *If a king is chosen, would you be willing to assist us in attempting to make it one of the two capable dukes?*

I feel strongly that outsiders should not interfere in the affairs of Kamm, Darzek said slowly. *I am obliged to do everything I can to prevent these other outsiders from raising a duke of their choice to the kingship, and I can't in good conscience replace their scheming with my own. But if I succeed, it may leave the way open for your candidate. And if chance placed me in a position to influence the outcome, I wouldn't hesitate to use it to benefit the People of Kamm.*

The captain smiled. *Bovranulz spoke truly. Your principles are not for sale, but I think you would not betray a friend for them. I pledge you my support and also that of the Sailor's League, of which I also am a captain.*

I accept with gratitude.

As soon as darkness fell, the captain left for home. He maintained a small dwelling and a mate in a sailor's village a short distance down the coast from the metropolis. Darzek followed him at a respectful three paces, a common sailor performing a duty for his master. He carried a basket of namafj. The namafj were noticeably overripe, and Darzek huffed all the way, breathing through his mouth.

In the captain's modest but brightly painted house, Darzek joined him and his mate for their evening meal. Kammian etiquette wisely prohibited conversation when the hands could be better occupied with other matters, and they ate their tastily prepared dishes of sea foods without exchanging a word. As soon as they had finished, the mate cleared the table and discreetly disappeared.

The captain leaned back meditatively. They were waiting for information about Sajjo—where she was, what kind of a guard she was under, whether she could be rescued.

Darzek, after half a day of furious activity and intense nervous strain, felt exhausted. The light, a crude lamp burning namafj oil, had a hypnotic effect on him. He caught himself dozing off, willed himself awake, and finally, it seemed only an instant later, he awakened himself again by almost pitching from his chair. As he straightened up, he discovered to his embarrassment that there were four more captains seated in the room. They had arrived, found him asleep, and waited patiently until he woke up.

Captain Wanulzk introduced his associates. *They are fellow officers of the Sailor's League,* he said. *You may trust them as you trust me. They are here to assist you.*

Is there news about Sajjo? Darzek asked anxiously.

We still wait for it. There are many difficulties in discovering what happens within the duke's castle.

Today, when the duke visited the fair, he had a companion in his carriage, Darzek said. *Do any of you know anything about that companion?*

Evil meets with evil in the duke's carriage, one of the captains remarked.

Bovranulz has told us that such as he are not of this world, another captain said. *The duke has been seen with two such companions. We know no more than that.*

Darzek nodded his understanding.

Captain Wanulzk's fingers flicked instantly. *You must not move your head. You either raise your shoulder—thus—or you must move your hand—so.*

Darzek grinned embarrassedly. *The head gesture is a common one among my people. I know that I should avoid it, but it is difficult not to move my head unknowingly. Is that how the black-capes became suspicious of me?*

It was the captain's turn to show embarrassment. *Probably not,* he said, with obvious reluctance.

I must have given myself away somehow, Darzek persisted. *A knight of the Winged Beast walked past, took a good look at me, and began to follow me. I can't understand it, because I have traveled far in your land, and until that moment everyone seemed to accept me for what I was pretending to be. Why would one of the black-capes of OO be able to detect my disguise?*

The captains exchanged glances. If Darzek could read anything of Kammian character—and he thought he could—all of them were embarrassed.

If there's a reason, I beg you to tell me, he said. *I must correct it, whatever it is. Otherwise, I can exist here only by hiding, and my effectiveness is at an end. I can't accomplish my mission and help the citizens of Storoz if I can't move about freely.*

Again the captains exchanged glances. Captain Wanulzk said finally, and his embarrassment was acute, *The reason the black-cape suspected you is because you stink.*

CHAPTER 14

Darzek, clothed in the black garments and cape of a lackey of the Winged Beast, looked up at the sheer wall that surrounded the Duke of OO's castle and contended with his seething impatience.

He was deeply worried about Sajjo.

He also felt deeply chagrined.

He should have guessed. Had he exercised an iota of the imagination and intelligence he hoped he'd been endowed with, he *would* have guessed. Terran animals recognized other animals by scent. He'd known that the deaf inhabitants of Kamm had powerfully developed senses of smell. Surely he should have been able to deduce that the human animal would have a characteristic scent, and that the Kammians would be aware of it.

There'd been an embarrassing abundance of clues.

That first day on Kamm, when he'd thought he was attracting attention because, unlike the Kammians, he was not wearing a personal perfume: It hadn't been the lack of a perfume that shocked the Kammians. It was a whiff of his revolting humanity that turned stares in his direction.

The phony black knight also had caught a whiff of his true self. He'd thought that Darzek, a perfumer, had mixed a bad batch.

And the fact that the fellow workers and superiors in the Duke Lonorlk's maz forest avoided his company so assiduously should have conveyed some kind of message to him.

On the other hand, Darzek had been reasonably safe when he was actively working as a perfumer—when he was actually handling and bottling various scents. These must have given him a powerfully blended protective veneer. When he traveled, his close association with the reeking nabrula and the foul wayside forums provided an additional measure of protection.

But in OO, where the forums were kept clean and the fair was immaculate, he had been functioning as a peddler. Obviously the perfume he'd selected as his personal scent hadn't been strong enough to cover his natural odor. All of these circumstances had combined to strip Darzek of every olfactory camouflage at the precise moment he most needed one.

He wondered how many of the vanished agents had been caught in the same way. Had the dukes alerted their knights to the presence in Storoz of creatures who looked normal but wore odors of unworldly foulness? The black knight had been suspicious of Darzek the moment he caught a whiff of him—suspicious but not certain. He had kept Darzek in sight and signaled for reinforcements before he decided to pounce. What finally made him certain? Darzek's meandering conduct?

Once Darzek got aboard the stinking namafj boat, he was safe. The black-cape, because of the power of the Sailor's League, did not dare arrest him without the certainty that his nose could not give him in that foul atmosphere. And the sailor's clothing had protected Darzek when he went ashore again.

Even so, Captain Wanulzk had given Darzek a basket of overripe namafj to carry, which meant that by evening his human scent had permeated the clothing. The captain probably found the smell of rotting namafj much less offensive.

And all the Kammians Darzek had come in contact with had been too polite to mention his unsociability—the danger Darzek carried with him, as Bovranulz had put it. Not even Darzek's Kammian family had told him. Sajjo must have suffered acutely on their long journey together, but she'd kept strictly to herself the painful fact that her adopted father stank.

Sajjo. Was it possible that the duke would subject a child to torture?

He wondered, with a chilling apprehension, whether she had been trapped by some residue of scent that he'd left about the cart.

In the wall opposite Darzek, a door opened. The fact that some duke now lost to history had breached his own wall with a door for the convenience of his employees was striking indication of how long it had been since this particular castle was besieged. A hand beckoned to Darzek, and he sprinted across to it. A young sailor—also attired like a black-caped lackey—waved Darzek through the door and quickly closed it.

The sailors had politely refused Darzek's offer to lead this invasion of the castle, no matter what magic powers he claimed for his amulet. Probably they thought his human scent would betray them. Darzek had not argued. From the ease with which the captain produced enough black clothing to outfit an entire company of sailors, he knew that they had done this kind of thing before.

But Darzek insisted on going into the dungeon himself, not only to rescue Sajjo, but to see whether any of the missing Synthesis agents were there. Once inside the wall, Darzek and the young sailor headed for a service entrance. They did not speak. The courtyard, lit only by a distant torch, was too dim for talk.

At the castle entrance a stout, barred portcullis had been raised, and just inside it, where a torch burned brightly, four guards lay unconscious. The black-caped figure inside gave the sailor's greeting and pointed, and Darzek raced down a ramp without waiting for the others. At the bottom he stepped over the figures of two prone guards. The black-caped sailor waiting there signaled, *Quickly!*

Darzek called out, "Synthesis! Galaxy! Primores!" He went from stone cell to stone cell, studying each occupant and speaking the words again. There was no response. The prisoners were only pathetic, broken Kammians. The sailors would not release them. To do so would bring reprisals against their friends and relatives.

There was no child.

Is this the only prison? Darzek demanded.

The sailor shrugged an affirmative. *We are trying to get information about the child through our friends in the castle.*

Darzek turned and hurried back up the ramp. At the top, he gestured a negative to the waiting sailors. *The cart,* he said.

Carts and wagons of all descriptions were parked in the courtyard. A sailor was waiting for them there, and they stumbled over another unconscious guard as they approached him.

Darzek jumped onto the nearest wagon, looked about him, and then went from one end of the park to the other, leaping from vehicle to vehicle. He returned the same way, on the far side of the park, and he paused to investigate several carts that seemed only vaguely similar to his.

Finally he swung down and signaled a negative. The sailors, crouched in the shadows, were looking about them uneasily. Their clothing would confuse the duke's men at first contact, but there were too few of them to fight a pitched battle, and they probably handled whips clumsily. It was time to leave.

They slipped out through the door in the wall, and they were halfway back to the harbor before processions of torches on the castle walls showed that an alarm had been given.

They went directly to the ship of Captain Wanulzk, where their sailor's clothing was waiting for them. So was the captain. He had not accompanied them—a captain of the Sailor's League was too well known to engage in breaking and entering at the duke's castle—but his evening had not been uneventful. He greeted them in his cabin with an amused pucker of a smile on his face.

The child was released this evening, he said.

Darzek asked quickly, *Where is she?*

We do not know. But she conducted herself well, and the knights found nothing suspicious about her. She said her father had left her at the fair to vend while he traveled about OO buying more stock. When the fair vendors sent the duke an official complaint concerning the arrest of a child innocently assisting in a family business, the duke ordered her release. They also released the cart and the nabrula, and she drove them away. No one knows where she went, but I'm confident she is safe.

Why was she arrested? Darzek asked.

The black-capes went through the fair looking for any display where a peddler was missing.

Is someone searching for her?

Of course.

The black-capes may have followed her, expecting her to lead them to me.

We've considered that.

Darzek dropped into a chair. His brief nap at the captain's house had done little for the exhaustion he felt.

The black-capes called at my home shortly after you left, the captain said. *They inquired after the sailor who behaved so awkwardly this afternoon.*

I've had much personal experience of police operations, Darzek told him. *Your black-capes are commendably efficient.*

The captain smiled again. *Not quite efficient enough—fortunately. I could only express my regret that they had not come sooner, if they did in fact have legitimate business with that particular member of my League. Because, of course, after I had reprimanded him for his behavior, I sent him back to his ship—which sailed at the half night. Such an investigation is contrary to the agreed procedures concerning members of the League. I asked for an explanation, and they refused to answer. I'll see the duke today. If he doesn't discipline those particular knights in my presence—as well as the lackey who went aboard a ship yesterday without first securing permission—I'll close the port.*

Darzek pursed his lips. *Isn't that rather severe?*

No. Rights not zealously guarded are quickly eroded. But it would be unwise for you to stay at my home. A ship would be the safest place for you.

I must look for Sajjo.

This particular ship will be loading tomorrow. All kinds of carts and wagons will come and go all through the day. We can arrange for you to come and go with them.

I would like to see your friend, Bovranulz.

The captain scowled. *He is at the fair. It would be unwise for you to return there—at least before another friend of mine, Nijezor, has done a certain job for you. He is waiting for you on the ship. He is a master perfumer.*

Darzek's hand cupped an exclamation.

He is eagerly awaiting you, the captain said. *An excellent craftsman always appreciates a challenge.*

Nijezor the perfumer was a stout little individual with a florid face. He carried his head slightly bent forward, and his eyes were perpetually squinting, as though he were peering at the world through distillation vapors. He prowled about Darzek for an hour, sniffing and making frightful grimaces, and then he returned to his factory to see what he could concoct.

Darzek went to the cabin that had been assigned to him and tried to sleep. But despite his exhaustion, and the fact that the motion of the gently rocking ship seemed superbly restful, his mind kept evolving plans for finding Sajjo and carrying her to safety.

Somewhere in OO there was an abandoned Synthesis headquarters, closed because of the danger to agents in OO, but Darzek did not know where it was or whether any equipment had been left there. He wondered if the transmitter was still there and whether it was functional.

He sensed the approach of a crisis in OO. If the black-capes were to persuade the duke that the sailors were concealing a wanted fugitive, his temper might prevail over his good judgment; and the duke was not known for his good judgment.

Darzek finally slept, only to be awakened at dawn by Captain Wanulzk, who wanted to discuss his plans for locating Sajjo. Their talk was interrupted by Nijezor, who arrived triumphantly with a flask of colorless liquid in his hand, the product of his night's work. He dabbed it onto Darzek in various unlikely places, and then both he and the captain retreated a few paces and sniffed thoughtfully.

No, Captain Wanulzk pronounced with emphasis. *You have blended one evil scent with another. They do not cancel; they reinforce each other.* He turned apologetically to Darzek. *No offense, my friend.*

Better you than the Duke of OO, Darzek told him.

It is difficult, Nijezor admitted. *One can always cover a stench with a powerful scent, but when the scent fades, the stench does not. I strive to neutralize the stench, after which friend Lazk will be able to display the most delicate fragrances with effect.*

A noble aim, the captain said. *Its achievement surely will be your masterpiece. If you fail, we can always make him a vendor of overripe namafj.*

Late that afternoon, Darzek lay in a covered cart that was proceeding slowly along one of the main surlanes of the city of OO. Moving from one side to the other, he peered through openings at the pedestrians they passed.

He was looking for Sajjo. The captain had assured him that his help was not needed. The sailors had many friends searching for her, and Darzek's presence would be a liability to them and a danger to himself. But Darzek was not convinced that the searchers could tell one child from another merely on the basis of a description. He, the adopted father, knew the child. He also thought he knew where and how to look for her.

Because he was certain she would be looking for him.

The cart's driver was a weaver, and his mate rode at his side. They had brought a load of fabrics to the ship, and they were on their way to pick up another load. If their route meandered far more than was strictly necessary, that was no one's concern but their own.

Darzek also wore a weaver's costume, just in case a black-cape got curious enough about the cart to look inside. He relied on the potent lingering odor of newly dyed cloth to cover his human smell.

They moved slowly, but without incident, on their trip from the harbor to the weaver's factory. Darzek helped reload the cart with short bolts of cloth, and then he climbed in on top of them for the trip back to the harbor.

They took a different route, and this time they were caught in a monumental traffic jam where their lane intersected one leading to and from the fair. Everyone seemed to be leaving the fairgrounds at once. Darzek continued to watch the passing pedestrians, and suddenly he saw the familiar figure and face he'd been searching for—Sajjo.

Keeping his eyes on her, Darzek caught the attention of the weaver's mate and pointed her out. Sajjo's conduct amazed Darzek. She moved along slowly, her head tilted back and continuously moving from side to side, but she seemed to be looking at nothing in particular.

The weaver's mate stepped to the pavement and intercepted her. They spoke for a moment, and then Sajjo turned and headed back the way she had come, and the weaver's mate followed her. From the cart behind them, a potter leaped out and followed the two of them, and another weaver appeared from somewhere nearby and set out after the potter—for the captain was taking great pains to make certain that the black-capes were not following Sajjo in the hope she would lead them to Darzek.

The traffic jam continued. The weaver left the cart and strolled as far as the intersection, and when he returned he leaned inside the tent and spoke to Darzek. *We didn't need to worry about the black-capes following your daughter. They've got more important work on their hands. The duke has closed the fair, and they're searching everyone leaving the fairgrounds and tearing apart all the merchandise displays. They must think the vendors are hiding you.*

He finally managed to turn the cart, and they headed for the harbor following a circuitous, roundabout route. Back aboard the ship, Darzek waited in a fever of impatience until finally his own cart arrived, with the potter driving and the weaver's mate seated beside him. Sajjo's pert young face peered out anxiously through the tent flaps.

A moment later the cart was aboard the ship, and Sajjo, on being led into Darzek's cabin, threw herself into his waiting arms.

When she had stopped sobbing, he asked her about her peculiar conduct on the streets of OO. *You weren't even looking for me,* he said jokingly. *You were just waving your head around. I think you had your eyes shut.*

I did, part of the time, she agreed. *I knew you'd be wearing different clothes and maybe have your face fixed different, and I wasn't sure I'd recognize you. So I was trying to smell you.*

Captain Wanulzk and Nijezor, the perfumer, were due at the ship shortly after dark. Their perfumer came alone. He gloomily reported that he'd been stopped three times by black-capes on his way there.

I, the most distinguished perfumer in OO! his hands exclaimed indignantly. *I cannot even visit the harbor to arrange a shipment without being harassed by knights of my religion!*

He applied his latest concoction to Darzek, while Sajjo looked on with intense interest. Then he stepped back, and both of them sniffed carefully. Sajjo grimaced, and the perfumer slumped dejectedly onto a chair. His dejection increased when he learned that Darzek intended to leave for Northpor at the first opportunity.

How can I disguise your odor if I do not have it to practice on? He protested.

Darzek explained that he had a novice perfumer in his own family who could work on the problem.

Bah! A beginner. Bah! When I, the foremost perfumer in Storoz, have tried twice and failed, you expect a beginner to succeed? Bah!

They discussed the possibilities open to them. Finally Nijezor suggested shipping an assortment of scents for Darzek to try on himself. His own family could perform the smelling test. Darzek approved.

The perfumer tucked away his flask and prepared to leave.

Then the ship's captain entered, accompanied by a young sailor. *Black-capes now are guarding the harbor,* the captain said. *They've stopped all traffic to and from the ships.*

I had trouble slipping past them, the young sailor said. *That's why*

I'm so late. They've been following me all afternoon, and when I finally escaped them, they'd cordoned the docks.

Darzek said politely, *I congratulate you on your diligence. Do you know what happened to Captain Wanulzk?*

I bring you a message from the captain. He has learned for certain that the dukes—all of them—have given pledges of faith to the Protector, and the Protector in turn has pledged to restore the old canons. There will be a new King of Storoz, chosen in the ancient manner. The captain thinks the king will be chosen by lot, and in a manner difficult to tamper with. Otherwise, the dukes would not trust the Protector.

I thank both you and the captain for the interesting news, Darzek told him. *Now see if you can think of a way for me to get a message to Captain Wanulzk. He is supposed to come here this evening, but with the black-capes guarding the docks, I think it would be best that he doesn't try.*

The young sailor spoke with engaging politeness. *Captain Wanulzk was arrested by the black-capes this afternoon—shortly after he gave me that message.*

CHAPTER 15

The ship's captain decided to sail at once. *Better to leave tonight with half a cargo than wait until tomorrow and not be able to leave at all,* he remarked.

Nijezor, the perfumer, had to choose between facing the black-capes again and sailing to Northpor. He said miserably, *I can't leave my family.* The young sailor refused to leave OO with Captain Wanulzk under arrest. The captain put the two of them into a small boat and had them rowed across the harbor to a ship whose captain was determined to wait out the trouble.

Darzek felt reluctant to leave himself. Captain Wanulzk had befriended and helped him—which was why he had been arrested.

The ship's captain said dryly, *There are hundreds in OO who will work for Captain Wanulzk's release. They know what to do, and how, and they aren't subject to arrest by the first black-cape who smells them. Surely you can be of much more assistance somewhere else.*

Minutes later they were underway, and the captain was performing the delicate job of piloting them out of the harbor in darkness.

The trip took them five days, in an unfavorable wind, and Darzek spent most of it in the bow with Sajjo, catching glimpses of Kamm's rich marine life. On her one previous ocean voyage she had seen nothing at all because she'd had to remain hidden in the cart. Now she delighted in the sights, and scents, and sensations. Her enthusiasm filled the five days; even so, the slow trip tried Darzek's patience sorely. He was eager to talk with Riklo, eager to find out if there'd been outside contacts, eager to consult the moon base file.

In Northpor, Darzek remunerated the captain liberally for their passage. At first he refused to accept payment, but Darzek asked him, *What pleasure is there in having money if one can't use it to reward friends?* It was a viewpoint alien to Kammian philosophy, and Darzek, when he drove their cart and nabrula ashore, left the captain staring after him perplexedly with his hand still uneasily clutching the money.

They headed directly for the Synthesis headquarters that now was home to both of them; and the city of Northpor, bustling, energetic, beautiful, seemed a shade or two less colorful, its mart decidedly provincial, its lanes narrow and poorly planned, its buildings much smaller, after the grandeur of the city of OO.

But the people were far happier, and the Winged Beast in the mart cast a shadow no longer than the height of its pole permitted.

Sjelk welcomed them home excitedly and took charge of the cart and the nabrula. Darzek and Sajjo hurried to the house, where Wesru greeted them with effusion and then went to double the portions of the stew she was preparing. Darzek hastened to Riklo's room. It was empty.

He returned to the kitchen. *Where's Riklo?* he asked.

Gone, Wesru answered indifferently.

Gone where? Darzek demanded.

Wesru did not know. *We could not keep her here. She said she had recovered and there was work to do.*

Did she say where she was going?

No. But she went by ship. Hadkez took her to the harbor.

Darzek retired to his own room, his anger tempered by his concern for Riklo's safety. She had seemed too ill for anything but rest, so he had given her no instructions. Even so, her departure without consulting him constituted insubordination, and she had disappeared at the moment he needed her most—needed the information she had acquired during her training.

And she did not know about the Kammians' sensitivity to alien odors. Her own body odor might be more or less offensive than that of Darzek —only a Kammian could tell her, and none would. By going off on her own, she probably had placed herself in certain jeopardy.

After his household retired that night, Darzek went to the moon base. There he found a report prepared by Riklo offering her own observations to supplement the report he had written. With it was a note Riklo had left for him.

"We need to find out what the other dukes are up to," she had written. "I'm going to make myself a suklonor, a peddler to females. The Synthesis headquarters in Southpor has a collection of luxury goods of the type all the dukes' wives covet. I'll travel up the east side of the island and call at all the castles. If the females know what their mates are up to, I'll find out. I'll report to you in Northpor and then return to Southpor down the west side of the island." She added, "At least, it's something to do."

Darzek nodded thoughtfully. If it wasn't for the fact that the first whiff of her, in the first castle she visited, would give her away, she might actually learn something.

But now she was gone beyond recall, and Darzek would have to educate himself. It took him half an hour to find the correct modules and get the response he wanted from the base's file computer, but eventually he was able to sit back and study the projection of a shallow slice of the galaxy that filled the communications room just above his head.

He enlarged it until those suns with planets had noticeable pinpricks of light circling them. Then he adjusted his chair to semi-reclining and lay back to let the computer play detective for him. The sector was thinly populated with stars. Ninety-five per cent of the inhabited planets were at the same technological level as Kamm or lower. Darzek described the Duke Lonorlk's crude electrical generator and asked which worlds in that slice of the galaxy boasted civilizations capable of supplying designs for it. Eight pinpoints of light began to blink rapidly.

Six were widely scattered. The other two were Kamm's neighboring solar systems. Scowling, Darzek punched buttons and put the file to work. The suns were Arrn and Zwentlax. Arrn had two habitable planets; Zwentlax had one, named Zruan.

"Interesting," Darzek muttered, "but I wish I knew why."

He described the strange metal detector he had taken from the phony black knights and asked which worlds could have created it. The blinking pinpoints of light dropped to four. Those of Arrn and Zwentlax were still among them.

He punched another question. "Which worlds have achieved space flight?"

The blinking pinpoints of light dropped to two: the worlds of Arrn and Zwentlax. Darzek amended the question to interstellar flight, and there was no response.

"Those blithering bureaucratic butanones!" Darzek said furiously. An Uncertified World with space flight capabilities required a crisis rating. Here were two that actually had achieved space flight without a change of status. As a result, they almost certainly had gone on to interstellar flight without the Synthesis's understaffed observation teams noticing.

He turned again to the projection. The three suns, Arrn, Gwanor, and Zwentlax, lay almost in a straight line, with Gwanor close to the midpoint. This meant that Kamm, the Silent Planet, could serve as a convenient halfway station on a space trip from the Zwentlaxian system to the Arrnian system.

Now he knew the source of the two kinds of aliens on Kamm and what they wanted there. It remained for him only to identify which aliens were in league with which dukes, and another question of the file accomplished that. The Duke of OO's guest with the massive, encircling ear came from the Arrnian Union, the two planets of the sun Arrn that possessed a single government. Darzek had not seen the Duke Merzkion's guests, but Captain Wanulzk's description of their high-set, circular ears was certain indication that they came from Zruan.

How could the Department of Uncertified Worlds have perpetrated such a massive blunder? No doubt the technologies of both civilizations were fumblingly inept by Synthesis standards, and someone in the department had considered them so remote from mastering interstellar travel that they were not even given the required crisis rating. The Department of Uncertified Worlds did not care how much an Uncertified World mucked about the ash heaps of its own solar system.

"Never underestimate the capabilities of *any* intelligence," Darzek murmured. Someone had, and now this quiet, technologically disadvantaged sector was in grave danger of becoming the setting for an interstellar war.

Unfortunately for the world of Kamm, its location almost midway between the budding space powers made it a potential battleground. No doubt the interstellar capabilities of both powers were limited. Neither could get at the home worlds of the other without Kamm, without a place to refuel and supply.

Darzek punched more buttons and found a mineral survey of Kamm. The planet's resources were mediocre, but there were uranium deposits in the central mountains of the island of Storoz. If one of the space powers gained permission to mine and process the uranium, it could attack the home bases of its rival. Each of the powers would realize that it had to control Kamm or deny it to the other, for its own protection.

Darzek turned his attention to the solar configurations beyond Kamm. If one of these powers occupied Kamm and managed to knock off the other, it might start on a rampage of spacial conquest that would carry it all the way to the sector boundary and beyond. The inhabited planets it would encounter were primitively civilized at best and would constitute easy pickings for a power with space capabilities. And when that power finally collided with a member of the Galactic Synthesis, it would be master of an interstellar empire and a conqueror to reckon with.

But the *if* was a formidable one, and so was the *might*. Considering the cost and tedium of primitive interstellar travel, few developing worlds would conceive of such a program of conquest or be able to follow through on it if they did. Subduing one world, even a world without technology, could take generations. Even if one of the powers produced a military genius, this Napoleon of the spaceways would not live long enough to do much damage, time and distance being the formidable factors they were in primitive space travel.

But the threat to Kamm was genuine. *Now* Darzek knew why Supreme had listed it as a potential trouble spot! The Galactic Synthesis took a rather aloof attitude toward the internal wars of Uncertified Worlds, but an interstellar war was a different matter. Kamm must be protected. Arrn and Zruan, neither of which was in a position as yet for overt military action, were attempting to secure the bases they needed through corrupt political maneuvering. They had to be defeated resoundingly and then dealt with on their home worlds.

"And that," Darzek told himself, "takes care of everything except the pazul." There was no evidence that the Duke of OO had one. Therefore it must have been brought from Zruan, by the allies of the Dukes Merzkion and Fermarz.

Without expecting any result, Darzek punched out the word, *pazul*, and the computer screen immediately flashed a memo from Rok Wllon himself that shocked Darzek.

Synthesis agents had failed to learn of the interstellar travel potentials on Arrn and Zruan, but when a suspected pazul occurred on the backward world of Kamm, they weren't so stupid as to overlook the possibility that it came from a neighboring solar system. Their department had gone to considerable trouble and risk to enter and search the most secret weapons and research and development centers in both civilizations, and their conclusions were irrefutable. Neither Arrn nor Zruan had a death ray.

The pazul, whatever it was, belonged exclusively to Kamm.

Darzek returned to Northpor, wrote more reports, tried to figure out how to make the communications equipment work, and waited for someone, anyone, to bring him a snippet of information he could act upon.

The news from OO was alarming. The Duke of OO had dared to challenge the Sailor's League. The port of OO had been closed permanently, and the sailors expected retaliatory measures against the Free Cities. Some of Darzek's Northpor neighbors were moving their families to Free Cities on the mainlands.

Reports from OO were tediously out of date and consisted mostly of gossip picked up by itinerant vendors who had been turned away by border guards but managed to acquire a rumor or two in the process. Darzek spread a net to pick up every scrap of information available, but in none of it did he find a useful snippet.

While he waited, he put Hadkez to work on the problem of his human scent, and he began to train Sajjo as a Synthesis agent. The child already had demonstrated an exceptional aptitude. Darzek told her to find out anything she could about the Dukes of Storoz or the Protector, and thereafter she prowled the mart, peeking in on conversations of visitors from other cities or provinces. Whenever she could, she asked questions. In this way they gradually built up character profiles of all of the dukes, but the Protector remained enigmatic. Sajjo never heard him mentioned.

Interesting as some of this information was, nothing actually intriguing turned up until Sajjo related an unexpected discovery about the Duke Borkioz, the elderly, senile duke of the southernmost province. It was rumored that he had moved from his own province to the Free City of Midpor and taken a palatial dwelling there for himself, his family, and his retainers.

Darzek reviewed his notes on the Duke Borkioz. He wondered if there was a coup in the process, and the old duke had been deposed or sent to safety. Either way it was an oddity, and he told Sajjo to ask travelers from the south about their duke.

Then a totally unexpected visitor arrived: a rather wan Captain Wanulzk.

Darzek greeted him warmly. *It grieved me to hear of your captivity,* he told him. *Especially so since I was responsible. I felt that I should stay in OO and do something about it, but your sailors thought I would be more hindrance than help.*

The captain gestured indifferently. *The Duke of OO has never loved the League. If the eruption set off by you and your daughter had not served as his excuse, he would have found another. But he moved against us impulsively, and it has cost him dearly.*

The League had closed the port of OO and assessed a colossal fine against the duke for his violation of agreements and his imprisonment of the captain and other sailors. The fine was increased daily. The duke defiantly refused to pay and demanded ransom for the release of the sailors he held. During this standoff, the economy of OO had disintegrated. The duke had to guard his borders—not against invasion, but against exodus. The artisans, in particular, were dependent on the export of their products, and they began to slip away surreptitiously with their families and set up their workshops in adjoining provinces.

Finally the duke's advisers prevailed upon him to make peace before his province was completely ruined. He paid his fines, for which he had to borrow funds from other dukes and his brother.

But it'll take the Province of OO years to recover, the captain said. *The artisans who escaped won't be returning soon. Those who remained will leave the moment they can do so safely. Customers for all of OO's products and produce have had to find other sources, and they won't be changing back at once. The duke professes not to care. He thinks that when he becomes king, he will close the Free Ports and bring the Sailor's League into subservience.*

Ah! Then he's convinced that he will be chosen king?

Those who are close to him think he will, the captain said gloomily.

And you think the king will be chosen by lot. Have you found out how this lottery will work?

No, the captain said. *It is thought that only the dukes know. And, of course, the Protector and his superior knights.* He paused. *So I really have nothing more of interest to tell you, except for an adventure of our friend Nijezor, the perfumer. And a message from our friend Bovranulz.*

Bovranulz? Darzek exclaimed. *Is he still in OO?*

Indeed he is. But he sends you a message, thanks to Nijezor. The message is that he anticipates with joy the reunion you and he will have in Midpor.

I regret that I cannot thank him in person, Darzek said. *Of course I have no intention of going to Midpor.*

The captain smiled. *Obviously some occasion for such a journey will arise, since Bovranulz says he will see you there. But let me tell you of the perfumer's adventure.*

Nijezor had been arrested by black-capes as he attempted to leave the harbor the morning following Darzek's departure from OO. But he had been treated with utmost consideration the moment he identified himself, and instead of being taken to the dungeon, he was taken to the presence of the duke himself, and the duke personally gave him a commission.

The strangest I have ever undertaken, the perfumer told Captain Wanulzk afterward. *The duke asked for as many varieties as I could contrive of the most unpleasant scents possible.*

Unpleasant? Darzek exclaimed.

That was the duke's very word, Captain Wanulzk said. *He specified the usual requirements for quality scents—especially that they must be long-lasting and of persistent strength. He told Nijezor that a scent that diminished in power quickly would be of no use to him. Nijezor had no choice but to comply. He was required to move his factory to the castle and work there. He says he never suffered so much in his life. He was constantly watched by black-capes, and he was required to deliberately produce and then test a long series of olfactory catastrophes.*

Darzek expressed his sympathy. *And was Nijezor able to please the duke?* he asked.

Only after arduous labor, the captain said.

Nijezor had prepared fifteen scents of horrendous unpleasantness. The duke took the samples overnight, and then he returned with the one that pleased him the most—it was number twelve—and he asked Nijezor to prepare several different varieties of that scent. Nijezor did so. The duke returned with one of them—it was number forty-seven—and made the same request again. And again.

Captain Wanulzk heaved a sigh of sympathy for his friend's ordeal. *It went on through three hundred and twenty-two samples,* his hands announced awesomely. *Number three hundred and twenty-two satisfied the duke completely, and Nijezor made a huge quantity of it—two full crock-measures. Enough scent to infuse the entire population of OO with ugliness. The duke rewarded him with enormous and unaccustomed generosity and ordered him to say nothing of his experiments to anyone. But why the duke requires such a stench Nijezor cannot say, and neither can I.*

Did Nijezor retain a sample? Darzek asked.

He retained the formula. He can make as much of it as you require. In fact, he made a full crock-measure for you, just in case you might be able to think of a use for it. This will show you what it's like.

The captain removed a small vial from a pocket in his cloak, unstoppered it, and offered it to Darzek.

Darzek took one whiff and reeled backward, choking. *Preposterous!* he exclaimed, when he was able to breathe again.

It is, the captain agreed happily. *It is almost as bad as your own scent, though of course completely different and with a far greater pungency. I have the crock-measure aboard my ship. Do you want it?*

Of course. And I appreciate your thoughtfulness, and that of Nijezor. I haven't the faintest notion of what the duke could use it for, but if we can find out, perhaps we can use it in the same way.

Excellent. Nijezor sends profuse regrets that he could not make progress with your problem, but the duke held him virtually in prison until the duke's commission was finished. But— The captain sniffed thoughtfully. *The scent you now wear almost disguises your odor.*

Unfortunately, it gives me only very temporary immunity. How is Bovranulz?

As far as we know, well. Did I tell you that he is a prisoner of the duke?

Darzek rose to his feet. *No!*

Nijezor had encounted Bovranulz quite by accident in the duke's castle. Bovranulz was left unguarded and his door ajar for a few minutes, and he was able to speak to Nijezor briefly. It was then that he had sent Darzek the message about Midpor.

Why would the duke do such a horrible thing to the Old Blind One? the captain demanded.

That's easy to answer, Darzek said. *The duke asked Bovranulz who would win the lottery and become king. Bovranulz refused to tell him. The duke intends to know, so he can take action to prevent another duke from winning. If imprisonment doesn't succeed, the duke may try torture. Couldn't the Sailor's League intervene in our friend's behalf?*

I will speak to the duke myself, the captain said grimly.

He took his leave, and Darzek sent Sjelk with him to bring back the crock-measure of the Duke of OO's special scent. When it arrived, Darzek scooped out a small measure of it, and he sat at the kitchen table contemplating it perplexedly. Sajjo and Hadkez entered, saw what he was doing, and leaned over to sample the scent. A single whiff made both of them retreat to the most remote corner of the room.

What is that? Hadkez demanded.

The Duke of OO's favorite perfume, Darzek answered shortly.

They sensed that he was in no mood for conversation, and they quietly withdrew. Darzek continued to contemplate the scent, and now and then he leaned forward and took a small sniff of it.

The smell was hideous, but it could not be dismissed simply as a ducal perversion. The Duke of OO had a highly specific use for it. Otherwise, why would he pursue its precise shading through more than three hundred samples?

It had to do with one of two things, Darzek thought: The duke's maneuvers to make himself king, or his attempts to detect alien agents. Darzek could not imagine how such a potent stench could possibly relate to the kingship. Neither could he imagine what relationship it could have to alien agents, but it made sense to him that the agents of Arrn and Zruan would have the same difficulties he did with his natural body odor. This scent could in some way be involved in covering up the odor of the aliens the duke favored—though Darzek, taking another whiff, found that difficult to believe. More likely this *was* the odor of the alien agents from Zruan, those who opposed the Duke of OO, and the duke intended to circulate the scent like a wanted poster: One hundred coins reward for anyone who smells like this, dead or alive.

But even that seemed scarcely credible. Darzek sniffed the scent again and shook his head. "An alien who smelled like that wouldn't be able to acquire any allies," he told himself.

And yet—the captain had considered the scent almost as bad as Darzek's. No wonder Darzek was sitting alone in a room in Northpor, making no progress whatsoever.

CHAPTER 16

He had the feeling of conducting a multifront war and losing on all of them. Every discovery seemed to take him into another blind alley. The Duke Lonorlk's electrical generator had led nowhere. His identification of the Duke of OO's companion as an alien should have solved the pazul problem; instead, it proved that the pazul originated on Kamm. He had learned that the dukes would soon be meeting to select a king, but he had no idea when, or where, or how that royal lottery would function.

Most serious of all, he had found no trace of Rok Wllon or any of the other missing agents, and he did not even know where to look for them.

There remained nothing for him to do but stay in Northpor and play games with Sajjo. These were serious games, involving elaborate stratagems for eavesdropping on newly arrived strangers, and Sajjo played them superbly well. In a short time she discovered that all of the dukes —except for the elderly Duke Borkioz, who already had moved to Midpor—all of the dukes were furiously occupied with preparations for something. No one knew what.

Bovranulz had said he would enjoy the reunion with Darzek in Midpor, but Bovranulz was still a prisoner of the Duke of OO. Darzek was tempted to go to Midpor anyway—but what could he accomplish if he went?

He returned to his glum contemplation of the Duke of OO's hideous scent.

Fourteen more days passed just as futilely, and then Captain Wanulzk returned. This time he brought a companion, a burly man clothed as a fellow sailor. When he uncapped on entering, a head of flaming red hair came to view. Darzek knew him instantly. This was the Duke Dunjinz, one of the captain's two favored candidates for the kingship.

The captain made no attempt at concealment. He introduced his companion as the duke, and he introduced Darzek as a visitor to the world of Kamm and a friend of its people.

The duke exchanged a sailor's greetings with Darzek. *The captain has told me about you. I have great admiration for one who braves the impossible.*

One must brave the impossible and succeed in order to receive admiration, sire, Darzek said with a grin. *There is little that is admirable about one who foolishly braves the impossible and fails.*

The duke responded with a grin of his own. *I think there is, if the cause is just. How may I serve you?*

Darzek looked questioningly at the captain; but Captain Wanulzk, having arranged this tableau, was intent on its running its course with no interference from him. He ignored Darzek's look.

I should like to serve you, Darzek told the duke, *by making you the King of Storoz.*

The duke's fingers flashed crisply. *Impossible.*

You would not admire me for braving this particular impossibility?

The duke burst into laughter. Darzek waited until he had quieted, and then his fingers spoke firmly. *Tell me how the king is chosen, and I will make you king.*

Impossible. Only the dukes, the Protector, and the highest knights of the Winged Beast know how the choice is made, or have ever known. Each of us has sworn his oath. The Duke Dunjinz does not break an oath. I cannot tell anyone.

Do all of the the dukes have an equal chance? Darzek asked.

The duke hesitated. *I rely on the Protector's integrity,* he said slowly. *Some think he will favor his brother, the Duke of OO, if the chance for a favor arises, but I know that he will not. He knows his own brother well, and he knows his brother would quickly betray his religion or anything else if it could be done profitably. No, the Protector will not favor the Duke of OO or any other duke. The principles of the old religion mean much to him. But most of the dukes are capable of turning the odds in their own favor if the opportunity is given to them. I don't know what schemes they may be contriving, but I do know that several are maneuvering for what they think will be an advantage. So I don't know whether all dukes have an equal chance.*

If you can't tell me about the lottery, what can you tell me? Darzek asked.

I can tell you that all of the dukes will meet in Midpor on the day of the third conjunction. They will travel together, each with his own party of knights and retainers and servants, to Surjolanz, which is the border town of the province of the Duke Tonorj. From there they will enter the Central Province, the Realm of the Holy Beast, and proceed to a small village called Veznol. There the knights, retainers, and servants will encamp, and the dukes will continue alone, each attended by his personal servants and superior knights, under the guidance of the

Protector, who will lead them to the place where the lottery is to take place. There the king will be selected; and then all will return to Veznol and the waiting followers, and the entire party will return to Midpor. That much I can tell you. It is secret, but we were only sworn not to tell anyone who does not need to know, and I consider that one who attempts the impossible needs to know.

Thank you, Darzek said. He turned to the captain. *Is that the information you wanted me to have?*

The captain raised a shoulder affirmatively. *That—and I also wanted you to know the Duke Dunjinz and I wanted him to know you. I sense, my friend, that you intend to be present at the lottery. The duke says you will die if you attempt it and accomplish nothing at all, and there would be no way he could assist you. Still, even though he has no authority in the province of the Protector, he might be able to aid you in secret if he knows who you are.*

In a time of need, Darzek said, *any helping hand is welcome. But I will attempt to conduct myself so that no aid is necessary.*

He removed the lid of the perfumer's crock, which still stood in the center of the table where Darzek could contemplate it frequently. *Does that scent mean anything to you?* he asked the duke.

The duke took only a small sniff before backing away. *It means only that something has died!* he exclaimed.

You've never smelled it before?

No. And I would not willingly smell it again.

Thank you. Darzek turned to the captain. *Have you any news concerning our friend Bovranulz?*

I spoke to the Duke of OO concerning him. The duke says my conclusions are entirely mistaken. Bovranulz remains at the castle as an honored guest, reporting his visions as the duke requests. Whenever he wishes to leave he will be free to do so, and when he leaves he will be handsomely rewarded for his services. But as yet he has not exhausted the visions the duke has requested. The captain gestured scornfully. *We know the duke lies, but there's little that we can do about it.*

Did you ask to see Bovranulz?

Of course. But he had just finished a trying work session and was resting—or so the duke said. The duke professes deep concern about the health of the Old Blind One, and he will not permit his rest to be interrupted. The Sailor's Council will discuss the matter at its next meeting, but by then the duke will have left for Midpor. Before we can take effective action, the king will be chosen and Bovranulz will have his liberty again.

I'll tell both of you this, Darzek said, working his fingers slowly and emphatically. *The Duke of OO means to be chosen king, and he knows how to arrange it. He has arranged it. I can't stop him without knowing how the lottery works.*

He looked at the Duke Dunjinz, who met his gaze firmly, a small smile on his face. His only other response was a negative gesture. He had pledged his word, and he meant to keep the pledge. He would, Darzek thought, make a good king. Perhaps too good—a sense of honor was a noble attribute, but one should be able to temporize when disaster threatened, and the Duke of OO as King of Storoz represented the ultimate disaster.

Darzek wondered if more than an oath was involved. The religion of the Winged Beast was ancient and harsh, and—Darzek remembered Rok Wllons poetry—it was a Death Religion. The duke's oath might be reinforced by ceremonies no decent Kammian would be willing to confess.

Do you approve of giving the lives of your fellow citizens to the Winged Beast? he asked bluntly.

The duke paled. *How did you learn that?*

There are many ways in which one may brave the impossible, Darzek returned.

No, the duke answered, *I don't approve. It is a sickening thing. But I cannot change it unless I do become king. If that happens, there will be many changes.*

Do you know of the two kinds of outsiders that are guests of the Duke Merzkion and the Duke of OO?

Both kinds called on me. They promised much. I ordered them out of my province.

Darzek turned to the captain. *Water passage is the best way to reach Midpor, isn't it?*

It's the only way, if you want to arrive there in time.

When do you leave Northpor?

At the half night.

I need to reflect on all of this, Darzek said. *I may see you on your ship before you sail.*

After they left, Darzek spent some time studying a map of Storoz. Then he doused himself with the special perfume Hadkez had prepared for him, told Wesru he wasn't to be disturbed under any circumstances, and descended to the basement.

And to the subbasement, from which he went to Midpor by transmitter.

The house used for a Synthesis headquarters had an air of musty dampness and desertion about it. Darzek first looked for a note from Riklo; but if she had successfully got this far north in her tour of the dukes' castles, she had been traveling far inland. The house's yard was a blight on an otherwise tidy neighborhood. Something would have to be done about that, but Darzek had more urgent matters to contend with.

Midpor was the smallest of the Free Cities, located at the head of a long, finger-like bay that cut deeply into the island. That indentation made it the port city closest to the Central Province, and it handled the imports and exports for the population of that province living east of the mountains, as well as those for the Duke Tonorj, whose province surrounded it. So rugged were the central mountains, and so difficult the passes, that a long haul from the coast was easier than a trip through the mountains. For this reason, the port of OO handled the commerce directed to and from the western part of the Central Province, even though Midpor was the nearest port.

So the dukes' destination obviously was on the eastern side of the mountains, or they would not have selected Midpor as a starting point. Darzek strolled from the Synthesis headquarters toward the harbor of the pretty little city and made a startling discovery. Midpor was being abandoned. Half the dwellings were empty already. Merchants were moving out their stocks, and many of the warehouses and commercial buildings were empty or being emptied.

He moved through a partially deserted mart and climbed the life pyramid to look down on the bustling activity of the harbor—all of it directed at loading ships. He saw no ship being unloaded. As he watched, the germ of a plan occurred to him.

Obviously the Sailor's League was abandoning Storoz. The number of empty houses in Northpor was increasing. Rumors had reached him of similar trends in the other Free Cities. The sailors were convinced that the Duke of OO, or another duke equally evil, would become King of Storoz, and that his first act would be to take the Free Cities by force and attempt to hold the sailors' families for ransom. As rapidly as possible they were moving to the Free Cities the League held on the continents.

The Duke Tonorj, whose province surrounded Midpor, had a foul reputation. The Midpor evacuation was being rushed. The Duke Lonorlk, whose province surrounded Northpor, was more highly regarded, and the Northpor evacuation was proceeding with less haste. In Southpor, a Free City long accustomed to being ignored by the senile Duke Borkioz, it had scarcely begun.

The implications were clear enough. By the time the new king was selected, the famed Free Cities of Storoz would be reduced to the status of ghost towns, and Storoz would be economically ruined.

The immediate significance to Darzek was that all of the Dukes of

Storoz were about to descend on this little city, accompanied by vast entourages—because on such an occasion no duke wanted to appear less
magnificent than his fellows—and no one in Midpor knew they were
coming! The city's merchants were emulating the sailors. They were
disposing of their stocks, salvaging what they could, and moving their
families. The dukes would find an empty city awaiting them, with
every kind of housing available and nothing to eat.

Darzek walked back to the business community and eventually
found the person he wanted, a sort of provision or commissary broker,
whose scribe filled a page with calculations while they talked. Darzek
rented warehouses and stables, bought wagons and nabrula, and then
went scouting around with the broker, picking up bargains in food
stocks that businessmen feared to be stuck with after the city was abandoned. In the process, they happened upon an entire warehouse of
dried namafj. On being assured that the price was a genuine bargain,
Darzek took all of it. He had been searching for the proper role for
himself, and the vending of dried namafj suited him perfectly. The
odor was less full blown than that of the overripe namafj he'd encountered in OO and not really an unpleasant smell, but it was penetrating
enough to conceal all traces of his human stench.

He left the broker to carry on for him and returned to Northpor.
There he conferred briefly with Sjelk, telling him to round up
unemployed youths who were experienced in driving and caring for
nabrula, and to start buying animals and wagons. Then he went to the
harbor to talk again with captain Wanulzk and the Duke Dunjinz.

A ship? Captain Wanulzk exclaimed. *You want a whole ship? Just
for yourself? I can easily arrange passage for you and as many as you
wish to take with you, but ships are in short supply.*

I know, Darzek said. *The sailors are leaving Storoz. So are most of
the merchants. But this is critically important.*

But why do you need a whole ship?

*Not a ship. Ships. I have no idea how many I'll need. I just want to
make certain that they'll be available.*

Critically important? the captain echoed, his hands fluttering doubtfully.

Critically, Darzek told him. *The future of Storoz depends on it.*

Very well. You'll have all the ships you need.

In the captain's cabin, Darzek had a long talk with the Duke Dunjinz.
He wanted to know the exact size of the party each duke was likely to
bring with him to Midpor. The Duke Dunjinz had not even decided on
the size of his own party, but when pressed by Darzek, he discussed his
fellow dukes astutely, and Darzek performed approximations, and they
arrive at working averages. Each duke could be expected to bring some

thirty knights, thirty knights' lackeys, and an additional thirty lackeys, retainers, and servants for himself. Rounding the total off at a party of one hundred for each duke, Darzek deduced that some eleven hundred people would be setting out from Midpor for the mountains.

Darzek took his leave of the two of them, having received the captain's promise that two ships would be available for him the following day. He went from the harbor directly to the business community, found another broker, and began buying stocks of food.

The dukes and their eleven hundred followers would arrive in Midpor, expecting to outfit themselves for their journey to the mountains, and such was their secrecy that there would be no one left in the abandoned city who could sell them a morsel of food or supply a single wagon or nabrulk.

No one, that is, except Jan Darzek, in his role as Lazk, the vendor of dried namafj.

CHAPTER 17

Darzek arrived by ship in the now almost deserted city of Midpor with Sjelk, Sajjo, and fifty newly hired wagoners, along with a shipload of wagons and nabrula. Wesru and Hadkez were left in Northpor, although Hadkez protested bitterly that the mart there was about to close and there was nothing for a perfumer to do—for the full tide of exodus now had struck Northpor as well. But Darzek wanted the Synthesis headquarters in Northpor to remain functional.

He immediately sent Sjelk and Sajjo to sift through the Midpor unemployed for those with experience in handling nabrula or foodstuffs. The unemployed were the one segment of the population that remained. They neither had a place to go nor a means of getting there.

Darzek put his wagoners to work moving the food purchases he had made in Midpor to his own warehouses, and as soon as ships began to arrive with purchases Darzek had made in Northpor, that food, also, had to be moved and stored. Already it was evident that more wagons and nabrula were needed, and Darzek sent Sjelk down the coast to Eastpor and Southpor; which also were in the process of abandonment, to buy everything available and also shop for bargains in food.

By the time the dukes began to arrive, Darzek had placed himself on the verge of bankruptcy, having spent all of the capital accumulated by agents of the Galactic Synthesis and in addition imposed a severe strain on his credit.

But with the arrival of the first ducal party, he was solvent again. The dukes brought their riding nabrula, as well as transport for the personal effects of their entourages, but all were accustomed to buying foodstuffs and nabrula fodder when and where they wanted them, and none had brought transport for that purpose. Neither had any of them considered the logistics of moving eleven hundred people from the coast to the mountains and the demands that this would make on the impoverished peasant villages along the way.

The number of nabrula required to move this procession over the rough roads of Kamm stunned Darzek. There would be more nabrula than people, and this route lay through long stretches of country where there was no edible natural food for the creatures. Darzek had to plan for an entire convoy of wagons loaded with nabrula fodder, which of course added to the numbers of nabrula that would have to be fed.

Darzek was able to meet the expedition's transportation needs from his stock of wagons and nabrula and his pool of unemployed wagoners. And once he had supplied the transport, he was ready to sell the dukes the necessary wagonloads of provisions for the trek to the mountains and back.

Going about with his daughter Sajjo—who seemed more like a partner to those watching, since Darzek consulted her deferentially about all kinds of transactions, and her astuteness pleased him as much as it amazed those he was doing business with—and his sons, which Sjelk and his leading assistants were assumed to be, Lazk the provisioner and family quickly became the most respected and sought-after business establishment in Midpor. Even Lazk's peculiar insistence on handling personally the dried namafj he urged upon the travelers was respected.

I got my start in business with dried namafj, he would say. *Can't eat the stuff myself. You buy and sell and store and process dried namafj for years and see what it does to your appetite. But there's more nourishment in it per wagonload than anything else you can transport. I say if you don't want to arrive where you're going hungry, carry at least a quarter of your provisions in dried namafj.*

As more dukes arrived, speculators began to appear. They had belatedly arrived at conclusions similar to Darzek's and hoped to make a killing; but the provisioner Lazk, with efficiency, service, and reasonable prices, already had established himself as the expedition's official provisions merchant. He was able to supply everything the dukes needed, and he—and he alone—had permission to bring his own train of wagons with the expedition to resupply the ducal parties along the way. So secure was Darzek's position that when the redheaded Duke Dunjinz arrived, he could only gape in amazement while his retainers transacted business with the famous provisioner Lazk.

Except for the senile Duke Borkioz, who had arrived early because his family feared that he might muddle his journey and lose his chance at the kingship, none of the dukes put their entourages in dwellings. They were ready to travel, and they moved into fields just beyond the Midpor city wall and set up their tents. By the time the eleventh duke, the Duke of OO, arrived, the tent city beyond the wall was far more populous than the abandoned Free City within it.

Captain Wanulzk himself brought the Duke of OO and his party, and after they had landed, Darzek slipped aboard the ship for a talk with the captain.

Bovranulz is with the duke, the captain said. *He's still a prisoner, but*

I managed a word with him. He says he is well treated and we shouldn't concern ourselves about him.

Darzek described his new profession. *I'll accompany the dukes with all the wagons I can acquire, equipped with double loading boards. And according to my calculations, that, plus the food the dukes are taking themselves, won't begin to get this royal mob to the mountains and back. None of the dukes has an inkling of the problems involved. When was the last time eleven hundred people went anywhere on Storoz?*

The captain couldn't remember such an event. *But why should they need so much food?*

Moving that many people over the lanes of Storoz is going to be slow. On the way out, I'll encourage the dukes to eat from my wagons instead of their own. The moment a wagon is empty, I'll send it back to Midpor for another load. That way there'll be a continuous stream of provisions overtaking us or meeting us on the way back. That's the only thing that'll keep this expedition from starving.

All the dukes are talking about you, the captain said. *They think you're a genius. Is there anything I can do to help?*

Yes. Bring in enough food to refill my warehouses after we leave for the mountains—and keep refilling them. Even if the expedition gets back here safely, I have a feeling that the dukes may wait in Midpor a long time for ships to take them home.

The captain smiled. *I'll do that.* Then he added slyly, *Will you be needing more dried namafj?*

Especially dried namafj, Darzek said firmly.

That was well thought of. Have you found a use for the special scent our friend Nijezor prepared for the Duke of OO?

No, Darzek said. *I brought the crock along with me, and I intend to take it all the way to the mountains, just in case I think of something. Thus far, the only thing I've been able to compare it with is nabrula manure.*

Darzek warmly bade the captain farewell and went back to the Synthesis headquarters, where Sjelk and a scribe were making lists of independent vendors and artisans Darzek intended to take along with him. Harnesses would break, clothing would wear out, wagons would break down, doctors would be needed both for Kammians and for nabrula, tools would be required—the immensity of the task of transporting eleven hundred people and their nabrula staggered Darzek. That evening he began to move his wagons and drivers, and those of the independent vendors and artisans, out beyond the city wall where the dukes had established their entourages.

The Protector had arrived, and Darzek studied him carefully from a distance—tall, lean, incisive in look and manner, a leader accustomed to command, an ascetic whose eyes flashed fanaticism. His character was indeed the mirror image of that of his self-indulgent brother, the Duke of OO, but to Darzek that simply made him a different kind of villain. He doubted that the Protector's victims felt any special consolation because the cruelty inflicted on them was sanctimonious.

The Protector was clothed in black and mounted on a solid black nabrulk, a creature so rare that Darzek had never seen one. With him was a retinue of a dozen black knights, and these priests of the Winged Beast, like their leader, disdained the luxury of tents. They unrolled their sleeping rugs wherever they chose to lie.

Darzek made his evening rounds carrying a basket of dried namafj, his trade-mark. Sajjo drifted along with him, sometimes the dutiful daughter following obediently at his heels, sometimes a wraith flitting unnoticed among the tents, seeing everything that happened, looking in on private conversations.

The rolling meadow was an incredible melange of tent-covered wagons, of caravans, of separate tents of all shapes and sizes and colors, of cooking fires and sputtering torches, of restless nabrula. Darzek moved slowly through the encampment, and the sheer confusion that reverberated everywhere seemed so magnificently contrived that Darzek felt for it the kind of affection he would have had for a singularly bad work of art. He felt the same way about the accompanying noise and also about the stench of the haphazard sanitary conditions.

At the enclave of each duke, he paused to talk with the duke's own commissariat. He was known to all the sentries, who allowed him to pass without challenge; but each enclave had an inner circle of tents and wagons where no outsiders were permitted, and these Darzek scrupulously avoided.

He had a long conference with the Duke of OO's commissariat, since the duke's entourage had just arrived and still hadn't purchased its needed supplies. Darkness had come on by the time they finished. Darzek promised delivery in the morning—he was getting rich, which couldn't have mattered less to him—and as he turned away he felt a soft touch on his arm.

It was Sajjo, and she tapped out a code they had invented between them so they could talk in the dark.

She had found Bovranulz.

Where? Darzek responded.

She motioned to him to follow her. They slipped between the shadowed tents and into the forbidden inner circle of the Duke of OO's enclave. Sajjo pointed. It was not Bovranulz's own distinctive tent but one indistinguishable from the others.

Darzek parted the flaps and looked in on darkness. Cupping his hands about his hand light, he pointed it at the interior and turned it on.

The gaunt, elderly form was seated on the edge of a cot. The wrinkled face grinned as its sightless eyes embraced Darzek.

Bovranulz's fingers were barely discernible in the dim light. *Greetings, my friend. Did you receive my message that we would meet at Midpor?*

Darzek's mind shaped the one question that mattered above all others. "Did the duke make you his captive because you refused to tell him who would be chosen king?"

No, my friend, the fingers answered. *He took me captive because I did tell him, and he feared that I would tell others. Bovranulz does not conceal the truth, nor does he fear to speak it. The duke made me his prisoner because I told him who would be chosen king.*

"Who?" Darzek's mind demanded.

The Duke of OO, the fingers replied.

"Is there no way to change that? No way to make another duke the king?"

None, the reply came. *The picture is drawn. The Duke of OO will be chosen King of Storoz.*

Two days later, the procession began to move westward at dawn. It was an interminable, utterly chaotic beginning because no one was in charge. The Protector and his personal escort of knights moved at the head of the line on their riding nabrula. Immediately behind them came the party of the Duke Merzkion, because his group was encamped at the extreme western edge of the meadow. The entourages of the other dukes contended for positions, and a knight of the Duke Suklozk fought a death duel with a knight of the Duke Pabinzk on the lane they were disputing and killed him. While they fought, passing wagons, carts, riders, even pedestrians—for there was no way to keep impoverished foot peddlers from tagging along—veered around them, showering them with clouds of dust as the heavy traffic churned the seldom-used lane to powder.

Few had thought to carry water, and though there were frequent small streams, the panting nabrula rushed into each one they encountered and fouled it for kilometers before drinking and cooking water could be drawn from it. Not until the third day did the dukes themselves realize that something had to be done to ease the water problem and settle the daily squabbles and duels that took place along the line of march. A capable knight of the Duke Rilornz was placed in charge, and after that things went much more smoothly. And there were no more duels.

But the procession continued to move slowly.

Each night, when the various entourages broke their line of march to encamp, Darzek made his rounds. He routinely took orders from those wishing to replenish supplies: crocks of flour, weights of dried meat or fish, bales of nabrula fodder.

And he watched and listened, and Sajjo flitted about everywhere, but they learned little. Evidently someone had seen Bovranulz with an unknown visitor, and the Duke of OO had been sufficiently alarmed to publicly whip a negligent sentry and place additional guards around the inner circle of his enclave. Darzek could glimpse Bovranulz's tent from a distance, through a narrow gap between tents—it was recognizable because a sentry now stood at its entrance constantly—but he did not dare attempt to approach it. And during the daily march, the covered cart carrying Bovranulz moved directly in front of the duke's carriage.

Darzek had his moments of stark despair, when it seemed to him that the selection of a king had nothing to do with him or the Synthesis, and he was wasting precious weeks of time on this outlandish trek. Even if there was something to be learned, the difficulties in doing so seemed insurmountable. It pained him to know that the Duke of OO and his closest advisers, the haughty black knights that accompanied him everywhere, were in secret conference beyond a thin expanse of canvas, and that Darzek—as the expedition's popular and efficient provisioner—could pass the tent closely without arousing a twitch of suspicion from the watchful guards; and yet he could not overhear a word. For there was no eavesdropping on the Silent Planet except when one could watch the hands of the talkers.

It bothered him even more when he realized that the Duke of OO was transporting a treasure. This thing of immense value had a wagon to itself and its own special guard of black-caped lackeys. The duke visited it every morning and every evening and sometimes during the day, but no one except the duke and its guard was allowed within twenty strides of it. At night, the treasure shared the inner circle with Bovranulz.

Darzek pointed this out to Sajjo, who considered it gravely and then went her flitting way through the night's encampment—she slipped unseen or unnoticed into places where even the distinguished provisioner Lazk would have been arrested at once—and she returned with the staggering news that *all* of the dukes were transporting treasures. Even Captain Wanulzk's friend, the redheaded Duke Dunjinz, had a thing of immense value in his entourage that was guarded as carefully as that of the Duke of OO.

Darzek wracked his imagination, came up with no answers, and finally dismissed the mystery from his mind. It was only one more imponderable among so many.

The daily march tediously crept closer to the mountains, which now could be seen on the horizon. Sajjo watched them uneasily as they loomed larger. When Darzek asked her why, she answered, *That's where my father is.*

He questioned her and discovered that the Central Province was called the Realm of the Holy Beast because Storozian religious mythology did in fact make that its lair. The Winged Beast perched atop the highest peak to look out over the world and select the next victim it would take to feed its young. Those who came close to the mountains were, in Sajjo's naïve version of the myth, much more likely to be seized. She seemed to have forgotten the reassuring words of Bovranulz.

Darzek reminded her of the villages they had passed along the way, and their apparently happy residents, subjects of the Duke Tonorj, whom the Winged Beast miraculously failed to molest; but she could not be convinced, and her uneasiness grew as the mountains loomed closer.

Darzek worried about her.

When they reached their destination, and the dukes and the Protector proceeded alone to their rendezvous, Darzek intended to follow them and learn what he could about the lottery. If it were in any way possible, he would prevent the Duke of OO from being selected king.

He knew that the chances were excellent that he would be captured. He also knew that retaliatory measures might be taken against his family helpers. He intended to alert Sjelk so that he could warn the others in time, and he felt that they could look after themselves. He already had told Sjelk to have every worker prepare a survival pack of supplies for himself.

But he worried incessantly about Sajjo. Therefore he struck up a friendship with a harness maker who had brought his wife and children with him. He invented a fictitious illness. The Winged Beast might spare him for a long time, he said; on the other hand—

The harness maker gestured wisely. His wife shrugged understandingly. They found his fatherly concern touching. In return for his personal wagon and nabrula, they would cheerfully add Sajjo to their family and raise her to maturity. And—they were fond of the child— they would give her a marriage portion equal to the value of the wagon and nabrula. Darzek thanked them profusely and told them he knew no nobler people on Kamm.

He knew they would reduce Sajjo to the role of an unpaid servant and there would be no marriage portion; but they would treat her kindly and provide a temporary refuge, and as soon as she reached a Free Port, any of the many sea captains who now knew her would return her to Northpor.

Now the mountains were close enough so that their precisely

stratified vegetation was visible, from the lush brown of the zarak forests to the vibrant blue of the izu meadows and finally the snow-capped
peaks. It was a formidable chain, and few would be the Kammians
hardy enough to trace the mythical Winged Beast to its lair.

As the land moved precipitously upward in their first really difficult
climb, they passed the village of Surjolanz, the last village and the last
wayside forum of the Duke Tonorj's province. A looming sculpture of
the Winged Beast announced what all of them already knew: From
this point, the old religion ruled. They stood at the border of the land
of death.

Their panting nabrula finally gained the narrow pass at the top of
the rise and pointed their bulging noses downward in long, steep descent. At the bottom was a broad valley, and on the far side of a shallow, swift-flowing, cold river was the village of Veznol—the only Central Province village on this surlane east of the mountains, it was said.

The long procession finally had reached its destination.

The Protector was there ahead of them, and he took personal charge
of locating the encampment. His decisions were incisive, but in the
inevitable disputes that developed he seemed infinitely patient and fair
in his judgments. He formed the enclaves in a vast circle on the floor of
the mountain valley below the village. He placed Darzek's establishment at the center of the circle, so that supplies and services were con-
veniently located for everyone. And he established a nabrula corral far
downstream where it wouldn't befoul the river's water before the needs
of village and encampment were taken care of.

Darzek was impressed.

As soon as Darzek's wagons were parked, he consolidated loads,
overloading as much as he could, and started the empty wagons on the
return lane to Midpor. That evening, coming back from the nabrula
corral, Darzek saw the long mounted column of dukes and their chosen
associates setting out up the narrow lane that led toward the high
mountain pass above the village. Night was coming on, but he could
see, in the zigzagging, torch-lit column, that each duke took his private
treasure with him, borne on a litter draped with costly tapestries and
surrounded by guards.

Where the lane left the village, and again halfway up the mountain,
were torch-lit sentry posts with armed guards. Darzek assumed there'd
be another at the top of the pass. Obviously the route was triple-
guarded; and at that very moment, black knights of the Winged Beast
were passing through the encampment warning all those left behind to
remain in camp. There was only one penalty for intruding into the
Realm of the Holy Beast beyond the village of Veznol: Death.

Actually, the situation seemed far more hopeful than Darzek had expected. The fact that the dukes continued their journey that night

meant that their destination was close at hand. The senile Duke Borkioz, who was in poor health, could not have tolerated a long night ride through the mountains.

The site of the lottery was within Darzek's reach if he cared to take the risk: a torturous night climb over the mountain, avoiding the lane all the way, and certain death if he were captured in the vicinity of that most secret ceremony that would decide the kingship.

He spoke tersely with Sjelk, reminding him of the agreed plan should Darzek disappear. Then he left the camp, strolling downstream as though he intended to visit the nabrula corral again. He stopped at a point where he could study the profile of the mountain against the darkening sky. He intended to take the risk; at the same time, he wanted to cover himself with some plausible excuse for getting lost on the mountainside, if he could think of one. He thought long and hard as he watched the last torches of the procession of dukes vanish into the high pass. If he waited much longer, the mounted party would be too far ahead to be overtaken.

He turned and found Sajjo watching him.

Suddenly he found the excuse he needed, but the experience would be a scarring one for her. He took her to their tent, lit a candle, and told her what he wanted. She agreed immediately, in the quiet, matter-of-fact way she accepted all of his requests. He looked at her doubtfully. He had to decide at once.

She got to her feet. *Shall we go now?*

Still reluctant, for he knew she would be terrified, he packed a lunch for her, dressed both of them in heavy clothing, and folded a rug and a blanket. He added a jar of water, telling her how to dispose of the jar, the rug, and the blanket when she was finished with them. Then he repeated his instructions again and had her repeat them back to him.

Moving from shadow to shadow, they slipped from the encampment, crossed the meadow, and started up the mountainside, moving quickly past the stabbing lights of the innumerable night creatures that so frightened Sajjo. Darzek again felt reluctant to go on; but when they reached the edge of the looming forest, she gestured a farewell at him and slipped from his sight.

He hurried back to the encampment and went directly to his friend the harness maker.

Have you seen Sajjo? he asked him. *I can't find her.*

The harness maker was instantly sympathetic.

I've looked everywhere, Darzek said. *She was afraid of the mountains. Would a child that age wander off when she's afraid?*

The harness maker, whose children were considerably younger than Sajjo, instantly constituted himself an authority. Of course she might, he said expansively. A child often wasn't afraid at all of the things she talked about being afraid of. But it seemed more likely that she would be found around the camp. There were plenty of things nearby to interest a child, even at night.

I've looked everywhere, Darzek repeated. He waved his hands despairingly. *I'll keep on looking.*

He hurried away.

Minutes later he was clear of the encampment himself and climbing the mountain. He saw no sign of Sajjo; but she would follow his instructions religiously and find a comfortable place for herself with as much concealment as possible but within sight of the encampment so she couldn't get lost. She was to make a bed of the rug and blanket and sleep if she could. At midmorning she was to cover rug, blanket, and water jar with leaves and undergrowth, disarrange her clothing, and come crying down the mountain, pretending that she had got lost and wandered about all night.

And that, Darzek thought, would give an anxious father excuse enough for wandering into the forbidden Realm of the Holy Beast. He doubted that it would save him, but it might keep the Protector's revenge from falling on his family.

He climbed stumblingly up the steep slope, through forest and thick undergrowth, and he was quickly exhausted; but he did not dare go near the lane for fear the watchful sentries would detect his movements through the luminous patterns of fleeing night creatures. Not until he approached the top of the slope did he veer sideways far enough to look down into the pass, and he found his suspicions confirmed. The torch-lit pass swarmed with black-capes. He turned away, plunged back into the forest, and finally came out on the downward mountain slope beyond the pass. He could look far into the valley beyond and see the tracery of night creatures on the distant valley floor.

His first discovery was that more torch-lit sentry posts barred the surlane to him. His second was that the party of dukes already had disappeared. He watched for some time, but he saw no moving torches anywhere—and they could not have moved quickly enough to cross the valley and gain the high mountain pass beyond.

Neither was there any sign of an encampment. He had lost them completely.

Rather than wait until morning, he chose to wander on in the dark. He reasoned that they must have descended as far as possible from the thin, chill air of the pass before they halted. He moved on, finding the steep descent relatively easy after the arduous climb and experiencing no problems with walking because the night creatures continued to light his every step.

As he walked, his puzzlement grew. He had expected an imposing religious temple, probably with a complex of buildings that befitted the headquarters of a prosperous religion. At a minimum, there should have been accommodations extensive enough to put up the parties of eleven dukes in the style to which they had let themselves become accustomed and in fact could be expected to demand.

And Darzek could see no building at all, not even a nabrula shed. Nor was there any trace of an encampment of tents. He found himself pondering the question of whether the dukes would accept the austerity of a night in the open as the price of a chance at the kingship.

He walked on.

Then, abruptly, he was falling.

He realized afterward that there'd been warning enough—a circle of darkness where no night creature scurried or even flew; but the exhausting climb and his need for sleep had dulled his responses, and until he stepped into it the hole looked like the rest of the dark mountainside. He absently walked up to an opening five meters in diameter and fell in.

He landed on a metal framework three or four meters below the surface and found himself in a caged airshaft. Before he could collect his confused senses, pain stabbed at his arm, and he jerked away and stood in the center of the cage, staring about him.

Beating at the bars of the cage, wings fluttering, fangs bared greedily, talons ripping at him, were the monstrous myths of the Kammian religion, terrifying in their enormity. At the same instant, an overwhelming wave of dizziness seized him.

He had fallen into a nightmare where the most farfetched fantasy became reality. He hadn't even considered the possibility that the hideous symbol of the death cult could be anything more than that—could in fact be real. But the gaping gullets, the slobbering jaws, the bared fangs, the knife-like talons of the Winged Beasts were reality's convincing horrification. His dizziness continued, and he feared he was about to faint.

A Winged Beast swooped up from below and slashed his ankle. Looking about him, Darzek saw that at two points the support bars formed a perfect ladder. It was his only chance, and instantly he made a rush for it.

He was forced back by slicing talons and ripping fangs. Both his arms and legs were bleeding, now, and his dizziness continued. He crouched in the center of the cage, ready to kick at any beast that approached from below, and fighting to remain conscious.

Then, in the dim light far below him, he saw, beyond another set of bars, a black-caped knight of the Winged Beast staring up at him. The knight whirled suddenly and ran.

CHAPTER 18

The time, Darzek thought, was dawn, though the only light that touched the small, bare, windowless, rock-hewn cell in which he had spent the remainder of the night came from torches in the corridor beyond. Footsteps approached; the barred door opened. A black-caped knight's fingers snapped an order.

Darzek sprang to obey, and they started along the corridor: one black-caped knight leading the way; two more following after Darzek. The corridor was chill, and Darzek, who had been shivering all night, continued to shiver. The low temperature in the system of caves perhaps explained why all the knights and lackeys wore some form of headgear. Darzek wished he had a hat.

The knights marched him directly to the Protector, who was seated on a dais at the center of a large audience room. He wore black robes and a hat with a twist to it that in such solemn surroundings looked positively jaunty. At his elbow stood a knight Darzek had seen several times during the trek from Midpor: a scribe, Darzek guessed, and perhaps an administrative assistant as well. Like all of the knights Darzek had seen there, he wore armor and a headpiece. In the temple of the Winged Beast, its knights always were girded for battle.

This is the provisioner? the Protector asked.

Yes, sire.

The Protector studied Darzek thoughtfully. *I have seen him.*

We all have, sire. He accompanied us from Midpor. He dealt in dried namajf.

The Protector sniffed and grimaced. *So I notice. Obviously he has dealt in dried namafj quite recently. Continue, please.*

Dried namafj and other things. He organized the food supplies, and also the system of repairs and services, for the entire expedition. He even has arranged to have supplies meet the expedition en route when we return, just in case the supplies brought with us are insufficient. All of the dukes speak highly of him. They agree that many would have been hungry but for him, and several say that the quest would have had to turn back.

It would seem that he has a commendable competence, the Protector remarked. His cold, flashing eyes bored at Darzek, who regretted that he could not meet them boldly. The Protector needed the experience of someone looking back at him, but Darzek was hardly in a position to supply it. He was about to experience one of life's most unpredictable occurrences: the judgment of a fanatic.

A remarkable administrative ability, the scribe agreed. *Further, he has priced his goods honestly, with no more than a fair profit to himself. He was seen to say that those who travel to the Holy Realm for a high religious purpose deserve to be commended, not robbed.*

A smile flicked on the Protector's lips; or perhaps it was only a nervous twitch. *Continue.*

He has a young daughter, to whom he is devoted, the scribe went on. *Last evening he called on a friend, a harness dealer, asking in concern where the child was. He feared she had wandered off. He said he would continue to look for her. Obviously he became lost in his search, trespassed the forbidden, and in the dark fell into the air vent.*

The Protector continued to scrutinize Darzek. *And the child?*

This morning she still had not been found. I have sent lackeys to assist in the search, and I have again warned those searching not to go beyond the east slope.

The provisioner seems to have told the exact truth, the Protector remarked, still keeping his eyes on Darzek.

Yes, sire. He has a high reputation for integrity with all who have dealt with him.

The child's mother?

The Winged Beast took her long ago, sire.

The Protector paused for a moment, lost in meditation, but his unwavering gaze never left Darzek's face. The Duke Dujinz had been right, Darzek thought. The Protector would favor no duke, and especially not his villainous brother.

A pity, the Protector said finally. His expression, as his hands formed the words, softened into one of genuine regret. *A pity, since he is a most worthy citizen and one meriting the thanks and esteem of us all. But he entered the Forbidden Temple uninvited. He has had the high honor of seeing the Holy Beasts. They already have tasted his blood. His life is forfeited to them. No other verdict is possible. Why did you ask?*

He is devout, sire. He wears an amulet of the Winged Beast. He is highly regarded for both his personal and his business dealings. He is a devoted parent, and his child has no other. I thought possibly, considering all of this, and especially the child—

There is no way to erase what he has seen. His life is forfeit. The Protector's hand fell casually on the scribe's arm. *But you have done well to ask. Since he has lived a commendable life, since he has rendered service to many, including ourselves, and since he has abilities our own service staff may find useful, I give you the privilege of postponement for him. If he serves us well, you may continue it indefinitely.*

Thank you, sire.

But no prisoner is excused from the selection of the king. He must share that honor with all of the others. See that it is done.

Yes, sire.

And throw some water on him. I don't object to the obvious marks of an honorable profession, but the odor of dried namafj lingers.

Yes, sire.

Darzek's escort of three stepped forward and led him away.

Unfortunately for Darzek, the strictures of the Protector were taken literally. He was drenched with icy mountain stream water, and the shock almost knocked him unconscious. And when, later that day, a knight chanced to take a deep breath while passing his cell and fancy that Darzek still smelled of dried namafj, the stricture was recalled, and Darzek was drenched a second time.

Otherwise, he spent the day in the same small bare room in which he had spent the last part of the night. But the pallet on the floor had been filled generously with straw, and the food brought to him was tastily prepared and ample. Whatever the knights of the Winged Beast ultimately did to their prisoners, they kept them well fed and comfortable.

He gave no thought to escape. They permitted him to keep his Winged Beast amulet, and he easily could have stunned his escort; but he would have had to find his way out of the system of caverns, past he knew not what obstacles, and if he succeeded, he would be on the outside. For the moment he preferred to be inside, even though he was a prisoner, because he had come there to find out how the king was selected and to influence the result if he could. Being condemned to participate in that selection looked like a stroke of luck to him.

He rested on his pallet most of the day—his mountain climb had exhausted him, and the slashes on his arms and legs, though the knights had tended them promptly and expertly, were still painful. He was fed again late in the day, and then night was announced by the simple expedient of extinguishing most of the torches in the corridor beyond his cell door. He was able to sleep well that night. In the morning he was fed another adequate meal, and then an escort of a knight and two lackeys took him to join the other prisoners.

Darzek was one of a group of ten that was led through a labyrinth of corridors: straight, curved, ascending, descending, branching. They passed through a series of barred checkpoints, and finally the group was turned into a long room that seemed nothing more than an extremely wide, barren, torch-lit corridor. Bars banged into place behind them; ahead of them, at the far end, were more bars. Half a hundred males of Kamm stood about, or squatted, or stretched out on the smooth rock floor. Sobs shook one male's huge frame—the only evidence of his silent weeping.

Instantly curious as to what lay beyond the barred opening at the other end, Darzek started to walk the length of the room. A few of his fellow victims looked up as he passed and then looked away again, thoughts turned inward, eyes dull with surrender or fear.

Then one looked quickly a second time as Darzek approached, and a third, and pushed himself into a sitting position.

And he spoke aloud. "Gul Darr. So even you have failed."

Darzek halted, staring down at him. It was Rok Wllon, though it looked nothing like him. He wore a form-fitting artificial covering, as did so many Synthesis agents, and it made him resemble a native perfectly.

Darzek knelt beside him. "I've been looking all over the island for you. How are you?"

"Weary. And eager. Death is failure's consummation, and I am eager for it. But I wish they didn't take so long about it." He looked searchingly at Darzek. "You came. I wanted to ask you to come, but I was afraid you wouldn't. Did you find the pazul?"

"I've been close to it. I know two dukes, at least, who have them. At first I thought it had been brought from another world—"

"No, no!" Rok Wllon protested.

"Then I found your memo. Since we know who has one, we'll soon find out what it is."

"You failed," Rok Wllon said. "You didn't find it, either. Death is failure's consummation."

He sank back against the wall, and though Darzek continued to talk to him, to ask him questions, to try to find out if he knew anything that might be useful, he would not speak again.

"It's no use," a voice said in Darzek's ear. "He's been that way ever since he came here."

Darzek looked questioningly at the young male who bent over him.

"I'm Kjorz."

"I'm Lazk," Darzek returned. "How many agents are here?"

"Six males and one female that I know of. You make the seventh male."

"Is the female Riklo?" Darzek asked quickly.

"Right. She's already told us about you. Expects you to gallop up on a nabrulk and put all the black knights to flight."

"She would," Darzek agreed grimly. "And instead, I came stumbling over the mountain at night, on foot, and fell into an air vent."

Kjorz said, a touch of awe in his voice, "You did? You actually found this place on your own? Maybe she wasn't overestimating you. The rest of us were hauled in here blindfolded, from all over Storoz. We've talked it over, and we know we goofed in some perfectly stupid way, but we can't figure out how. Do you know?"

"Yes," Darzek said. "But there isn't much we can do about it. Certainly not here. The problem is that you stink. All of us stink."

"Nonsense. The Synthesis has been on Kamm for at least a hundred years. If aliens smell so offensively, how come the natives never noticed it until now? We never had any trouble before. I've been on Kamm for five years without making anyone hold his nose. Suddenly I was picked up. All of us were picked up, one after the other, and more than half of us were killed."

"You got picked up because someone smelled you," Darzek told him. "Ever hear of worlds named Zruan and Arrn?"

"I guess so. They're in neighboring solar systems, aren't they?"

"Right. They're in the two nearest solar systems to Kamm's. Both have achieved a primitive interstellar travel. Kamm is located almost midway between them, and it's occurred to both of them that they need a base here. So they're meddling in the local political situation on Storoz because Storoz has the uranium ore they need."

"What does that have to do with our smelling?" Kjorz demanded.

"There are two kinds of aliens on Storoz besides us—Arrnians and Zruanians. Each is trying to do in the agents of the other. One group supplied its Kammian allies with metal detectors—only an alien is likely to be carrying metal objects about. In retaliation, the other group discovered that its rivals have a personal odor that stinks to the natives of Kamm, so they have their supporters going around smelling everyone. Between the two groups, they managed to trap our agents along with the aliens they were looking for. Until the other aliens got here, the Kammians ignored our body odors out of politeness."

"Then they really weren't trying to catch us?"

"No. But you were caught just as surely as though they had been. What do you know about this place?"

"Come and have a look," Kjorz said.

Darzek got to his feet, and Kjorz frowned and fingered his blood-stained sleeve and looked with concern at a blood-stained rip in his trousers.

"My introduction to the Winged Beasts," Darzek said.

"Then I don't need to explain."

"About the Beasts, no. Though I must say a face-to-face encounter with a monstrosity I'd considered the abstract symbol of a myth is the kind of shock I'd prefer not to experience twice. The black knights must have been raising them in captivity since the early days of their religion. What can you tell me about the layout of this place?"

Kjorz led him to the far end of the room, and they stood looking out through the bars upon an enormous, domed, circular arena. It was dimly lit from barred openings in the ceiling of the type Darzek had fallen into. At intervals around the sides were pairs of barred openings the size of a large door—one at floor level and one directly above it. Resting on the floor in the center of the arena was a large cage.

"It's a cathedral," Kjorz remarked. "It's the site of the most important religious ceremonies of Storoz. It's also the place where religious questions are decided—including the selection of the king. The barred openings on the upper level are royal boxes—there's one for each duke and one for the Protector. When there's an important question to be decided, the arena is filled with Winged Beasts, and a victim is placed in the cage. Then the lower doors are opened and the cage is hoisted to the dome, leaving the victim unprotected in the center of the arena. All he has to do is get to the safety of one of the lower doors before the Beasts tear him to pieces. The first few victims don't manage more than about three steps apiece, but eventually the Beasts have their hunger satisfied, and they lose interest. Even then, they enjoy the chase so much they'll attack and kill anyway if the victim tries too energetically to escape. But finally one makes it, and whatever door he escapes through decides whatever issue is under consideration. Today, it'll decide which duke becomes king. Pleasant little game, isn't it?"

"You've seen it happen?" Darzek asked.

"Unfortunately, yes. Not for the choice of a king, of course, but for lesser matters. And I've got friendly with one of the young lackeys, a student priest, and he's so pleased to have someone to talk with that he's been violating his vows to tell me about the history and ritual of the death religion. If I ever get out of here, I'll have a lovely report to write."

"How do they decide which of us to use?"

"By lot."

"Have any of our agents died in the arena?"

"Thankfully, not yet. Not that I know of. But you've seen the director's mental state, and the other four males have been tortured. They're in bad shape.

"I've seen a lot of worlds, and a lot of primitive practices, and a lot of violence," Darzek said. "But this—" He shook his head.

"Generations ago they changed to animal subjects. That was before the old king was deposed. But the present Protector is reviving the old customs—the restoration of the kingship and the reversion to what they call 'citizen sacrifice,' as though it's a special form of taxation. The victim that escapes has a very nice thing going for him. The duke he makes a king will give him honors and rewards. He might be elevated to the knighthood and even allowed to marry the duke's daughter, if the duke happens to have one available. It won't be so nice for the victims that don't make it. The unnerving thing is that they take so long to die. The Beasts like to tear their meals from living animals, and they craftily avoid administering a fatal wound as long as possible. It's pretty gruesome."

"Is there any way I could see Riklo?"

"No. The women are kept on the other side of the arena, and women victims are sent in through the door opposite this one. I managed one brief talk with her and got two lashes for it from the knight who caught us. I don't even know if Riklo is the only female agent there. I suppose you haven't any idea of how to get us out of here."

Darzek patted his Winged Beast amulet. "This is a stun gun. But the charge is small, and I'd be silly to try to take on the army of knights and lackeys guarding this place. If I'm the chosen victim, I might possibly be able to use the lowest setting and keep the Beasts away long enough to choose myself a king. I know which duke to choose."

Kjorz pursed his lips thoughtfully. "If you actually injured a Beast— or seemed to injure one, even if you only knocked it unconscious—the priests would tear you apart even if the Beasts didn't. It'd be risky. There's no way of telling what the lowest charge would do to a Beast, or whether it would affect it at all."

"Perhaps not. But using this thing would be no more risky than standing out there and doing nothing," Darzek pointed out. "The other alternative is to knock off my guards when I'm being escorted somewhere. There are never more than three. But I was brought into this place blindfolded, too, and there seemed to be a lot of barred passageways, and I have no notion of which way is out. Do you?"

"No. So what are you going to do?"

"I don't know. I'll snoop around and talk to our fellow victims and see if I can learn anything."

He moved back along the room, stepping over a prisoner who lay prone on the stone floor wracked with terrified shudders. A wizened oldster who sat nearby grinned cheerfully at Darzek, so Darzek stopped to talk with him.

Don't get discouraged, the oldster's hands said. *Maybe you'll be lucky, like me.*

Lucky in what way? Darzek asked him.

My number doesn't come up. Been here four years, and I'm still

here. Food is good, quarters aren't bad, and they don't give you much work to do. It isn't a bad life if you don't mind being herded down here on Holy Days and the like.

Darzek gestured at the arena. *Do you enjoy what goes on in there?*

I don't let it bother me. Sure—I know it could be me, in there. But it isn't, and I'll die of old age before my number comes up.

Four years, Darzek mused. *How many lives have you seen given to the Beasts?*

Don't know. Never bothered counting. A lot. But usually it's only one or two at a time, and my number doesn't come up. Of course I never saw a Choice. Today's the first time there's been a Choice. The knights say they'll use a lot of us for a Choice.

Darzek walked on. He found the other four Synthesis agents, talked with them briefly, and left them. They had been brutally mistreated. One had been whipped almost to death, and his body was a sickening network of scars. They also had been starved before being offered to the Protector as victims, and they were still weak. They might be led out of the place, but no vigorous action could be expected from them.

Suddenly a familiar odor caught Darzek's attention—a vile, pungent odor. He turned toward it and identified the source—a young Kammian who was seated against the wall in an attitude of relaxed indifference. Darzek could not recall seeing him before, but the stench he emitted was unmistakable. Darzek had a jar of the stuff himself, in his wagon, and he had been sniffing it and puzzling over it ever since Nijezor, the OO perfumer, had sent it to him.

With a sudden flash of insight, Darzek knew how the Duke of OO expected to become King of Storoz.

He also knew how he was going to prevent it.

CHAPTER 19

Darzek continued to prowl about, and he managed to examine the bars securing the exit door before a black-caped lackey chased him away. It could be opened only from the outside.

The females had been brought into the passage opposite theirs. Darzek peered across the area at the torch-lit opening until once again he was chased away, but he was unable to identify Riklo.

Finally he seated himself along the wall and considered his surroundings. This vast and complex network of natural caves had been altered and improved and extended by generations of priests. Probably there were kilometers of passageways, on a multitude of levels. Considering the frequent barriers and the ease with which one could get lost in the place, fighting one's way out would be impossible. It would have to be done by subterfuge.

He was confident that he could escape by himself; but how to get the others out?

There was a sudden flurry of activity at the end of the corridor. The barred door swung open, and a procession of black-robed, black-hooded knights and lackeys marched in. The prisoners were summarily lined up against the wall, and a young lackey moved down the line painting on each prisoner's forehead a glyph that served as a Kammian numeral.

A knight accompanied him and signaled each prisoner's number as it was applied. *The paint rubs off easily,* he kept saying. *Anyone found with a bare forehead will be given to the Holy Beasts immediately.*

Perspiration trickled down many foreheads, but Darzek, number thirty-three, noticed that no one brushed it away.

There was movement in the arena. A Beast dived hungrily at the barred door and then swooped upward. Momentary panic followed as the prisoners fled to the other end of the long room and the knights angrily sought to restore order.

Darzek fled with the others. He could not account for the sudden wave of terror that swept over him, but he experienced a dizziness he could only attribute to uncontrollable fright, and his pounding heart set his pulse booming in his ears. He wondered if there was some primeval impulse in all life forms that reacted with stark terror to the threat of being eaten—a threat both human and Kammian ancestors once had to contend with daily.

One of the few prisoners who seemed unaffected was the youth who reeked of the Duke of OO's special scent. When the others fled, he strolled nonchalantly after them. Now he drifted back to the other end of the corridor to peer into the arena, and Darzek followed him. But Darzek's uneasiness, and his pounding pulse and dizziness, continued.

A pair of lackeys began to haul on a rope that pulled the central cage toward the barred door.

Suddenly the Protector himself entered and strode the length of their room with a retinue of black knights trailing behind him. He stood for a moment looking out into the arena. If he felt triumphant at this, the moment of restoration of the Storozian kingship for which he had labored so long, he gave no sign of it. A knight spoke to him with fluttering fingers, the Protector delivered a shrug of approval, and marched away, still trailing his escort. Around the arena, a new row of torches flared, lighting the upper barred openings from which the dukes and their parties were to watch. A group of faces peered from each, but Darzek was too distant to identify any of them.

The outer door opened again, and a black knight strode into their room carrying a ceramic jar. When he reached the opposite end of the room, he stood for a moment peering into the arena. A lackey stood beside him with a torch. He waved it. In the opening across the arena, a torch answered.

The knight turned. He reached into the jar and pulled out a wood disc. *Thirty-seven,* he announced. He tossed the disc to the lackey with the torch, who pocketed it. Number thirty-seven, a large, beefy individual, toppled to the floor in a dead faint.

Lackeys dumped water on him, revived him, and hurried him to the arena door. The cage stood there, hauled into place by waiting lackeys. It was as tall as the door, and when the door was opened, it completely blocked the opening. Number thirty-seven was shoved into it. The cage's door was closed; the arena's door was closed and secured. The lackey waved his torch again, and there was an answering wave from the opposite door. Lackeys there hauled on the rope that would pull the cage back to the center. The moment it arrived there, the torch waved again, and the cage jerked upward. The victim was left crouching in the arena in helpless terror.

Darzek watched with a compulsion born of horror as wave after wave of dizziness swept over him and his pounding pulse produced both faintness and nausea.

For a terrible moment nothing happened. Number thirty-seven, suddenly imbued with hope, got slowly to his feet, looked about him, and bolted for the side of the arena. The first Beast to plummet downward raked his back and sent him sprawling. He rolled over, lashing out with arms and legs, as the Beasts swarmed onto him. Somehow he managed to clutch a wing, and there was a momentary stir of alarm among the watching knights and lackeys; but another Beast found his eyes, and another his throat. The feast had begun long before his struggles weakened. And while the Beasts squabbled and gorged, the cage was lowered and hauled back toward the waiting victims.

The knight reached into his jar again. *Number forty-two.*

Lackeys dragged him forward, and four years of luck ran out on the wizened little male who thought to die of old age. Fear paralyzed his legs, and the lackeys had to support his body while they rudely stuffed him into the cage.

When the cage was raised, he had slumped to a kneeling position, covering his face with his hands. A Beast circled slowly and landed on his back. Pain goaded him into a furious struggle, but he had waited too long. He never did regain his feet.

Already those grotesque horrors seemed to have dulled Darzek's sensitivity. His dizziness was lessening; his nausea decreased; his pulse seemed to be returning to normal; and all the time the Beasts squabbled and threatened each other with bloody fangs while they tore at the dead bodies, which now were being dismembered. One Beast flew off triumphantly with an entire leg.

The third victim was female. She behaved more courageously and resourcefully than either of the males. While the cage was being hauled to the center of the arena, she had removed her billowing skirt; and the moment the cage went up, she ran, twirling it about her head.

For a long, suspenseful instant the Beasts seemed befuddled by this, and she actually got two thirds of the way to an open door. But when they finally descended on her it was with the irresistible force of a ravenous horde. Again the nausea and dizziness swept over Darzek, and his pounding pulse returned, as he watched the Beast shred the unfortunate female's flesh.

In the room where Darzek waited, the knight announced another number: *Seventeen.* Darzek, still standing beside the youth who reeked with the Duke of OO's scent, was ready. He had set his amulet stun weapon at full power and positioned himself so that no one else would catch the beam. Now he pointed the gaping snout of his amulet and triggered it. The youth collapsed instantly.

No one thought anything of that. One victim already had fainted that day; no doubt it happened often. Lackeys dumped water on the youth, dumped more water, finally became curious. They examined him and called for a knight, who looked him over perplexedly. Probably few victims had been frightened completely to death when their numbers were called, and this one was dead.

But no one gave the oddity more than a moment's thought—the dead male was doomed to die anyway, and there were other victims waiting. There was, in fact, a prisoner who had carelessly wiped the sweat from his forehead and removed his number—as a chorus of his fellow prisoners indicated with urgently fluttering fingers. It was not even necessary to hold another drawing. Knights seized him and rushed him toward the cage.

Darzek, feeling smug over his successful disruption of the Duke of OO's sordid plot, stiffened as the subsitute was hurried past him. This victim, too, smelled of the duke's special scent—and Darzek could not get a shot at him without hitting at least two knights. He was in the cage before Darzek could think of a way to take action, and Darzek could not get close enough to the barred opening for an unhindered shot at him in the arena.

Cursing himself for underestimating the duke's resourceful perfidy, he could only watch helplessly as the reeking figure acted the part of a terrified victim. He ducked and dodged, stumbled and fell, struggled to his feet, lashed out helplessly at the swooping Beasts. But the scent repelled them, as Darzek suspected it would. They dove, but each time they veered away, and the duke's stooge finally worked his way to one side of the arena and darted through an open door.

The door swung shut. At the same instant all the torches in the ducal boxes save one were extinguished. In this revival of an ancient Holy Custom, the Duke of OO had been chosen King of Storoz.

Tension in the victims' room relaxed immediately. The prisoners wiped the numbers from their foreheads, and knights and lackeys began organizing them for the return to their cells.

Darzek spoke tersely to Kjorz, and the two of them managed to keep the Synthesis agents, including Rok Wllon, together. The other prisoners had been living in dormitory rooms, ten to a room. There were no room assignments; the lackeys simply counted the prisoners off in tens, and each group of ten was marched off to one of the rooms. By holding back, Darzek and Kjorz managed to get themselves, Rok Wllon, and the other four Synthesis agents counted into the last group, which contained only nine prisoners.

Their turn came, and a knight and two lackeys marched them away. Darzek studied their route with care and searched for clues as to the way out of the place, and Kjorz was doing the same. The took a corridor that slanted upward steeply; then a walk of fifty paces and the climb of a corridor slanting upward in another direction brought them to the level where the prisoners were kept.

A lackey moved ahead and opened a door. The two non-Synthesis prisoners entered obediently. Darzek, at the head of the Synthesis group, calmly plucked the door from the lackeys hands, swung it shut, and dropped the bar in place.

Lackeys and knight were thunderstruck. They were unarmed—probably no hint of rebellion ever had occurred in that place. The rebel would have been fed to the Beasts at once, and all the prisoners knew that.

Darzek dropped the knight and one lackey with a single shot from his amulet. The other lackey turned to run and was cut down before he'd taken a step.

Kjorz hurried down the corridor and found a remote room that was empty. With Rok Wllon and the other four agents looking on in bewilderment, Darzek and Kjorz dragged the knight and lackeys into the room. While Kjorz removed the clothing from the knight and one lackey, Darzek checked the three of them over carefully. He had set the amulet at medium charge. He saw no need to kill them, but he wanted time to get the Synthesis agents beyond pursuit before they woke up.

He donned the knight's clothing, carefully perching the helmet at the proper angle, and Kjorz took that of one of the lackeys. Then they barred the door, and they started the Synthesis agents back the way they had come—Darzek, the knight, leading the way, followed by five prisoners, with Kjorz bringing up the rear as a lackey.

After the first barrier, Darzek was confident that everything would be all right. A grating spanned the corridor, with a lackey in charge of its central door. He opened it without hesitation, closed it after them. They walked on.

But it took them more than an hour to find the exit, and Rok Wllon and the four mistreated agents were becoming tired and increasingly difficult to handle when Darzek finally reached a fork in the corridor, caught a draft of chill, fresh air coming down one branch, and turned in the right direction.

None of the lackey guards at the main entrance looked twice at them. They were trained to obey a knight instantly and without question, and probably the Protector had instilled in them more concern about unauthorized persons entering the sacred precincts than about escaping prisoners. Darzek, knight of the Winged Beast, led his detachment of prisoners away under a warm afternoon sun; but the moment the lane curved out of sight of the entrance, he hurried everyone up the mountainside and into the trees. There they paused to rest.

"From here on, it's up to you," Darzek told Kjorz.

"You're not coming?"

"I'm just getting a glimmer of what this is all about. If I can understand that glimmer, I may be able to accomplish something. Take them over the crest and down the other side as far as they're able to travel. Watch out for air shafts on this side of the mountain. When they can't go any further, find cover for them and wait until dark. Then go down to the encampment and get help."

Kjorz looked at him doubtfully. "You're sure you'll be all right?"

"No," Darzek said. "But I sense an opportunity here that may never happen again, and I'm not about to run off and leave it."

"You'd better tell me about this encampment. Where do I go to get help?"

Darzek described the encampment and the positions of his own wagons and tents. As he talked, he began to feel doubtful himself. It wouldn't do to take this bedraggled group of agents into the camp—the black-capes would know about it within minutes. They'd have to make a wide circuit and hide near the surlane until Sjelk could arrange to pick them up at night and smuggle them out of the central province in one of his returning empty wagons.

A sudden movement in the undergrowth brought him to his feet. An instant later a small figure hurled itself at him.

It was Sajjo.

When her tears had subsided, he presented her to Kjorz and the others. Then, speaking slowly with his hands, he told her precisely what had to be done. *Quickly!* he said. *There's no time to waste. Their lives depend on you.*

He embraced her again and stepped back. She smiled and turned to the others, motioning them to follow her.

The other agents and Rok Wllon got to their feet bewilderedly. Kjorz turned again to Darzek.

"You're sure you'll be all right?"

"When I leave this place," Darzek said, with more confidence than he felt, "I expect to be traveling in a much finer style than you will. Now get going."

He watched them move off into the forest, with Sajjo bounding along ahead of them. Just before they disappeared, she turned and waved at Darzek. Then they were gone. Darzek turned and moved laterally, following the lane at a safe distance. The forest drew close to it where it met the surlane coming down from the mountain pass, and Darzek settled down there to wait. Whether it would be for an hour or a week he had no idea. He hoped the religious ceremonies for the new king would be brief.

While he waited, he examined with care the glimmer he had seen, and focused and amplified it; and when he finally had his thoughts arranged, only a few confirming details were lacking for him to shape the final solution to the mystery of the Silent Planet.

Or so he hoped.

He continued to wait.

Finally he saw the procession coming. Again the Protector led the way, mounted on his solid black nabrulk, with his retinue of black-caped knights riding behind him. Next in line came the red-caped party of the Duke Merzkion. Darzek scrutinized it with care. The duke was there, and all of his retainers, but the duke's treasure was missing. He knew that the Duke Merzkion had taken a treasure over the mountain with him. He had seen him fluttering about it anxiously as the outgoing procession got underway. Now the Duke Merzkion was treasureless.

Following him came the silver-caped party of the Duke Rilornz—with no treasure.

And then the purple-caped party of Duke Fermarz—with no treasure.

And the parties of the Dukes Pabinzk and Tonorj, oranged-caped and brown-caped, both treasureless.

Then, in the center of the procession, came the new King of Storoz, formerly the Duke of OO, with his gold-caped followers. And the new king still had his treasure. It rode on a litter carried by four mounted black-caped lackeys; and the treasure chest, covered by elegantly embroidered cloths, was at least two meters high, two meters wide, and three meters long.

Darzek studied it calculatingly. "A little large for diamonds," he murmured.

He pointed his amulet at it.

As it came opposite him, he touched the trigger, giving it an unusually long blast of maximum power.

The sudden *clump* was audible even at his distance, but the procession of deaf Kammians moved along serenely. Darzek remained where he was, watching the parties of the remaining dukes: The Duke Borkioz and his deep blue-caped followers, no treasure; the redheaded Duke Dunjinz and his pink-caped followers, no treasure; the Duke Suklozk and his gray-caped followers, no treasure; the Dukes Lonorlk and Kiledj, with followers cloaked in pale blue and white, both treasureless. None of the remaining dukes possessed the treasure he had started out with.

When the end of the procession reached him, Darzek turned with a grin and loped off through the forest until he overtook the Duke of OO's party. By the time he reached it, the entire procession had halted. The new king, his knights and retainers, and black-capes from elsewhere in the procession had gathered about the treasure. As Darzek watched, the Protector rode up.

Darzek turned away, climbed higher up the mountain to be safely out of sight, and hurried back toward the caverns. His next hunch was that the entire procession would be returning to the underground temple of the Winged Beast, and he wanted to get there well ahead of it.

CHAPTER 20

If the lackeys guarding the entrance remembered Darzek and thought it odd that he was returning without his work party, they said nothing. Neither did those at the barricades. Darzek's principal problem was in finding the dormitory rooms: He had to mimic the sedate pace of a knight while searching with frantic haste.

He lost his way several times, and he was fighting a sensation of panic when finally he located the correct ascending passage. He first looked in on the knight and the two lackeys. They were still unconscious and showed no signs of reviving. He took the trouble to dress the knight in his armor. Then he barred that door, opened the door of the last occupied dormitory, and closed it after him, trying to coax the bar into dropping partially into place as the door slammed. It did—barely. His two cell mates were asleep after their emotional exhaustion of the morning, and they didn't see him enter. He stretched out on an empty pallet and quickly fell asleep himself.

He was awakened abruptly and herded into the corridor with a crowd of bewildered prisoners.

What is it? the prisoners were demanding.

It's another Choice, a knight told them maliciously.

But we just chose a king!

So we did. Now we're going to choose another king.

He turned away. The prisoners were marched off, one dormitory at a time, and if anyone noticed that Darzek's room was short six prisoners, no mention was made of it. They retraced their route of the morning, winding their way down to the long room reserved for prisoners.

Darzek hurried to the opposite end and looked into the arena. The torches already had been lit, including those in the ducal boxes, with one puzzling exception. The box that had been occupied by the Duke of OO was dark. The door under his box was closed. All of the others doors were open—except, Darzek assumed, the one occupied by the Protector, who was not eligible for the kingship. That door must have been the one adjacent to the one the victims entered, for Darzek could not see it.

The prisoners' bewilderment was pathetic as the knights backed them against the wall for numbering. As a lackey painted a glyph on Darzek's forehead, and the knight's fingers announced, *Twenty-seven,* Darzek stepped forward protestingly.

I don't like that number, his fingers informed the knight. *Give me another.* Deliberately he wiped it off.

The knight stared at him for a moment. Then he signaled the lackey to continue, and they finished the numbering.

The knight with the jar of numbers made his entrance, and the Protector soon followed. As he turned to leave, his gaze fell on Darzek. His hands snapped a question. *No number?*

A knight answered apologetically. *His mind has become addled. It happens frequently, especially after several of the prisoners have been given to the Beasts. He wiped off his number, but we remember it. It's twenty-seven.*

It's the namafj vendor, the Protector said. He sniffed. *He smells worse now than he did when I saw him yesterday. Didn't you dump water on him?*

It was done several times, sire. Do you wish it done again?

No matter. He wiped off his number, and you have a rule. Take him first.

The Protector left. Knights and lackeys converged on Darzek. He made them drag him to the cage and push him in. Then the cage moved, and he found himself walking toward the center of the arena. While he walked, he set his amulet at the lowest intensity and the broadest beam the little weapon could supply. Then he looked about him. He had picked out the Duke Dunjinz's box as soon as the cage moved out into the arena—its door was the second on the right from the one used for the prisoners.

Beasts were flapping excitedly far above, and several dived on the cage as it moved. Dizziness swept over Darzek, and he had to will himself to be steady, to concentrate, to think. The first moment after the cage went up would be decisive. "Just give them a touch to start with," he reminded himself. "See how they react. To kill one might be fatal." Even if such a death seemed a mysterious act of providence, there already had been too many peculiarities about this particular namafj vendor. The Protector would exact a horrible vengeance.

The cage jerked upward.

Darzek stood at the center of the arena, pivoting slowly, with both hands extended above his head. His posture was that of one invoking the gods. His audience was about to witness a miracle, and Darzek hoped to convey the impression that the miracle was a holy one.

The first Beast plummeted downward, and a new wave of dizziness enveloped Darzek and staggered him. He kept his feet with difficulty, tracked the Beast with his amulet, pressed the stud.

Nothing happened, except that the Beast leveled its screaming dive at the height of Darzek's head, and Darzek had to duck to escape the slashing talons.

A second Beast followed the first down. Darzek's dizziness continued. He aimed his amulet again, pressed the stud—and again nothing happened. Before the Beast had finished its dive, Darzek despairingly abandoned the amulet and tensed himself to dodge. For the amulet—after the day's activity and especially after the long full power blast at the Duke of OO's treasure—the amulet had a dead power supply.

But the second Beast also pulled out of its dive at the level of Darzek's head and veered off.

Darzek turned. A sudden dash would bring out the Beasts' killer instincts, so he walked slowly, one small footstep at a time, and set his course for the Duke Dunjinz's box. The Beasts continued to dive on him, but now they did not even come close before they veered off.

But the dizziness came in mounting waves, his pulse pounded wildly in his ears, and he wondered how much longer he could remain conscious. His head became a throbbing, tearing agony. He staggered on, closer and closer.

A report rang out across the arena, and blood spurted as his left arm was struck. He lurched and almost lost his balance; he knew he had been shot, and to fall would be fatal. With his final, failing strength he dashed for the open door below the redheaded Duke Dunjinz, and he collapsed as he burst through it.

A black-caped knight caught him. Another swung the door shut behind him. The two of them escorted him, supported and half carried, up a curving ramp to the box above, where the Duke Dujinz stepped forward to meet him.

You! the duke's hands exclaimed. *It is a miracle!*

Darzek slumped when the knights released him, and the duke himself caught him and made him comfortable on a cushioned bench. The duke gripped Darzek's arm and felt the gushing blood.

You're hurt! he exclaimed. He called for a doctor and immediately began shredding his own ducal robe to make bandages. One of the knights bent over Darzek to tend to the wound.

You shall be rewarded! the duke promised. *Anything you ask—*

Do you have any perfume? Darzek demanded.

The duke stared. Then he produced his personal flask, unstoppered it, offered it to Darzek. Darzek took a sniff. It was a strong, masculine scent. He took the flask and poured some on his head. Then he drenched his hand, reached under his tunic, and rubbed some on his chest. The duke watched openmouthed while Darzek proceeded to anoint himself, liberally, all over his body, with the duke's personal scent.

He was tired of having people tell him he stank.

As soon as Darzek could stand erect, he was made the subject of a brief religious ceremony. If the making of a king brought rewards, it also imposed responsibilities. Darzek found himself invested as religious adviser to the new king and sworn, in a solemn oath with the most fearsome consequences if he violated it, to reveal nothing of what he had learned and to undertake with zeal a course of religious training.

Then, in resplendent robes hastily draped over his shabby namafj vendor clothing, he had the high honor of leading the new king into the presence of the Protector.

The Protector had a problem of his own to cope with. He was seated on his high dais, and an angry petitioner stooped over him, confronting him as an equal: his brother, the bloated Duke of OO.

The Beast was sickly! the duke's fingers proclaimed.

The Beast was young and in perfect health. It was the responsibility of the Keeper of the Beast to protect and preserve it. The law speaks clearly.

The duke's fingers jabbered on, furiously, but the Protector broke off the argument with a scornful gesture, got to his feet, and descended to greet the new king.

When he had done so, he turned to Darzek. *It's the namafj vendor,* his hands said. *Surely the Winged Beast was guiding me in my decisions. Because you were worthy and devout and a devoted parent, I could have released you, but my instinct was to follow the law. And when your mind became addled and you erased your number, again I could have excused you because your will was not your own, but instead I followed the law. And by following the law, I have raised you to high honors.* He sniffed Darzek. *You smell much better already. Has your mind fully recovered?*

Darzek affected the wildest stare he was capable of, fixing his eyes on the Protector. His arm ached fiercely from the gunshot wound. He had lost blood. He was exhausted and hungry. His natural pallor and fatigue could only serve to enhance the effect he wanted to create: Lazk, the namafj vendor, in the throes of a religious delirium.

The frenzy he actually was experiencing was one of wrath. He resented being shot, and that gunshot meant that alien invaders had been present in the arena and were still attempting to influence the choice of the king. He was furiously angry over the persecution the Synthesis agents had received at the hands of the aliens and the treacherous dukes allied with them. Now he was his own instrument of revenge.

His hands spoke to the Protector. *I have touched Death, and I have seen—things.*

The Protector scrutinized him intensely. *What sort of things?* he asked finally.

Darzek made his fingers speak slowly, as though each word were torn with difficulty from his tortured vision. *Death's heavy shadow, unseen, unfelt, unsmelled, ripples no awareness, heeds no sanctuary. It enters and touches, and there is light. And by that light, I have seen.*

The Protector was staring at him incredulously. Whatever the source of Rok Wllon's poetry, few namafj vendors would be capable of such flights of thought. His retranslation of a translation should have been different enough, yet similar enough, to electrify the Protector.

It was. The Protector was too much a priest to ignore the possibility of a genuine miracle and too much a politician not to attempt to make use of one. *Tell me what you have seen,* he commanded.

All eyes in the room were fixed on Darzek's hands. *A Holy Beast, dead,* Darzek's hands said. He burst into sobs. *I saw a Holy Beast, dead. I saw it killed.* Cringing, he covered his face with his hands.

The Protector stepped forward. He embraced Darzek, and then, with infinite gentleness, he removed Darzek's hands from his face.

Fear not. Describe your vision. What killed the Holy Beast?

I do not understand, Darzek pleaded.

It is not the visionary's duty to understand. You have only to see and to describe. Others will interpret. What killed the Holy Beast?

Things, Darzek answered.

The Protector echoed perplexedly, *Things?*

Things I do not understand surrounded it and breathed poison on it. The same things surround us now and breathe poison. There is poison all around us, and all around the Holy Beasts. He sobbed his terror. *All of them will die. And all of us. There are things—*

He turned and began peering into faces. All winced and drew back as he approached. *Things—*he sobbed again. *Things—poisoning—*

He peered into the face of the Duke of OO, and that individual, still livid with rage and totally uninterested in religious visionaries, took an angry step backward and tried to get the Protector's attention again.

But the Protector was intent on Darzek, whose fingers continued to flutter. *Things—*

Darzek had encountered a familiar face. It belonged to one of the Duke of OO's companions, and he had last seen it in the duke's carriage at the OO-Fair. In one swift movement he stripped the alien's hood aside.

He pointed tremulously at the enormous single ear that curved around the entire back of the head. *Things—poisoning—*

The Protector strode forward. The alien tried to replace his hood, but two knights already had seized him. The Protector stared and continued to stare. He moved slowly behind the alien, scrutinizing the utterly inexplicable organ whose function he could not guess at.

He turned to Darzek. *Are there other—things?*

Darzek was no longer acting. Weakness and exhaustion had overwhelmed him; he felt as stricken as he must have looked. *Yes. Things —poisoning—look for them.*

As he slumped to the floor, a dozen hands caught him and helped him to a cushioned resting place and made him comfortable. He lay there contentedly, eyes open just wide enough to watch an argument between the Protector and the Duke Dunjinz, the new king.

I will have no more of my subjects killed, the duke was announcing. *Even this—this thing. I will not have him killed.*

You are not invested, the Protector told him. *You are merely chosen. Until you are invested, I am the custodian of the sacred premises, and I will render proper and legal punishment to any who profane them and make mockery of the holy ceremonies.*

He turned to one of his knights. *Several ducal parties have members who are hooded. Remove the hoods. All of them.*

Darzek sank back contentedly and closed his eyes.

But when, a short time later, the Duke Dunjinz bent over and asked if Darzek felt like accompanying him, he permitted himself to be helped to his feet. He was feeling indescribably lousy, but he was much too curious to know what was happening to remain where he was.

Once again he found himself looking out into the arena, but this time he was seated comfortably in the Duke Dunjinz's private box. And when the cage went up, there were seven aliens in the arena—three of the massive single-eared type from Arrn, and four of the double-eared Zruanians.

Three of the ducal boxes were empty. The Protector had made no pronouncement concerning the fates of the Duke of OO and the Dukes Merzkion and Fermarz, who had brought these—things—into the sacred precincts in violation of their holy oaths. Probably no one except the Protector and his knights would ever know what had happened to them. Certainly none of the other dukes was in a mood to ask.

The Protector had ordered a new flock of unfed Beasts, and they circled cautiously as though waiting for the victims to move. Then they began to dive. Dizziness again swept over Darzek, but he could not tear his eyes from the arena.

None of the Beasts struck. They dove, they zoomed upward again or veered away; but the aliens, one after another, collapsed and lay twitching or threshing in agony. Blood spurted from mouths, noses, eyes, ears, as the monstrous Beasts dived on them again and again.

But the Beasts did not touch them. Perhaps, as with Darzek—once the fish smell had been washed from him—they were repelled by an evil scent. Or perhaps, also as with Darzek, they sensed that things with such odors were not of this world and should be shunned. So they circled and dived, but they did not touch.

Finally it becomes obvious that the Beasts would not eat these victims. Then priests entered the arena in the cage to carry them away, and the Protector mercifully permitted those watching to leave the boxes.

Darzek had long since retired to the most remote corner of the Duke Dunjinz's box. In that place his dizziness lessened somewhat and could be replaced by the euphoria he felt he was entitled to. His work on this planet was finished.

Because he finally had identified the pazul, the mysterious death ray of Kamm.

CHAPTER 21

Rok Wllon said weakly, "The pazul—you say the pazul—"

"On the Silent Planet," Darzek said firmly, "the pazul is silence. Probably it's the most deadly silence in the universe."

They were seated in the tastefully furnished sitting room of the Synthesis headquarters in Midpor: Rok Wllon, Darzek, Kjorz, Riklo, and —comfortably relaxed in the distant corner of the room with an expression of sardonic amusement on his face, Bovranulz.

The dukes and their entourages had returned to Midpor and gone their separate ways. The new King Dunjinz was residing there temporarily, in one of the more palatial of the abandoned residences, for conferences with Captain Wanulzk and other leaders of the Sailor's League. The refugees already were returning to the Free Cities. A period of peace and prosperity seemed in store for the island of Storoz.

And in the Synthesis headquarters, the Director of the Department of Uncertified Worlds was trying to comprehend what had gone wrong.

"First," Darzek said, "the Winged Beasts didn't get to be the legendary death monsters of Kamm by accident. Folklore claims that they once ruled the planet. Back in the mists of a forgotten prehistory, probably they did. They developed their own unique method of catching their prey. They stunned it with blasts of ultrasonic energy."

Rok Wllon said perplexedly, "Blasts of ultrasonic—"

"We won't know for certain what it is until the right scientific equipment arrives. I'm guessing that it's a peculiarly oscillating ultrasonic wave of enormous power. It functions entirely above the normal range of hearing, which is what makes it such a deadly silence. The victim never knows what hit him. And it's a *directed* ultrasonic beam—the Beast is able to focus and aim it at the intended victim. As this strange power evolved and developed, it had a tumultuous effect on the course of evolution on this planet. The Beasts' prey had to evolve also, or become extinct. As is so often the case with evolution, the more powerful this sinister weapon became, the more immune the intended prey became. Finally the Beasts became all powerful and completely ineffective as the surviving life forms first lost their hearing and then their ears. Probably there were internal compensations in all of the vulnerable organs. At that point the clumsy, slow-moving Beasts had a survival problem of their own, especially when the dominant life form began to develop a civilization and weapons. On Storoz, the Beasts were driven back into the mountains. They would have become extinct themselves if the dominant life form hadn't made them a religious symbol and bred them in captivity."

"But you were given to the Beasts," Rok Wllon protested. "You survived. Several of us were close enough to be exposed to that deadly silence. We survived. I wasn't even aware of it."

"True. But remember—I said a *directed* beam. The waiting victims weren't exposed to the full deadliness because it wasn't aimed at them. For another thing, you may be immune. The physiologies—and therefore susceptibilities—of various life forms vary drastically. The Kammians are virtually immune, but they must have some racial memory of a time when they weren't that's reflected in their terrified reactions to the Beasts and in their fear of darkness. The Beast is a nocturnal hunter. I felt dizzy even in the adjoining room, and so did Riklo. In the arena, where I was subjected to repeated direct blasts, I came awfully close to fainting. Riklo got one very brief direct blast, and she did faint and suffer some internal bleeding. Prolonged exposure would have killed her. Wenz received a short blast and died horribly. Probably some of the missing agents died the same way. The aliens from Arrn and Zruan were highly susceptible."

Kjorz said doubtfully, "I can understand all that. But how did you depose the Duke of OO? He'd just been chosen king, and suddenly they demoted him and ran the lottery over again."

From his place in the corner, Bovranulz laughed softly. The clairvoyant had been interested in the same question, and Darzek had attempted to inform him, through a series of mental images, of the reasoning process by which he arrived at an understanding of the Kammian tradition of kingship. When he finished his explanation, Bovranulz embraced him as a fellow seer.

It was Captain Wanulzk who had given Darzek the vital clue, though at the time Darzek hardly noticed it. The captain mentioned that the King of Storoz traditionally had *three* titles: Ruler of Storoz, Protector of the Faith—and Keeper of the Winged Beast. Belatedly it had dawned upon Darzek that a king with such a title must actually have a Winged Beast in his possession.

But Darzek hadn't been able to account for the quantum leap by which he formed his next deduction. He knew that the kingship was not hereditary. He guessed that it was not for a fixed term of years, or someone would have mentioned that fact. He knew that the kingship rotated among the dukes, and therefore there had to be a limitation on the king's term of office. But his conclusion that the king reigned only as long as his Winged Beast lived was less a conjecture than an inspired hunch.

"The Duke Merzkion had a Winged Beast," Riklo objected. "It killed Wenz and almost killed me."

"All of the dukes had Winged Beasts before the new king was chosen," Darzek said. "That was because the tradition of a king reigning as long as a Winged Beast lived seemed highly suspicious and risky to them. Most of them had never seen a Winged Beast. The first step in the Protector's groundwork for re-establishing the kingship was to give each duke a Winged Beast of his own to care for. Naturally this ownership was highly secret, and most dukes kept their Winged Beasts in guarded rooms in a castle tower. After a year, all of the Beasts were alive and in good health, so phase two of the Protector's plan went into effect: The kingship lottery would be held at the end of the second year, and all the dukes able to return living and healthy Winged Beasts to the Protector at that time would be eligible.

"While that was going on, agents from Arrn and Zruan were attempting to manipulate things to their own advantage, offering the dukes bribes like electric generators, and promising the more susceptible dukes the kingship. Probably an agent from Arrn gave the Duke of OO the idea that a scent would repel the Beasts, and his own black knights helped him plant his stooges among the prisoners.

"In the meantime, the Synthesis agents became curious as to what the dukes were hiding. A few found out and were killed by the ultrasonic cries of the Beasts they discovered. Their attempts alarmed the dukes, who thought that other dukes were trying to eliminate them from the lottery by killing their Beasts. They reacted by putting the Beasts under heavy guard, leaving us to wonder why this death ray that killed anyone coming near it had to be protected.

"It finally occurred to me that the dukes' treasures must be Winged Beasts when I saw how the Duke of OO rigged the lottery. In order to come up with a scent that repelled the Beasts, he must have had a Beast to try it out on. Then I had my hunch about the king's term of office, and I killed the new king's Beast to try it out. I didn't find out until later that the Duke of OO wasn't eligible to succeed himself."

"It was brilliant," Kjorz murmured.

Darzek indulged in a Kammian shrug. "Maybe, but what followed was rather stupid. I didn't know that I'd exhausted the charge in my amulet until the Beasts were diving on me. I only survived because the natives of Kamm think I stink, and because the Winged Beasts must think I stink revoltingly. And fortunately my physiology is such that I could temporarily survive the ultrasonic bombardment. From first to last we blundered through this thing."

Sajjo came dashing in and went directly to Darzek. *The king says yes. Send Kjorz to him.*

Darzek turned to Kjorz. "Congratulations. Go to the king and make like an ex-namafj vendor."

"As long as I don't have to eat any namafj," Kjorz said with a grin. He went out.

The opportunity to have a Synthesis agent installed as religious adviser to the King of Storoz was too glittering to be passed up, but Darzek was not about to prolong his stay on Kamm for any kind of opportunity. He recommended that Kjorz, who resembled him superficially, take his place. The king was reluctant to part with a genuine miracle worker, but finally he had assented.

"And that winds things up," Darzek told Rok Wllon. "We'll see that Arrn and Zruan land no more agents here, and if they persist in making interstellar nuisances of themselves, you can deal with them directly. Is there any reason why we shouldn't leave on this supply ship that's due tomorrow?"

Rok Wllon said blankly, "No. No reason."

Riklo came over to Darzek. They hadn't had a chance to talk since he'd secured her release from the underground temple. Now there was nothing left to do except exchange farewells, and she seemed acutely embarrassed.

"If you think you behaved stupidly," she said, "I should tell you what I did."

Darzek grinned at her. "I already heard. Forget it. Sometimes it takes a generous measure of stupidity to make things work out."

Riklo's tour as a peddler had been brief—her scent gave her away at the first castle she visited. She could have escaped at once by using her amulet, but she let the opportunity pass and waited for a better one that never came.

But her crowning humiliation had come in the arena. She had been so revolted by the kingship lottery that she placed herself in the rear ranks of the female prisoners and refused to look at it. As a result, she saw nothing at all of Darzek's performance. She didn't realize until her release that he had been the successful victim—and that she could have been standing by ready to help him with her amulet if she hadn't been too squeamish to watch.

"Be grateful for mistakes that aren't fatal," Darzek said. "Sometimes it's possible to learn from them."

She said slyly, "Your own vast learning must be the result of a great many non-fatal mistakes."

"An enormous number," Darzek agreed.

"Are you really taking Sajjo with you?" Riklo asked.

"Of course. She wants to go. She wants to grow up to be an interplanetary agent like you."

"But—with her being deaf—"

"There may be a way to correct that. I think she'll be able to learn to speak, too. She's already reading lips—and in Galactic, too. See her smiling at you? She recognized her name. She has a natural talent, and she deserves an opportunity to develop it. Bovranulz approves. He foresees a long and happy life for her."

"I'm afraid to ask what he foresees for me," Riklo said. She touched Darzek's hands in farewell and took her leave.

Darzek looked after her with a frown. "She's a talented agent. Unfortunately, she's too stubborn to take orders."

Rok Wllon flashed a superior smile at Darzek and gestured expansively. Here was a problem that properly belonged in the familiar territory of his own administrative expertise, and he was prepared to enjoy it. "Your violation of regulations disturbed her. Also, she has her own sound intuition to follow. I've just decided to promote her—she'll be the new team leader for Kamm."

Darzek nodded. It felt good to nod. He'd had a repressed urge to nod his head all the time he'd been on Kamm. For all he knew, Riklo would make an excellent team leader.

He nodded again, at Sajjo. "Ready for the galaxy?" he asked. She couldn't have understood, but she smiled and nodded back at him.

Rok Wllon was watching him expectantly. It pleased Darzek that he was his old, argumentative self, but Darzek did not want to argue about Riklo. "If you want to promote her," he began and broke off abruptly, scowling.

"What's the matter?" Rok Wllon asked anxiously.

It had just occurred to Darzek that every problem he had encountered on Kamm had been resolved successfully—except one. "I still don't know what Riklo looks like," he remarked.

Rok Wllon puckered his face inquiringly.

"I've never seen her outside that artificial Kammian body she wears," Darzek explained. "I have no idea what her real form is. I know she's a native of Hnolon, but I don't remember ever seeing one. So I don't know what she looks like. I've been tempted to ask her to take off that synthetic epidermis so I could see her as she really is. But now I think it might be better not to know."

"That's very strange," Rok Wllon observed thoughtfully. "A little earlier today she said exactly the same thing about you."